Deceiving D'Artagnan

By

Fi Whyms

Copyright © 2023 Fiona Whyms

ISBN: 9798391632269

All rights reserved, including the right to reproduce this book, or portions thereof in any form. No part of this text may be reproduced, transmitted, downloaded, decompiled, reverse engineered, or stored, in any form or introduced into any information storage and retrieval system, in any form or by any means, whether electronic or mechanical without the express written permission of the author.

This is a work of fiction. Names and characters are the product of the author's imagination and any resemblance to actual persons, living or dead, is entirely coincidental.

The views expressed in this work are solely those of the author and do not necessarily reflect the views of the publisher, and the publisher hereby disclaims any responsibility for them.

Chapter One

I was so looking forward to celebrating New Year's Eve with Darth Vader and the Arch Bitch, not to mention Randy Uncle Harry.

No, we weren't going to a fancy-dress themed NYE party, we were going to D'Artagnan's sister's house for the annual gathering of my husband's extended family. Apparently, our attendance was non-negotiable.

'Because it is the tradition, Nicole,' D'Artagnan said haughtily. 'I do this every year.'

The cold that I'd acquired just after Christmas had, rather disappointingly, not developed into something more serious like bronchitis or pneumonia or the plague. I forced a cough that was intended to project terminal-stage Brontë-esque consumption but didn't quite hit the mark. 'But I'm really not well!'

He turned the imperial brown gaze on me and blinked a few times. 'Yesterday we walk all the way to the *boulangerie*, Nicole, and you do not die. So you are fine to come to Bordeaux.'

I scowled. 'But I'm probably still infectious – I'll probably end up killing half your family!'

He gave a sly grin. 'I tell you which ones to cough at, okay?'

'Seriously, Guy! I have a horrible cold!'

'Seriously, Nicole! I know you are trying to find an excuse not to come to Bordeaux!'

I was sitting on the chaise longue in Heaven, my purpose-built dressing room, wrapped in my fluffy dressing gown. Mrs Muffin was sitting on the arm of the chaise longue, gradually customising it with her claws and purring happily as she pursued her artistic endeavours.

It was the 30th of December. I watched as Guy pulled his jeans on carefully over the long, jagged scar on his left thigh. It was still pink and inflamed, though it was healing remarkably well given that it was only just over two months since he'd attempted to remove the lower half of his leg with a chainsaw. That had resulted in his near death, three blood transfusions and a spell in the ICU of Cognac hospital; it had made the end of our first year together in rural France rather more exciting than I'd been anticipating.

He zipped up his jeans and pulled his T-shirt back down without taking his eyes off mine. 'I don't understand why this is such a problem for you, Nicole. You have met my family and you are close to Françoise – why is this difficult?'

'Because there'll be a lot of people and I'll get anxious,' I muttered.

'*Bah* – take some of your tablets, then. This is why Doctor Malin give you these tablets, *n'est-ce pas?*'

I gazed at him steadily. I had not told him that lately I was getting through rather more diazepam than I was comfortable with. My hyperactive little brain had taken to replaying the goriest images from the day of the chainsaw demi-massacre, specifically the one where I was sitting in a pool of his sticky blood, his head in my lap and his lips turning blue as I watched the life drain from his face. It was distressing when it flashed up on the screen of my consciousness as I went about my daily business. Diazepam dulled it – and the nightmares.

I didn't answer. He sighed deeply and sat next to me, then slipped an arm around my shoulders and pulled me close. D'Artagnan is incredibly physical; it's almost as if he can't communicate unless he's touching the person he's talking to, even if it's only his fingertips on their arm. It makes *les Anglo-Saxons*, as he insists on calling the English, very uncomfortable. He is well aware of that; the less he likes an *Anglo-Saxon*, the more he touches them. It amuses him to see them try not to recoil.

I sneezed moistly into his shoulder, which pleased me.

'Nicole,' he said patiently. 'It is our first New Year together and I want to celebrate it with you, my beautiful wife. I also want to celebrate with my sister and my nieces, like I always do. Please don't make this a choice for me.' His voice was quiet, and he stroked my neck gently with his thumb.

Ergo the non-negotiable, non-fancy-dress NYE party.

***

'What should I wear? What's the dress code?' I asked the next morning as I slid back the mirrored sliding doors of my wall-to-wall wardrobe and perused my beloved collection of designer clothing.

'Sexy.' He smirked seductively. 'This is the code.'

I raised an eyebrow. 'Not a huge amount of info there.'

Nonchalant Gallic shrug. 'Wear one of your beautiful dresses. It is a big *fête* this night – everyone will dress up. This should make you happy, Nicole. You are always telling me you never have a chance to wear nice clothes any more.'

This was true. Ever since Guy had orchestrated our move from central London to the Duchess, the slightly dilapidated seventeenth-century château he had inherited in rural south-west France, there had been worryingly few calls for party frocks and evening gowns.

All my Louboutins had scurried away into the depths of their soft, monogrammed shoe-bags inside their immaculately preserved shoe boxes around the time I'd acquired my first pair of Wellington boots. But even though I knew the Louboutins are terrified of mud, I was fairly sure I could coax a pair out of hiding for a party.

***

We descended the stairs towards the crowded salon in Françoise's home, a beautiful old white-shuttered, ivy-clad stone *longère* set amongst the estate's Bordeaux vineyards.

'For fuck's sake, I'm completely overdressed,' I muttered out of the corner of my mouth.

'You are ravishing in that dress, *mon trésor,*' D'Artagnan murmured, his hand smooth on the base of my naked back.

I was wearing an ankle-length, dusty-pink, silk Valentino that plunged between my breasts at the front and latticed with thin silk ties at the back. It was the dress I'd worn when Guy and I had married at Chelsea registry office the previous March, exactly five months to the day since he'd first swaggered into my life. I remembered feeling shell-shocked at the speed with which he had seduced me, as I stood next to him in front of the registrar. Shell-shocked and mesmerised.

He'd spent an exquisitely long time removing the Valentino afterwards.

Darth Vader and the Arch Bitch – Guy's brother and wife – had not got the memo about it not being a fancy-dress party and had come dressed as undertakers. They were the first fellow partygoers we encountered.

'Stephane! Catherine! How lovely to see you again!' I channelled Richard-and-Judy levels of enthusiasm as I leaned forward and exchanged kisses with them. They channelled Spanish-inquisition levels of enthusiasm in return.

Stephane's lip curled distastefully. He leaned forward from the waist, his gnarled hands hovering a good distance from my shoulders as we kissed. I was unsurprised to note that he was still in full Darth Vader mode, inhaling all joy in the immediate vicinity and exhaling disdain and disapproval in its place.

Catherine was even less thrilled to see me. Her gaze travelled disapprovingly down my cleavage (such as it is – 34B doesn't offer a whole lot of cleavage, TBH) then back up again. 'Nicole. You must be freezing cold,' she said as we exchanged kisses. Her dry, un-moisturised lips (because God disapproves of moisturising one's lips, apparently) were like sandpaper against my cheek.

'Oh no, I'm fine, thanks, Catherine. I'm actually quite warm.' I smiled at her. D'Artagnan and I had shared a bottle of rather good Champagne in our room after we'd showered and dressed, and I'd swallowed another 10mg of diazepam to forestall any uncontrollable anxiety.

D'Artagnan exchanged kisses with his brother. 'Stephane. *Ça va?*' The look that passed between them was insolent from D'Artagnan's side, icy from Stephane's.

'Guy. *Oui, ça va. Et toi?*'

I wondered whether they'd always disliked each other, even when they were kids. There was a picture of the four siblings amongst Françoise's collection of family photographs on the enormous oak dresser in the kitchen diner, and I'd spent some time studying it when we'd visited the previous year. It was taken in front of the Duchess, who had somehow seemed a lot less forbidding than she was in my limited experience.

The four of them were lined up in height order: Stephane at one end, a dark-haired, angular, frowning teenager; plump, blond, cuckoo-in-the-nest Antoine next; Françoise, so pretty with her dark bobbed hair (unchanged some forty years later), and finally Guy, all dark-blond curls, big eyes and the most angelic smile. He was completely aware of his powers of seduction, even at the age of five.

I loved that photo of him. And, although it made me sad, I also loved the one of him and his best friend, Laurent, their darkly tanned torsos covered in beach sand and the sun glinting in their hair, Guy's arm around his friend's neck and Laurent's blue eyes wide as they laughed into the camera. They looked so ... young, so beautiful. I couldn't imagine how Guy had felt losing his best friend, or how Françoise had survived losing her beautiful young husband when he died of cancer at the age of forty.

I knew that Stephane and Catherine, being fervent Catholics, had disapproved of Guy's first marriage to non-Catholic Isabelle, and that they had disapproved equally of their subsequent divorce. Apparently divorce outside of The Faith did not cancel out marriage outside of The Faith.

As for Guy's second marriage to me, the too-young, ex-model arm candy (unsurprisingly, also outside of The Faith) – well, that was just risible. Hence the glacial reception I received from Darth Vader and the Arch Bitch on the mercifully rare occasions we met.

D'Artagnan's insolence was not muted as he exchanged kisses with his sister-in-law. Her resting expression was one of puckered disapproval; it must have been painful to have maintained it for most, if not all, of her life. '*Catherine, comment vas tu?*' he asked smoothly. 'And God? How's He doing?'

I turned away and coughed to cover my snort of laughter. I understand French pretty well – it's just my spoken French that causes D'Artagnan to suffer slight facial tics. It's my grammar, he assures me, not my accent. I'm still not quite sure whether that's a compliment or an insult.

He squeezed my hand as I coughed and winked at me slyly.

'I am fine, thank you, Guy,' said the Arch Bitch.

Thankfully Françoise had spotted us and she crossed the room, her face lit with a lovely smile. I was pleased to see that she was wearing an elegant, off-the-shoulder evening dress; I was not as overdressed as I'd feared. Her shiny hair brushed her delicately boned shoulders as she took my hands. 'Nicole, it's so wonderful to see you again! You look lovely!'

I smiled and squeezed her hands 'So do you, Françoise. It's so good to see you again, too!'

She held my shoulders gently as we exchanged kisses, then fixed me with her brown eyes. They aren't as dark as D'Artagnan's, although she has the same long eyelashes. 'How are you? How was Christmas? I hope my brother bought you a very expensive Christmas present after what he put you through last year!'

Christmas had been ... mostly muted with diazepam. D'Artagnan's son and daughter and their partners had joined us for Christmas at the Duchess. It was our first Christmas together and I was nervous about spending it with twenty-four-year-old Emmanuel and twenty-one-year-old Charlotte. Theoretically, they were now my step-children. Sometimes I was acutely conscious of the twelve-year age difference between their father and me, and at thirty-seven I was definitely *not* old enough to be their mother. Unless we'd regressed to the thirteenth century. Or twenty-first century Afghanistan.

But Christmas was less stressful than I'd anticipated. Guy did all of the cooking, assisted occasionally by Charlotte who had inherited her father's love of food. I simply followed instructions about what went where and when, we consumed a fair amount of wine and Champagne, and everyone seemed to enjoy themselves. Guy and Isabelle had divorced long before I was in the picture, and Emmanuel and Charlotte had never shown anything other than warmth towards me.

'It was lovely, thank you. And he did spoil me – this is my Christmas present.' I touched the Chaumet Bee My Love necklace around my neck, which matched the wedding rings I'd chosen when we married. 'So I've forgiven him, I suppose.'

Stephane and Catherine clearly thought the necklace was unforgivably sparkly because they both frowned deeply.

I caught D'Artagnan's eye and he smiled at me before turning to Françoise. He held out his arms and gathered her up in an enormous hug, lifting her off the ground and kissing her resoundingly on the cheek. '*Ça va, ma beauté?*' he asked, grinning.

She was laughing as he put her down again and she touched the side of his face tenderly. '*Ça va, mon petit frère.*'

I realised that the stupid grin was very present, the one that appears unconsciously on my face whenever I watch people who love each other.

After Françoise had excused herself in order to circulate, we moved away from the Vortex of Misery (of which Stephane and Catherine were the epicentre) and did a circuit of the elegantly decorated salon with its ancient stone fireplaces at each end. We exchanged kisses with Françoise's daughters and their partners and congratulated Guy's eldest niece, Emma, on her pregnancy and her engagement to Conor, he of the soft blue eyes and dreamy Cork accent. Then we exchanged kisses with Guy's weird racist brother Antoine and his Spanish boyfriend, and with quite a lot of other people. I smiled graciously, said '*enchantée*' a lot and instantly forgot their names.

We ended up back with Emma and Conor near one of the fireplaces. Unfortunately the Vortex of Misery had joined them, and Conor looked relieved to see us. Emma was explaining to Catherine that her pregnancy had been unplanned and that no, it wasn't going to be possible to get married before the baby was born.

This did not please Catherine *at all*. 'But you are only three months pregnant! You have plenty of time to marry. It is not appropriate to have a child when you're not married!'

'No, Aunt Catherine, I'm *five* months pregnant. We planned the wedding for April, but that's when the baby's due so we're going to get married a bit later,' Emma explained.

I admired her patience and the kindness in her voice. She looked really lovely, positively glowing with health, and I felt a mixture of happiness, envy and sadness as I glanced surreptitiously at the slight bulge of her belly. I had only ever managed just over three months, and I hadn't known I was pregnant at the time. If I had known, I might not have gone hiking that day. My life might be very different now – if I'd known.

But anyway.

Françoise was thrilled that she was going to be a grandmother, but she was also a little concerned because Emma and Connor's meticulously planned wedding would have to be postponed until June, or even July. 'I don't want it to get in the way of your wedding,' she had said in a low voice earlier that evening. 'Do you have a date for it yet?'

When D'Artagnan and I had married the previous March, it was very low key with only my best friend Jules and her husband Mark as our witnesses. Following D'Artagnan's triumphant return to the motherland with his newly captured bride, however, he was adamant that we needed to get married all over again. And this time it would be in front the Duchess in full French style: marquees; floral arrangements; horse-drawn pumpkin coaches (probably); flower-draped aisles; wedding frocks; wedding vows in front of loads of people; speeches; toasts, and a formal sit-down meal...

Whenever I tried to focus on the prospect, I felt slightly overwhelmed. I don't like being the centre of attention. I know that sounds odd, given that I spent ten years walking up and down the catwalk being stared at and photographed, but I could absent myself from that because it wasn't about me – it was about what I was wearing. And I was very good at being absent if I needed to be. But for our wedding I would have to be very much present because I would have one of the two starring roles.

I'd had to admit to Françoise that we hadn't decided on a date, but I promised to let her know as soon as we did.

The Arch Bitch turned to me and her mean little eyes flickered over my flat stomach. Guy had gone to get us another glass of Champagne. 'What about you, Nicole? You've been married for a while now. Surely you'll be having children soon?' Stephane and Catherine had produced six children because that's what Good Catholics do.

I stared at her. The subtext of her prying was clear: why on earth else did Guy marry you, if not to produce children?

Everyone was suddenly looking at the floor, as if a new and wildly interesting pattern had appeared in the carpet.

'Oh, we're not going to have children.' I smiled at her. 'I can't, and Guy's had a vasectomy. Actually, I only married him because he's incredibly good in bed.'

Conor snorted loudly and Emma tried to disguise her laugh with a polite cough. The collective glare from the Vortex of Misery radiated with the fury of a thousand suns.

I realised D'Artagnan had returned and overheard what I'd said, because I felt him slip his arms around my waist, still holding both glasses of Champagne as he fastened his mouth very insistently on *that* spot, the one on the side of my neck where it curves into my shoulder – the spot that he knows makes my knees go weak.

I leaned back against him and raised my hand behind me, gently rasping my nails against the nape of his neck. His arms tightened around me, his breath hot on my ear. '*Toi aussi, mon amour, tu es incroyable...*'

Conor turned abruptly to Stephane and started discussing the economic situation in France very earnestly.

The diazepam had fully kicked in. Everything was lovely. Waiters and waitresses circulated with trays of delectable *canapés*, all of which I waved away politely on the grounds that (a) it was New Year's Eve, (b) it was France, and (c) it was inconceivable that the *canapés* would not contain *foie gras*, i.e. kryptonite for vegetarians.

I turned to face D'Artagnan and he smiled his slow, sexy smile. '*Je t'aime, mon ange.*'

I gazed into the fathomless depths of his beautiful brown eyes. '*Je t'aime aussi*, darling man.'

'*Également,*' he said.

'Okay.' I leaned into him. His body felt wonderful: hard and strong and very desirable.

'That's what you say, Nicole.' He blinked slowly at me. I could feel the palm of his hand and every one of his fingertips splayed warmly on my naked back.

I shrugged languidly. 'Okay.'

He frowned. '*Non*, I mean that's what you say when I say "*je t'aime*". You don't say "*je t'aime aussi*" You say "*je t'aime également*".'

I gazed into his eyes and took another sip of Champagne. 'Okay. Sorry, I wasn't aware that we were also going to have a French lesson tonight.'

His frown became more quizzical. 'Did you take some of your drugs, Nicole?'

I nodded. 'Uh-uh.'

'How much?'

I shrugged. It was another indolent shrug. 'Oh, you know. Enough.'

He glanced at my glass. 'Is it okay to drink more Champagne with the drugs, Nicole?'

In the early days of our relationship, I'd explained that it wasn't a good idea to mix diazepam and alcohol. But following the chainsaw demi-massacre and what were now becoming fairly regular blood-soaked nightmares, I'd found that the combination was good for keeping them at bay.

'*Pffff.*' I expelled a little air from between my pouted lips. I had mastered this ubiquitous French exclamation, the one that ought to have its own alphabetical symbol because it's such a part of everyday speech, usually preceded or followed by '*bah*'. I was still working up to inserting '*bah*' into my discourse for fear of sounding inauthentic. 'Of course! So long as I don't drink too much.'

He pursed his lips. His mouth was so perfect it made me want to kiss it, so I did, very softly.

His eyes narrowed. 'How much is too much, Nicole?'

The twenty questions were becoming tiresome.

'Look, darling *également* man, I'm fine. I'll only drink water from now on, okay?' I made big eyes at him.

He gave me a little smile, but it was sceptical.

As well it might be. Because he wasn't where I'd left him when I returned from the loo, and I'd happened to meet a very charming waiter on my way back who'd persuaded me that another glass of Champagne was just what I needed.

I decided that sitting down while I drank it might be a good idea as the crowded salon was becoming a bit blurred and my eyes were feeling heavy. There was a sofa in the far corner of the room and I glided over to it, smiling serenely at anyone I passed too close to. It was bliss to sit down after standing for so long, and I thought perhaps no-one would mind if I slipped the Louboutins off and tucked my feet under me. I glanced at my watch and saw it was 11.25. I yawned. I felt very sleepy.

Suddenly the sofa depressed heavily next to me and I felt a hand grasp my thigh in a very proprietary manner. Then I heard it, the nasal Glaswegian whine in my left ear. 'Eeeeeh, heeelloo there, gorgeous gerrrrrrrrellll.'

Randy Uncle Harry's impenetrable Glaswegian accent assaulted my eardrums. His bulbous red nose and watery blue eyes were unpleasantly close to my face as I turned to him and simultaneously removed his hand from my thigh. He put it back immediately.

'Harry.' I stared at him. 'Please take your hand off my leg.'

'How are ye, lovely gerreelllll? I didnae see ye a' feerrrsst, sittin' 'ere all o' yer ooown.' He was now running his hand up and down my thigh, squeezing it quite hard.

I decided that merited the broken-finger method of discouragement. I grabbed the middle finger of his intrusive hand tightly and bent it back as far as I could, smiling sweetly at him as I did so. Pain moved swiftly across his face, he opened his mouth to exclaim – and was suddenly hauled off the sofa by D'Artagnan.

Harry's feet did not touch the floor as my knight in shining armour (limping heroically, of course) transported him across the room and into the nearest wall, dislodging a picture in the process which fell on the floor, smashing the glass.

I was *so* thrilled. What had previously been a situation that I'd been perfectly in control of was now a major incident that everyone in the room was aware of.

Guy's cousin Benoît crossed the room quickly to rescue his father when he saw D'Artagnan in full alpha-male mode. It was irritating; I am very accomplished at avoiding unwanted attention, and Harry's version of it was very amateur. One of my earliest memories of the glamorous world of modelling was when I'd been booked with a (notoriously lecherous, I later found out) photographer for the first time. While the make-up artist had been attending to me, he'd unzipped his jeans and quite casually, as if it were completely normal, buried his penis in my hair at the back of my neck. The make-up artist had rolled her eyes at me in the mirror but I'd been horrified; I'd instinctively elbowed him in the balls and he'd collapsed on the ground.

Everyone told me that was a stupid thing to have done, that it would harm my career, that he would refuse to work with me again if the agency booked us together. But he *did* work with me again, and his penis and I never had any other altercations after that.

I was seventeen.

After the initial excitement, everyone in the room lost interest in D'Artagnan's defence of my honour. The volume of music and noise increased. My husband was still oozing testosterone as he returned to the sofa and held out his hand. I took it reluctantly and he pulled me up, holding me under the elbow while I slipped on the Louboutins again. When I finally stood up and glanced at him, he was scowling at me.

'Why are you sitting there, Nicole? Why did you not come to find me?'

I blinked at him wearily. 'I was a bit tired.'

His eyes narrowed.

'Oh do stop with the alpha-outrage, D'Artagnan.' I sighed. 'It's Harry, for fuck's sake. I can handle him.' I gave a dismissive wave.

'You are drunk, Nicole, and I don't want another man touching my wife, *merde*!'

I tried to control my eyeroll. 'It's New Year's Eve, sweetheart. Everyone's a bit drunk.' He continued glaring at me.

A waiter passed tantalisingly close by with a tray of lovely, sparkle-filled glasses. I lifted my hand to signal to him, and D'Artagnan grabbed my wrist. Suddenly I was very wide awake. 'Don't you dare do that!' I hissed.

He did not let go of my wrist and I locked my eyes furiously on his. 'I *want* a glass of Champagne, Guy.'

He released my wrist but his mouth was in a tight pout. 'You are drunk, Nicole,' he repeated. 'And you have taken Valium. You should not drink any more – you are not in control!'

I made wide 'what the fuck did you expect' eyes at him. 'It was your idea that I should come to this party, remember?'

'This is my fault that you are drunk?' He inclined his head to one side, eyes wide.

I looked away and shrugged. The anger dissipated as quickly as it had risen. 'It's no-one's fault, Guy. It just is what it is.'

He didn't say anything for a long while.

'*Cinq minutes!*' someone shouted. Several people whooped loudly.

I did not meet his eyes as I thought, not for the first time: *How is this ever going to work between us? Insanely addictive sex aside, our world views are vastly different. He treats a near-death experience as if it were a bothersome paper cut, while I'm sinking in a mental quagmire, over-medicating myself to suppress what seems an irrevocable slide into some sort of breakdown, triggered by something that happened to him – not me – more than two months ago!*

'*Je t'aime*, Nicole,' he said quietly. He touched the side of my face with the back of his hand so softly that my eyes instantly pricked with tears. 'Please, *mon amour*, please let us not start the New Year angry with each other.'

I looked up at him. His dark eyes were so serious. The ten-day stubble around his expressive mouth was just starting to grey and his light-brown hair was brushed back off his temples. He was so gorgeous.

The countdown to the New Year began. We stared into one another's eyes as everyone chanted the numbers '*dix, neuf, huit, sept, six, cinq, quatre, TROIS, DEUX, UN... BONNE ANNÉE*!!'

'I love you so much, Nicole. I can't live without you.' His eyes were mesmerising, shiny with moisture.

And I succumbed because, even though it was all so complicated, I couldn't imagine my life without him either. I touched his face gently and I said, '*Également, mon amour.*'

That made him smile the loveliest smile, and we kissed, very softly, and he said, '*Bonne année, ma belle, merveilleuse femme*,' and I said '*Bonne année*, D'Artagnan, my love.' We kissed again and his arms tightened around my body. I slipped my arms around his neck and the kiss became more intense, and then it became *very* intense indeed, and by the time we finally broke off I was glued to him. I could feel his heart beating against my breasts and I could feel him hard against my stomach.

'Shall we go upstairs, *mon amour*?' His voice was slightly breathless against my ear.

We did. It was a very pleasant way to start the New Year.

***

The following day was New Year's Day brunch. Guy and Françoise spent the morning in the kitchen with much scuffling, giggling and occasionally heated arguments about the best way to cook whatever traditional French dish was obligatory on New Year's Day. In any event, it was going to involve *foie gras* and oysters. The rest of us helped set the table in the formal dining room, carried through the serving dishes and placed them on the mahogany sideboard so that we could all serve ourselves.

Happily, Darth Vader and the Arch Bitch had left early to drive back to Paris, and Randy Uncle Harry had returned to the *pied-à-terre* his family kept in Bordeaux, so the opportunities for New Year's Day conflict were significantly reduced.

By the time we sat down to eat it was nearly one o'clock and D'Artagnan was circulating with yet another bottle of Champagne. I put my hand over my glass when he motioned towards it with the bottle. He smiled smugly at me. '*Un peu fragile ce matin, mon petit trésor?*'

I made withering eyes at him. 'No, just a bit tired, light of my life.'

His smugness did not falter. 'Would you like some *jus d'orange* instead, *mon petit ange?*'

The sarcasm was beginning to fog up the room so I ignored him and reached for the jug of tomato juice. I had already imbibed more than enough sugar-coated sweetness.

D'Artagnan sat next to me after he'd passed me a bowl of soup from the tureen. 'I make you the special soup that you like, *mon amour.*'

His eyes were soft. The stubble suited him. For some reason (I suspected it was because he'd turned fifty in early December), he'd decided just before Christmas to shave off the beard that I had always known him to have, and my skin was tender in several places that morning as a result of his stubble and the rather spectacularly good sex the previous night.

'What soup is it?' I smiled lazily back at him.

'Butternut and truffle.'

'Sorry, what?'

He frowned a little. 'Butternut and truffle soup, Nicole. You know this soup. I make it for you often.'

'Really?' I tried to suppress my smile.

Confused frown. '*Bah* – of course! I make it for you last week, for the Christmas dinner!'

'Oh! Sorry – I thought that was broccoli and blue cheese.'

'*Mais non*, of course it was not! It was butternut and truffle!'

I wondered how many more times I could get him to say 'butternut', because in French it's pronounced *'beurternert'* which I find hilarious and also rather sexy. I am mystified as to why the French, a nation that it is fair to say are pretty much food obsessed, have not invented a word for a vegetable that is popular and widely consumed in late autumn and early winter.

When I'd finished the bowl I set it aside. 'Mmmm, that was lovely soup. Thanks, my darling. I love leek-and-potato soup.'

He glanced at me suspiciously. I waited. He did not say it.

I put my mouth close to his ear. 'Go on, say it again. Say *"beurternert"* in your sexy *Frrrrench* accent.'

I didn't quite end up all the way under the table in order to get away from his expertly targeted tickling, but it was close.

After the sexy soup, I ate salad and some of my favourite cheeses with lots of walnuts on the side. Everyone else ate dead animal or dead seafood, and they all ate not-dead oysters. One eats them live, apparently. Early on in our relationship, D'Artagnan had shown me how the oyster shrivelled up at the edges when he squirted lemon juice on it before slurping it into his open mouth. I had felt ill for quite a while after that.

***

D'Artagnan's other bugbear, apart from constant musings (viz. this is a better idea, this is *my* idea and I am French *and* I have a penis) about my plans for the château renovations, was my need to learn to speak Académie Française French. I can confidently swear, sex-talk and order food in restaurants in French, but my language skills are a long way off Académie Française French. They always will be, something D'Artagnan didn't seem to be capable of absorbing.

The French that I learned to speak as a child, the language that I soaked up by hanging around with Jules and her family when they came to live in the apartment block where dear Tiffany, my alcoholic ex-mom and I lived, was nowhere near Académie Française French. I understand most of what I hear and can communicate reasonably successfully when I need to; on occasion, I can even add something useful to a conversation – but I do not, in any sense of the phrase, speak grammatically correct French.

'I think you must have some French lessons, Nicole. Proper ones to learn grammar and *conjugaison* of verbs. I will ask Benoît if he know someone.'

I resisted the urge to point out that there was an 's' on the end of knows. Ah, such fun we could have correcting each other's imperfect language skills.

Guy's cousin Benoît, the progeny of Randy Hands Harry and Aunt Sylvie (who had largely absented herself from day-to-day contact with Harry for fairly obvious reasons), lives not far from the Duchess. He owns and manages a small Cognac-producing *domaine*. He is utterly charming, has a lovely smile, curly dark hair and D'Artagnan's brown eyes. He's married to the perfectly coiffured Veronique, who I'm pretty sure is a direct descendent of the Vikings, such is her sharply bobbed blonde hair and her impressive, thrusting, 34DD chest.

As they were sitting opposite us at lunch, D'Artagnan didn't waste any time in his dual-guardianship capacity; in the first case as guardian of the sacred French language, and in the second as guardian of his ill-educated wife and her woefully lacking French language skills.

'Nicole needs to have French lessons,' he announced, breaking off a piece of baguette and popping it into his mouth.

Benoît looked a little puzzled. 'But Nicole's French is fine. She understands, and she speaks it quite well.'

I gave him a big smile and he smiled back at me. He has delightful, mischievous eyes.

'No,' said my governor. 'She doesn't understand *conjugaisons* and her French is not grammatically correct. She need to have proper lessons.'

'I know a French teacher who lives in Cognac,' offered Veronique. 'He's quite young and he taught French to my English friend's children.' She smiled at me and wiggled her eyebrows suggestively. 'My English friend thought he was *very* charming.'

D'Artagnan frowned deeply. 'No, she needs someone who teaches adults, not children.'

I raised an eyebrow and turned to him. 'Surely it's the same language, whether it's adults or children?' I knew full well that it was the '*very* charming' bit that was bothering him.

A pout was forming. He ignored me and reached for another oyster, dousing it in lemon juice before levering it free of its shell and sliding it into his mouth. I inadvertently shuddered.

'I know someone else,' said Benoît slowly, 'but I don't know if she's still taking students. She's a very old friend of mine.' His gaze dipped a little and then slid away and travelled across the room. 'She is very interesting. She taught French all over the world but now she is back in France. She lives quite close to you, about twenty minutes' drive.' There was a slightly wistful tone to his voice and his unfocussed gaze was soft, almost dreamy.

Viking Veronique frowned at him hard. She'd heard what I'd heard.

'That sounds like exactly what she needs.' D'Artagnan gave one of his approving smiles; he clearly liked the idea of a very old woman being my French teacher. I sighed inwardly and wondered if there were any yoga classes in Cognac I could go to while D'Artagnan assumed I was repeating French verb conjugations by rote under the strict gaze of a tyrannical French teacher.

'She sounds as if she will be perfect. Will you speak to her and ask her to take Nicole as a student, please, Benoît? I will pay her well.' D'Artagnan was pleased that his *My Fair Lady à la française* project was going to be realised.

I rolled my eyes and sighed – and then I caught Benoît's eye again. He was wearing that mischievous little smile that he has, and he gave me a sly wink, and I thought, *Well ... that's interesting*.

I wondered what that wink meant.

Chapter Two

We arrived back at the Duchess later that afternoon just as the winter sun was setting. It had been a beautiful winter's day with clear skies and bright Van Gogh sunshine.

The Duchess, when first glimpsed through the trees that line the meandering driveway, is quite enchanting. Her fairy tale, slate-roofed towers at either end of her sixteen-windowed façade make her almost Disneyesque in her perfection. Close up, though, it's clear she's been asleep for a while and that she's been snoring and dribbling a little in her slumbers. Her beauty is slightly tarnished.

She has not been in the best of moods since I woke her up from her last snooze, which began sometime around 1967, the last time she'd suffered an attack of 'interior decorating' at the behest of some member or other of D'Artagnan's family.

The Duchess does not like me. She was pretty pissed off about my audacious mucking about with her innards during Phase One of Project Bonjour Twenty-First Century! (subtitle: Château Renovation for Beginners: Well, *That* Was Unexpected!). Despite her ire, and D'Artagnan's inability not to interfere in every decision I made, I was very happy with the results of Phase One, which had been the creation of our luxurious bedroom suite (including Heaven) on the first floor.

I was girding my loins for Phase Two (a), (b) and (c) of Project Twenty-First Century: Still Here! (subtitle: Yes, More Than One Bathroom Per Château Is Perfectly Normal Nowadays).

We were sitting in the library that evening, Guy sprawled at one end of the cracked leather chesterfield with his bare, long-toed feet in my lap. He had stripped down to his T-shirt even though it was −3° Celsius outside. The wood-burner was burning brightly and Mr and Mrs Muffin (they had elected to retain their English titles rather than become Monsieur and Madame) were sharing the beanbag in front of it, languishing in the 28° Celsius heat that was blasting out.

Guy looked up from his phone. 'So, *mon amour*, what date are we going to have our wedding on? Françoise want me to tell her a date because she need to move the *mariage* date for Emma.'

'Immediately after Phase Two of the renovations are complete,' I said.

Some long-lashed blinking. 'What Phase Two? What renovations?'

Deep, calm breath. 'I've told you about the renovations, Guy. Replace the Peach Panoply. Create a new ensuite shower-room in the first-floor guest room. Create a new bathroom on the second floor. Redecorate the bedrooms.'

'The peach what?'

'The existing bathroom. It's vile. We've already talked about this.'

More blinking and an elevated eyebrow. 'But we have our *mariage* in front of the château, not in a bathroom.'

I pressed my lips firmly together and counted to five. 'Do you think, Guy darling, that perhaps some people might come and stay with us in the château when we have the wedding?'

Small shrug. 'Yes. It's possible.'

'And might it also be possible that in the future friends and family might come to stay?'

'Of course, Nicole.' Frown. 'Charlotte and Emmanuel already come to stay for Christmas.'

'So they did, and it was embarrassing having them in bedrooms that were last decorated when floral wallpaper was all the rage. Plus they had to share a bathroom that probably swung a bit too far, even when it was installed in the swinging sixties.'

Narrowed eyes. 'You have a little bit of an obsession with bathrooms, Nicole.'

'No Guy, I do NOT have a '*leedle beet*' of an obsession with bathrooms! But one vile, ancient bathroom for four guest rooms is not enough! Surely you remember your promise about renovations to the château? That I could do whatever I thought necessary?'

A little shrug, a little expulsion of air. '*Ouais mais...* You have spent a lot of money on the bedroom and the dressing room last year – and on the bathroom. *Mon dieu,* Nicole, you have spent a fuck of a lot of money on the bathroom!'

I gazed at him steadily. We had already had the discussion about '*ze furck*' of amount of money I had spent on our ensuite bathroom, the aftermath of which had resulted in possibly *the* hottest sex we had ever had on the ancient, sturdy medieval dining-hall table. It still made my eyes close involuntarily and an electrical charge pulse through my body whenever I thought about it.

'Once again, my angel,' I said, taking that image and shoving it unceremoniously to the back of my mind, 'we've already had that discussion.' I took a deep breath. 'And I'm sorry, but if people are going to stay with us for the wedding – or even just visit – then I don't feel comfortable about them having to share one bathroom. We need to renovate the château – we need to bring her into the twenty-first fucking century!'

Long, insolent stare. 'A château is not a "her", Nicole. It is masculine, it is *le château* not *la château, mon ange*.'

There was nothing within my immediate grasp to throw at him so I raised my slippered foot instead, intending to ram it into his groin. He grabbed it and grinned.

'This is why you need to have some French lessons, Nicole! Benoît promise me he will phone this woman tomorrow to make a rendezvous for you.' He did not let go of my ankle.

'Guy, you're deliberately changing the subject! You know what you said – I know you know what you said!' I paused and frowned. 'Is there a problem with that now? Is there a problem with money for the renovations?'

'*Pffff, mais non*! Of course there is not a problem with money!' He paused. 'Except now I decide to sell the flat in London so that I can invest more equity in the joint venture.'

Once D'Artagnan had snared his unsuspecting new wife, he had unilaterally decided it was time to return to *la belle France*. He took early retirement from the League of Masters of the Universe (aka investment banking) and invested his fortune in a joint property development business with Guillaume, an old school friend, who was also an ex-Master of the Universe.

Their initial development project was the conversion of several old wine-storage warehouses that Guillaume had inherited, into apartments. The warehouse development was in a very trendy part of Bordeaux and happily, we would be keeping one of them. D'Artagnan wanted an apartment in his birth town, with which I had very rapidly fallen in love. It had pavements and shops and yoga studios and vegetarian restaurants – and a distinct and very welcome lack of mud. What wasn't to love about Bordeaux?

I gazed at him. 'So what does that mean? Is there no money to do any more renovations to the château?'

'*Mais non*! Of course there is money, *ma chérie*!' He blinked a few times at me, and then removed my slipper. His hand was warm against the underside of my foot, his other hand still clasped strongly around my ankle.

'But Nicole, no more bathrooms that cost sixty thousand euros, okay? Promise me that, otherwise I tickle you.' He grinned wickedly as he gently ran his fingers across the arch of my foot. I yelped and tried to yank it out of his grasp. I'm very ticklish. 'Promise me, Nicole, no more expensive bathrooms and dressing rooms, okay?'

'Okay, okay!' I eventually managed to wrestle my foot away from him. I settled back against my end of the sofa and pulled my slipper back on. But I still felt that I needed to say it. 'Should I use some of the money from the sale of my flat for the renovations if you're tying up all your money in the joint venture with Guillaume?'

'*Non*!' he said crossly. 'Nicole, stop asking me about money! There is plenty of money, *mon ange*, just don't be ... *archi-extravagante* with the renovations, okay?'

I didn't really know what *archi-extravagante* renovations meant. Since he seemed unwilling to discuss actual numbers, I decided that as long as the renovations to the rest of the château came in below what I had spent on our bedroom suite, it was all good. If I needed to, I'd make up the difference with the money from the sale of my London flat, even though that made me a bit anxious. What if everything went tits up between D'Artagnan and me at some point? The money in my savings account was all I had in the world; although in theory the Duchess belonged to both of us, it was only because he'd orchestrated our marriage a few weeks before he'd inherited the château. The idea that I 'belonged' in the Duchess – or even more laughably that the Duchess in some way 'belonged' to me – was faintly hilarious.

I was also aware that the Duchess had no intention of being coaxed quietly into the twenty-first century. I knew she was plotting something unpleasant for me in the Peach Panoply; on several occasions there had been a large, yellowy-orange puddle smack bang in the middle of the hideous lino that covered the bathroom floor. Try as I might, I could not find its source. I tried to keep from my mind the very vivid image of the Duchess in human form lifting the slightly tattered skirts of her ballgown and squatting in the middle of the floor to pee, because that was uncannily what it looked like.

True, I do have an active imagination, but I'm quite certain of the Duchess's presence. I reckon she hangs out with the musketeers in the medieval dining room – and she's *very* bawdy.

***

'Yeah. No, he's fine. Much better. He's still limping around like Quasimodo, but he doesn't seem bothered by it. You know what he's like, Jules, he doesn't seem to understand that he's mortal.'

I was lying on the chesterfield in the library and the Muffins were, as usual, sprawled in front of the wood-burner. I gazed into Jules' blue eyes on the computer screen. We had been best friends since the age of seven; I pretty much don't have any other friends. I missed her so much – her easy laugh, her irreverent sense of humour, her spontaneous hugs – and I missed her funny, awkward husband Mark. I missed their kids Katie and Josh, the tight, unconditional embrace of their small bodies, the soft perfectness of their cheeks when I kissed them. I missed their happy, uncynical enthusiasm for life, for the world.

'Well, that's brilliant, Nicky darling.' Jules blinked at me and smiled. 'And you? How're you feeling?'

'Oh, you know ... fine?' I took a sip of my wine. 'A teeny bit anxious at the moment but I'm, y'know, medicating that away. I have a brilliant doctor here – actually, he's D'Artagnan's family doctor. I just have to tell him that I need diazepam and he goes "Okay, how much?" and writes the prescription. Then we have a long chat about life and his latest exotic holiday. It's *so* much better than all that bullshit I had to go through in London to get a prescription.'

I took another sip of wine. Some of it sloshed out and dribbled down my chin. I rolled my eyes and grinned as I wiped it away.

Jules took a controlled, non-sloshy sip of her own wine and asked softly, 'Are you taking a lot of Valium, babe?'

She knows almost everything about me. She knows about Tiffany, my alcoholic ex-mom. She knows about Karl, my heroin-addict ex-boyfriend, who broke my heart in a trillion places after he'd conscripted me into his velvety underworld. Jules knows it took nearly two years for me to get clean, and she also knows how devastated I was when the first and the second and the third IVF treatments failed after Karl and I started trying for the children we'd always talked about. But there's some stuff Jules doesn't know because sometimes there's a limit to how much trauma and misery you can ask your best friend to bear.

'Not "a lot" exactly,' I said, frowning. 'But, well, sometimes... It's kind of weird, Jules, but my brain flashes up shit when I'm just – I dunno – sitting on the loo or putting the Muffins' bowls down or just walking from one room into another. It's kind of annoying.' I took another sip of my wine, being careful not to spill any of it this time.

Jules blinked; it was slightly delayed as the video-call streamed. In the background I could see their kitchen, the layout of which I knew so well. I'd stayed with them in deepest, darkest Bucks (actually, it's only about ten kilometres from Marlow) for about six months after I'd returned from Ireland after the hiking incident nearly five years earlier. I'd looked after Katie and Josh when they were little; it had been a bittersweet experience. I had accepted that I was never going to have children and at the same time I delighted in them, in their inquisitiveness, in their innocent beauty.

'What sort of shit, Nicky?'

I did a big '*Pfffff*'; I even considered doing a '*bah*' to make her laugh. Juliette is French; her family are from the Ile de la Reunion. Even though English is her first language, she has absorbed all of the French linguistic mannerisms.

'Oh, you know, the favourite one at the moment is when I'm sitting on the floor in the *salon* and D'Artagnan is unconscious in my lap, and there's blood like... *everywhere*.'

As I sipped the last of my wine, I realised my eyes were glassy. I looked away while I reached for the bottle on the floor next to the sofa.

Jules was blinking very rapidly at me; either that, or the streaming was struggling. 'Nicky, babe, you're suffering from PTSD,' she said. Her blue eyes are very violet blue. She looked so pretty with her heart-shaped face framed by dark ringlets.

I frowned and tried to pour some more wine into my glass without spilling any. 'Really? You think so?'

'Yes, babe, you are. It's normal.'

I put the bottle down again and successfully raised my rather full glass. I took a deep sip. 'It wasn't me that nearly died, Jules. It was D'Artagnan.'

She shook her head firmly. 'It was very traumatic for you. Everything happened so quickly last year. One minute you're living quietly on your own—'

'—with the Muffins. Don't forget the Muffins.'

She smiled. 'Okay, you're living quietly with the Muffins, working nine to five in an office and having hardly any social life. The next thing, you're married to the world's most bombastic Frenchman who persuades you to leave everything that's familiar to you and move to rural France where you don't know anyone and you don't really speak the language. And then he almost dies in the most dramatic way possible.'

She raised an eyebrow as she took a sip of her wine. 'That's quite traumatic for anyone to cope with, so I'm really not surprised that you're struggling to process it.' She paused. 'Particularly since you already have some major anxiety issues.'

I stared at her. 'But Jules, D'Artagnan is completely unaffected by what happened! Seriously, he's just annoyed because he's not going to win the Tour de France this year!'

She pursed her cherubic lips in a perfect Gallic pout and raised an eyebrow to indicate her deep scepticism. 'Guy deals with things differently to you. You had such a shitty childhood that your – your standpoint when you're required to deal with trauma is very shaky. But Guy's upbringing was very solid, so not a lot frightens him. He intrinsically believes that he's in control of his world.'

I snorted. 'And then some!' I frowned deeply. 'Sorry, Jules, but I'm confused. When did being a business analyst enable you to develop such a finely honed knowledge of psychology?'

She laughed then, which made me smile. I love to make her laugh. 'Ah, Nicky, well might you ask. Well might you ask!'

'I am asking Jules.'

She smiled. She has such a lovely smile; it makes her eyes go all soft at the edges. 'D'you remember I mentioned last year that I was thinking of retraining, of doing something different?'

I nodded. 'I remember. We were on the beach at Saint Palais.'

'So, I've started reading up on psychology. I've always been interested in it, but I'm getting kind of tired of working with arseholes so I'm seriously thinking of retraining as a counsellor or a CBT therapist. It'll take about four, maybe five years, and I'll do it part-time, but by the time I've qualified the kids will be in secondary school and we'll have paid off quite a lot of our mortgage.'

My eyes opened wide. 'Wow, Jules! That's excellent! You know I've always thought you'd make a brilliant therapist! Seriously, I often wonder if I'd still be here if it wasn't for your counselling skills.'

She grinned. 'Thanks, sweetheart. But I think you'd still be here with or without me. You're a fighter, Nicky. A survivor.'

I raised a very sceptical eyebrow.

She nodded firmly. 'You are. You just need some professional help, maybe CBT to help you deal with the PTSD flashbacks. Therapy is so much better than medication. Medication just dulls everything but CBT – or even just talking about what happened – can ultimately help you to get over the issue.'

She scrutinised my face. 'And you need to start dealing with your shitty childhood, Nicky. I know it's difficult for you to think about that, but you have to. It's a large part of the reason why you struggle so much with anxiety.' She paused. 'You promised me that you'd call that therapist I told you about. Please, sweetheart, I really do think you should. She's very good. My friend recommended her highly.'

I tried hard to sound sincere. 'I'm gonna do that, Jules. Seriously, next week, when everything's back to post-New Year normal, I'm gonna ring her.'

She smiled gently. 'I think it'll really help you.' She drew a deep breath. 'But on a less serious note, when are you and the gorgeous D'Artagnan going to have the big wedding? Katie's constantly pestering me about what she's going to wear, and I need to have a date, babe, so we can plan for the summer. Pleeeease tell me you've decided on a date – you can't just keep saying "when the Duchess is presentable"!'
I grinned. 'Actually, we have decided on a date. It's the last Saturday in August.'
She clapped her hands gleefully. 'Yay! I'll book the ferry tonight! Are you nervous? I bet you are!'
I nodded. 'Yup. Dreading it.' I took another sip of wine.
She rolled her eyes. 'Oh, silly girl, it will be *wonderful*! It'll be like a fairy tale... Who would have thought it. Nicky? You, that scrawny little kid with permanently grazed knees, marrying your prince in front of his ancient French family château!'
'Who hates me,' I added.
She frowned. 'Who hates you?'
'The château. The Duchess. I've told you how much she hates me.'
She rolled her eyes again. 'You and your overactive imagination. God, I remember you and your imaginary menagerie when you were a kid... D'you remember all that? D'you remember your imaginary rabbit that went everywhere with you?'
'Yes, of course I do,' I said. 'His name was Julian.'
'Yeah, Julian, I remember now.' She shook her head. 'Man, you were a weird kid.'
'Well, you were my best friend, so you were probably a bit weird too.' I smirked at her.
'Yeah, we were both weird. Both misfits.' Her voice softened. 'But you know, Nicky, D'Artagnan is so crazy about you. He just wants to celebrate your wedding a bit more romantically than you did in that rather austere civil ceremony in Chelsea last year. I really don't think you should be dreading it. It'll be fine, it will be absolutely wonderful, and we'll all be there with you to celebrate! And Katie is *so* dying to be your flower-girl!'
I gave her a big, soppy smile. 'Y'know, Jules, if for no other reason, I'll do it just so that Katie can wear a bridesmaid's dress.'

She smiled back at me. 'It will be wonderful, Nicky. You'll see.'

***

I didn't call the therapist like I'd promised I would; instead, I Googled PTSD, symptoms and cures. I was not at all thrilled to learn that not only could recent trauma cause flashbacks and nightmares, but PTSD could also dredge the subconscious for other, older traumas.

That was already happening; apart from the various D'Artagnan Soaked in Blood scenarios, my subconscious had started serving up trailers for forthcoming features. The current two-for-the-price-of-one nightmare was where my mother, Tiffany, yanked me roughly away by the arm just as the dying, blood-covered D'Artagnan reached out for me. I woke from that one with a start as her raised hand connected with my face.

And the night before, there'd been the most terrifying one, the one that I had managed to bury for a very, very long time, the one that wasn't a nightmare. It was a flashback, a flashback sequence, the Marble Villa in Hell sequence. I'd sat up suddenly in bed, rigid, like a reanimated cadaver in a horror film, covered in sweat, wide-eyed and gasping for air. Crystal clear in my mind was the beaked, bejewelled mask and the hard black eyes behind it, the force of the slap stinging my face and ringing in my ears as if it had just happened.

I'd even woken D'Artagnan, who hardly ever wakes. He'd slipped his arms around my waist, pulled me firmly against his body, murmuring *'Doucement, doucement chérie,'* and I'd wanted to crawl into him, to bury myself in the familiar safety of his strong, warm body.

I felt a wave of nausea wash through me every time I remembered it.

***

Don't get me wrong – it wasn't all psychological drama in the Duchess that winter; there was psychological mystery, too. I was still mystified as to how the yellowy-orange puddle on the floor of the Peach Panoply kept appearing.

'It is a leak, Nicole,' said D'Artagnan dismissively, when I dragged him in to show it to him one morning.

'Yes, but a leak from where?! There isn't a trail for the leak and there's no mark on the ceiling. There's just the puddle, as if it came from nowhere – like someone peed there. That's what it looks like.'

He frowned at me in consternation. 'Nobody is doing a *pi-pi* in the middle of the bathroom, Nicole.' Pause. 'Unless one of your Muffins is doing this.'

It was my turn to frown. 'No, the Muffins don't do that. They go outside, or they pee in their litter tray. Also, it doesn't smell like cat pee. I smelled it. Cat pee has a distinct smell.'

He raised an inquisitive eyebrow. 'You smell it? How?'

'In the most obvious way one would smell something – I got down on my hands and knees and I smelled it. And it doesn't smell like cat pee.'

He started laughing then, slipped an arm around my neck, pulled me against him and kissed my temple. 'Ah, my crazy wife. You know you are a bit crazy, Nicole, if you are going around the château on your knees sniffing all of the things you do not understand. Please, *mon amour*, please tell me you are only sniffing these things, that you are not also—'

I tried to push him away but his grasp was firm 'No! Of course I didn't taste it! That would be *disgusting*!'

He carried on laughing at me, then spent the next few days suggesting that I might like to sniff everything I happened to ask a question about. I suggested he might like to sniff my raised middle finger instead.

I was still not convinced that the Duchess wasn't peeing in the middle of the Peach Panoply.

***

D'Artagnan finally accepted that there were going to be further renovations.

I called Gabriela and Camille, who had expertly and professionally done the work on Phase One, and asked if they would consider doing Phase Two. I had so enjoyed working with them; they had listened carefully to my ideas and made sensible and useful suggestions where changes were necessary. All of the stress – and there had been plenty of it – had come from D'Artagnan and his two, three, five, ten, twenty centimes' worth of opinion, advice and general interference.

And the Duchess, of course. She had made her feelings about Phase One abundantly clear.

Gabriela and Camille were due to come around to the château that morning to discuss making Phase Two happen. 'Perhaps, Guy darling,' I said sweetly, 'you should let me have the first meeting with them alone?'

'Why, *mon amour*? I am talking to the architect in Bordeaux for my project and she have some interesting ideas. I think I have some good ideas for things you want to do in the château.' He smiled that self-satisfied smile, the really annoying one.

Deep, deep joy.

Gabriela and Camille arrived around 10.30 and D'Artagnan made us all coffee. We sat around the table in the dining hall after we'd exchanged New Year's kisses. 'First,' said Gabriela, her narrow, slightly sallow face very serious, 'Camille want to propose something important to you.'

I sat up. Camille normally *never* speaks, she just mesmerises you with her deep black eyes, framed by the extraordinary wheat-blonde ringlets that fall to her waist. I had never met anyone like Camille; she is fae, magical, as if she isn't really of this earth. But as she started to speak hesitantly, I realised that she was actually very shy and that was why her partner Gabriela normally did all the talking.

Camille looked down while she spoke and fidgeted with her hands. Occasionally she fastened her black eyes on mine or on Guy's then instantly looked down again. She spoke in French with a heavy *Occitanie* accent (she's from the Camargue region) but slowly, for my benefit. I was thrilled that I understood most of what she was saying because, on the rare occasions I'd heard her talking to Gabriela, I had been completely mystified as to what language she was speaking. It hadn't sounded French or Spanish or Portuguese (Gabriela is Portuguese); it had been indecipherable.

'I have two horses,' she said, hesitantly. 'They are with my brother in Camargue, but he is selling his land and moving to Spain. I don't want my horses to go to Spain. I miss my horses. I want them to be here with me, but Gabriela and I don't have land for them. I want to know if you would consider letting us keep the horses here at the château. We would repair all the fences around the paddocks and make a new shelter for them. We would pass by the back of the château so that we do not disturb you when we come to look after them. In return, Gabriela and I will look after your château and your cats when you are not here, and we will pay you for their keep in the paddocks.'

'No. Never,' Guy said instantly, as soon as she stopped talking. '*Hors de question,*' he added.

I turned to stare angrily at him.

'You will not pay anything. I am very, very happy to have your horses come to live at the château, Camille. My grandfather always had horses here, and I had my own horse for many years.' I thought he looked a bit wistful. 'We would be very happy to have your horses here, but you may not pay anything. Although it would be very useful if you would look after the château and the cats when we are not here.'

Camille's eyes widened and she started to smile. 'Really, Monsieur du Beauchamp? You would really be happy with this?'

'It's Guy, Camille. Please call me Guy.' I could hear the warmth in his voice.

She regarded him intently. 'Are you sure you would be happy to do this, Guy?' She tried out his first name hesitantly.

He frowned a little. 'Of course, Camille. I would not say it otherwise! I told you, when I was young there were always horses here at the château and I miss not seeing horses in the paddocks.'

That was news to me.

Camille's expression was still slightly concerned. 'So why don't you have horses now, Guy?'

Big Gallic shrug. 'It's difficult, Camille. The horse that I had ... she was very special, and I had to leave her when I went away to Paris to study. She got sick one day, a very bad colic, and my grandfather had to put her to sleep.'

Their gazes were locked. 'That must have been very hard for you,' Camille said finally.

I watched D'Artagnan's face. He looked more vulnerable than I'd ever seen him, which was *really* weird. I had not known he'd had a whole Hi-Ho-Silver! childhood. Then again, there was so much I didn't know about him. But being on the planet for fifty years, he must have experienced quite a lot of stuff by the time I met him. I was only thirty-seven and I'd experienced way more stuff than I'd wanted to, stuff I hadn't told D'Artagnan (or anyone) about, so it wasn't surprising there was plenty I didn't know about him.

I kind of liked that.

Guy gave another shrug. 'It was, but it was a long time ago. Now I am living in the château with my beautiful wife—' he turned and smiled softly at me and I smiled softly back at him '—sometimes I think about getting another horse, even though I know it's a lot of work to keep horses.' He paused. 'My son has a horse that he keeps outside Paris. We've been talking about going to Argentina one day to ride across Patagonia on Criollos. Do you know this breed, Camille?'

She nodded. 'Yes, I know them. They are descended from Spanish mustangs.'

D'Artagnan inclined his head. '*Ah bon*? I didn't know that.' He paused, and then asked, his voice curious 'And your horses, what breed are they?'

Her black eyes shone as if they'd been lit from behind by a galaxy of love. 'They are Pure Race Espagnole.'

'Oh.' It sounded like he'd had almost had a little orgasm. I stared at his profile, at the aquiline nose and the slightly hooded eyes. His full lips were slightly parted. 'The most beautiful horses in the world,' he breathed.

'Yes, they are,' Camille breathed back at him.

I glanced at Gabriela across the table and she lifted her eyes to the ceiling.

D'Artagnan and Camille then started speaking a new foreign language where only the occasional words – *cheval* or *chevaux* – were discernible. It was very intense and passionate. I knew nothing about horses apart from that they are very big, they run fast, they jump things, they live in stables and my God, can they poo!

Karl and I had once seen the Changing of the Guard at Buckingham Palace. (I'd memorised the poem as a child and can still recite it in its entirety; I'd always longed for an Alice of my own.) We'd staggered out of a Brixton nightclub at about 7am, completely off our faces, still wired on E and coke, and barely able to hear after a night of deep house. We went for breakfast in a greasy-spoon caff in Vauxhall then decided to walk home to his flat in Mayfair. We happened to wander past the palace just as the Changing of the Guard was happening. One of the horses passing close to us had lifted its tail and an *enormous* amount of poo had come out.

Voilà, the sum total of my horse expertise. D'Artagnan and Camille clearly had a lot more experience than that.

Eventually they shut up and we got back to the important topic of renovations. I was delighted at the thought that we would be seeing more of the two of them, probably on a daily basis. I felt so comfortable around them, even though Gabriela could sometimes be quite dour and disapproving and Camille was – well, weird most of the time. But I loved their female warmth and their knowingness when we exchanged glances about whatever inappropriately sexist assumption D'Artagnan had just unconsciously expressed. I loved the camaraderie that I felt with them, even though we didn't share anything close to a common cultural background. My instincts are highly honed, and I'm very sceptical about the human race, but they were good people, people that I felt instinctively would be friends for life.

And they *loved* the Muffins and would look after them when we went away! Yaaaaaaay!!

After yet another coffee, we went upstairs to discuss how we might further disembowel the Duchess. At that point, D'Artagnan started being annoying and opinionated again. I lost count of the number of times he said, '*THREE* extra bathrooms Nicole?!' and the number of times I replied, '*NO*, Guy, *TWO* extra bathrooms and the *replacement* of the peach-coloured horror!' without losing my temper once.

Gabriela's subtle arbitration skills resurfaced during our chat; she knew exactly how to handle D'Artagnan. By the end of the morning we had agreed a timetable, starting with the dismembering of the Peach Panoply, the creation of a new ensuite in the largest guest bedroom and the redecoration of all the guest bedrooms on the first floor. Thereafter, the second floor would be gutted, a new bathroom created between the two bedrooms and all of the corridors and stairwells redecorated.

'How soon do you think you can do it all?' I asked anxiously. 'By the summer? July? August? Late August?' I was gnawing the edge of my thumbnail.

Camille looked at Gabriela, Gabriela looked at Camille, and Guy made a face at me like I was some crazy bitch that had just escaped from the asylum.

Gabriela fixed me with her dark eyes. 'I think it is possible to do by August, Nicole, but it is quite a lot of work. We can probably start early in February after we have made the paddocks ready for the horses. But you will need to order the fittings for the bathrooms – you will need to choose the showers, the baths, the basins, the tiles and all of the things we will need as soon as possible. These things can take some time to be delivered.'

I could not help but smile at that. My level of cynicism when it came to French deliveries was higher-intermediate by now; I wasn't yet an expert, but I wasn't far off. I had already spent hours researching online and days leafing through catalogues. I was *summa cum laude* on bathrooms, and I was ready to push the 'buy' button on the many bookmarked websites.

'But yes, it is possible,' Gabriela continued. 'I think it can be done. We will make it happen for you because you have made Camille so happy with this possibility of bringing her horses here to Charente to live close to us.'

She gave a big smile, the biggest smile she had ever given me. She smiled at Guy too and, as she turned her melancholy Portuguese eyes on him, I knew he was really pleased to be on the receiving end of one of her rare expressions of pleasure. Camille blinked her black, sparkling eyes at us and grinned; she looked thoroughly delighted.

I was so happy that day, and I floated around the Duchess on a little cloud of serenity. I didn't even get stressed when she spat the washing-machine hose out from its housing and all the soapy water in the wash cycle spewed over the utility-room floor. I gaily mopped it up and I even winked at her. I knew she was sitting up there on the old oak beam that crossed the room, glaring at me, her hair escaping untidily from the ragged confection on top of her head.

Chapter Three

'Well, unless she lives in the middle of a *fucking* vineyard, you wrote the address down WRONG!' I shouted down the phone at Guy. I had put the address he had given me for Bérengère, my new French teacher, into the satnav and my car was insisting that a dirt track in the middle of a field of neat, bare vines was her home.

I contemplated further sarcastic phrases about very, very tiny houses and even tinier people living in them, but instead just breathed angrily down the phone. I was already late for my first lesson with Bérengère, and I hate being late for things. It gives a very bad impression and I hate giving bad first impressions.

'*Bah,* Nicole, I will look again but I am sure it is right...' D'Artagnan sounded relaxed, his voice mild, unbothered.

That just made me more cross. I would rather that he was shouting back at me, that he was equally annoyed.

He read out the address to me in French because numbers are always easy to understand in French when you're annoyed and late. '*Quatre-vingt-onze rue des Vignes. Donc, t'as raison,* Nicole. There will almost definitely be some vines there.'

'In English, please, Guy. Numbers are difficult in French,' I growled.

'Ninety-one, *mon amour.* You know, Nicole, this is why you need to have some lessons in French.' He sniggered at his own joke.

I contemplated bashing my phone's (or indeed my own) brains out on the steering wheel with frustration. I might not have very regular periods but by God, I am capable of epic PMT.

'You wrote down ninety-fucking-*SEVEN*.'

Snotty, now. 'No, Nicole. I know how to write numbers down. Numbers is what I do, what I do all of my life. I write ninety-one down.'

'Well, it looks suspiciously like ninety-seven when I look at it – and I am looking at it! The one looks like a seven, it has a long sweep in front of it.'

A sniff. 'That is how we write "one" in France, Nicole.'

'Oh my God,' I breathed down the phone. 'As if the language isn't difficult enough on its own, you have to muck about with ordinary Roman bloody numbers as well?'

'They are not Roman, Nicole, they are Arabic. The origin is Arabic.'

I raised my eyes to the leaden sky and prayed, begged, *prostrated* myself for just one tiny bit more patience.

'Actually my darling husband, light of my life, I don't really have time for a discussion on the history of numbers and where they come from because *I AM ALREADY FUCKING LATE FOR MY LESSON*! What I really need to know whether it's ninety-one or ninety-seven, Road in the Middle of Nowhere with Vines?!'

An annoyed inhalation, as if the conundrum might be starting to irritate him, too. 'It is ninety-one, Nicole.'

'THANK YOU.'

It is very unsatisfying hanging up angrily on a mobile phone. One just presses a button and there is silence. I resolved to find a way to add the sound of a volcano exploding or a meteor hitting the earth whenever I hung up angrily in future.

***

Bérengère was *wild*. She had long silver-grey hair that hung to her waist and she was wearing a floaty purple cheesecloth top, a loose, sheepskin-lined suede coat, and a long dusty-pink skirt over scuffed cowboy boots. Her dogs – four, maybe five of them – ran around us as she embraced me when I finally arrived.

I apologised profusely for being twenty minutes late and explained that I had got a bit lost without going into detail. She did a perfect, languorous Gallic shrug. '*Ça n'est pas grave*, Nicole,' and she smiled a lovely slow smile. Her pale grey eyes were friendly and warm. I guessed she was in her forties. Or maybe fifties? Sixties? It was impossible to say. The long grey hair was misleading because her face was youngish and her easy smile was youthful, charming.

She introduced me to her dogs. There were five, three big ones and two smaller ones. They all bared their teeth at me, their tongues lolling out of their mouths. One of the bigger ones, white and black with a black patch over one of his blue eyes, brought me a ball and dropped it onto my polished Saint Laurent boot, where it left a large globule of saliva. He/she looked up at me expectantly as I smiled gingerly at it. There was no way I was going to touch the slimy ball.

'Come, come inside. It is cold outside, Nicole.' Bérengère took my arm and led me into her house. I suppose it could be described as rustic – very rustic. There was an enormous open fire in the stone fireplace in the kitchen and a collection of copper pots and saucepans hanging off the low wooden beam over the chipped cooking range. The dogs came in with us too and sat on their various beds at the other end of the room.

She motioned to me to sit down at the kitchen table and I chose a chair next to a fluffy sleeping cat. I stroked it gently while Bérengère disappeared through a low door into a dark room and returned with a bottle of amber liquid. 'We take an *apéro*. You look like you need one, Nicole. Have you tried this drink, *Pineau*?'

She showed me the label: *Pineau des Charentes*. I shook my head. 'No, I don't think so.' I frowned. 'Is it alcoholic? I mean, I am driving...'

'*Bah ouais*, of course it is alcoholic, but it is normal to take an *apéro* now, Nicole. You need to learn about France, about how we do things here. This is what I spend a lot of time teaching my students about.'

She poured me a glass of the amber liquid; it was thick and coated the sides of the fluted glass. She raised hers to mine, I raised mine to hers, and we clinked glasses. I took a sip. It tasted lovely – rich, sweet but not too sweet, with a woody undertone.

'*Santé,* Nicole. I am so pleased to meet you, to help you to learn about my country and my language, *la langue française*, the language of diplomats, of lovers.' She smiled at me again, a slightly flirtatious smile, and raised an eyebrow. 'I hope I will teach you many things in French and about France, about my wonderful, crazy country, and that you will learn some *chouette phrases en français!*'

She sipped her drink. 'From now on, we speak only in French. No more English. When you come here, we speak in French, *d'accord?*'

I smiled back at her and nodded. Feeling at ease, I took another swallow of the amber nectar. It was really nice, even if it was only 10.30 in the morning and my stomach was empty (I do not do breakfast).

Fuck it, D'Artagnan could come and fetch me from ninety-one rue de Middle de Nowhere, if necessary. I was already a little in love with Bérengère, my cool, hippy French teacher. I had an inkling that she would not be drilling me in French verb tables anytime soon, and that thought was very pleasing.

I was right. Instead, I learned how to say, '*Ah bah, dit donc,*' which basically can mean anything and also nothing, and is useful for making it sound as if you really are French. I also learned how to say '*Merde alors!* I am a vegetarian and ham is not a vegetable, no, not even in a salad!'

We laughed a lot, and I really, really liked her. A lot.

***

D'Artagnan was less impressed. 'No c*onjugaisons*? Not even of *aller, venir, faire*? I am not sure, Nicole, that this Bérengère is a good teacher. Maybe Benoît is wrong.'

I gazed at him. The only French teacher I wanted was Bérengère. 'She said we would do that the next time. This lesson was just to get to know each other. We're going to do all the *conjugaison* stuff next time. Loads of it, she said.'

'*Ah bon,*' he nodded, relieved.

'Yeah, all of that. She's really very strict! I think she only gave me some of that drink – what is the drink? She said it's the drink of the region?'

'It's *Pineau,* Nicole, *Pineau des Charentes.* It is made with *eau-de-vie* and grape juice. Benoît makes a very good one aged in the Cognac barrels. I will get some for us.'

'Yeah, so she only gave me some because she thought I was a bit stressed. Because I was late. Thanks to *you*, darling man.' But I was incapable of being angry with him any longer. I was feeling pretty chilled. I'd had only had one glass of *Pineau* so I probably hadn't been over the limit, and Bérengère had assured me that driving after alcoholic *apéros* at 10.30am was '*totalement normale*' before we'd done big Kissies and I'd left.

***

We were walking to the *boulangerie* early the following week and I was trying to be upbeat, despite having had what felt like one long, continuous nightmare of a night. I was tired, and I wasn't really looking forward to lunch with Guillaume and his girlfriend, who were stopping off on their way up to Paris. I'd met him the previous year and I hadn't liked him much. He'd been a bit creepy.

We bought croissants at the *boulangerie* to eat on the way back, and fresh, crusty *baguettes* and a *galette des rois* for dessert, even though it was the third week in January and the Epiphany, when the *galette des rois* is traditionally served, had long since passed.

D'Artagnan pointed to the cake he wanted then turned to me with a little smile. 'Maybe you get the *fève*, Nicole, then you can be the queen!' Apart from being yet another obligatory food tradition in the packed culinary calendar that is an intrinsic part of French culture, the *galette des rois* is the puff-pastry equivalent of traditional British Christmas pudding inasmuch as it also has the potential to kill you. There is always a porcelain (or sadly more often plastic) figurine called a *fève* hidden somewhere in the frangipane paste inside the sugar-coated *feuilleté* pastry.

But it was a bright, sunny winter day and I found myself smiling when I saw Marion walking towards us over the hill on her way towards the *boulangerie*. Her dog, the small black-and-white one that looked like it had been plugged into an electrical socket and never stopped barking when it met us, was running ahead exuding happiness and joy (it hadn't seen us yet). Her two boys, Kevin and Thibault, were scooting about behind her on their bikes. As usual, skinny little Nina was trailing far behind, her head down and her dark hair obscuring her face. She was brushing at the grass with a stick.

Marion and Thierry live about a kilometre away from the Duchess and are our closest neighbours. Marion has curly brown hair that is greying quite rapidly and soft blue eyes. Thierry has long blond hair that he ties back in a ponytail; it is also greying. They have an air of kindness, of gentleness, about them. They're a '*famille d'accueil*' or foster family. D'Artagnan had explained to me that it is quite common for couples to foster children in order to supplement their income, usually when their own children have grown up and left home.

At first it made me sad to think that the children had been abandoned by – or removed from – their biological parents. Then I thought that actually, they probably had quite an enjoyable life here in the countryside. Whenever we bumped into Marion, the boys seemed really happy, laughing and kidding about with one another. Little Nina less so; she was much more withdrawn, though Marion was always very gentle with her.

That morning, as every other morning when we crossed paths, we stopped and did the Kissies ritual. Guy and I exchanged kisses with Marion and we made small talk about the lovely weather, then we exchanged kisses with Kevin and Thibault who tilted their soft-skinned cheeks towards us brazenly because it's such a natural part of their learned behaviour to exchange kisses with adults. Nina was much less forward. As usual she kept her head down and did not look at us when we leaned down to her, and she looked away when I touched her silky dark hair.

My heart ached when she did that, but she didn't move away from Marion when she touched her skinny shoulder tenderly to reassure her.

***

I am fascinated by the Kissies ritual in my new country. Quite soon after we moved to the Duchess, I stopped at traffic lights in Cognac. Two groups of adolescents, mostly boys but including a couple of girls, met up at the bus stop. Without skipping a beat, they exchanged Kissies in greeting, boys with boys, girls with girls, girls with boys. I was so fascinated that the car behind had to beep as the lights had changed and I was still sitting there, gawping like an anthropologist observing a new tribe for the first time.

I love this aspect of French culture, this innate, physical acknowledgement of the presence of one's fellow human beings. Everyone does it, even the very young ones. The Kissies ritual is compulsory; it happens automatically in offices and supermarkets, on factory floors and car assembly lines. (I can't be absolutely sure it happens on car assembly lines, but it's nice to imagine that it does.) The sound of kisses being exchanged between parents, children, colleagues, in greeting and on departure is an integral part of every French morning.

In the UK, touching someone on the arm that you've just met: unacceptable.

In France, kissing someone on both cheeks that you've just met: normal.

However, something I absolutely *hate* about French culture is that immediately after you've done Kissies, you ask them how they are and they tell you that they have just been to the doctor and have been diagnosed with the plague. Or flu. Or they have a terrible cold. Full disclosure *before* Kissies, people, and a polite Kissies refusal if one is contagious. Is that so difficult?

***

I was setting the table in the medieval dining room when Guillaume and Léa arrived, so D'Artagnan limped to the door when the solid metal knocker echoed in the hallway.

Guillaume seemed taller than I remembered as he walked into the dining hall ahead of D'Artagnan. His high cheekbones accentuated his full mouth, which was fixed in the same slight sneer that I remembered from our first meeting. Had it really been our first meeting? I was suddenly certain that I'd seen him somewhere before I'd met him and Léa in Bordeaux the previous summer.

'Nicole.' His voice was so low that it almost vibrated as we exchanged kisses in greeting. 'How are you?' His hands gripped my shoulders proprietarily, and it felt like he was nuzzling my cheek when he did that creepy breathing-in thing that he'd done the last time we'd met. It felt as if he were sniffing me. I suppressed a shudder and tried to disengage myself from his touch as quickly and unobtrusively as possible.

I turned to his girlfriend and smiled at her. 'Hello, Léa, it's lovely to see you again. How are you?'

She raised her big, long-lashed eyes to mine and smiled nervously. She looked even younger than she did before: younger, skinnier and more – fragile. 'Hello, Nicole, it's nice to see you again, too.' She smelt of honeysuckle, and she looked down shyly after we'd embraced.

D'Artagnan hobbled off into the kitchen to get the wine.

'So,' Guillaume took a slow look around, 'this is where you live now, Nicole. How are you enjoying living in rural France in an old French château? This must be a very different life to the one you had before. You were a model, weren't you?' He finished his disdainful sweep of the room and fixed me with his eyes again, top lip slightly raised in the faintest approximation of a smirk.

'Yes.' I smiled brightly. 'But that was a long time ago. Now I'm very happy living here in France, thank you.'

Objectively, Guillaume is an extremely attractive man. He is tall and athletically slender, and his features are classically sculpted; the Italian half of his heritage is much more in evidence than the French half. But there's something cruel about him. He's not a nice man. Very charming, very seductive, but not very nice.

D'Artagnan has known him forever, apparently. 'We go to school together in Bordeaux, the three of us, Laurent, Guillaume and me,' he'd explained when I'd asked how long he'd known Guillaume.

A wistful, nostalgic little smile had spread across his face. 'We spend all of our holidays together, sometime at Laurent's grandmother in St Tropez, watching all the beautiful girls on the beach, sometime at Pyla with my family. And every year in February we go to Venice for the carnival, for a *big* party at Guillaume's family home.' He shook his head, his gaze slightly glazed with memories. 'Those were crazy parties. All these beautiful girls and everyone wear a mask and we have a party for three days – it was crazy! A crazy time!'

As I watched him, I had a vivid image of the three of them together. 'So the three of you just shagged your way around Europe, did you?'

He pouted slightly sheepishly. '*Bah*, Nicole, we were young – seventeen, eighteen. It is before we finish school. But after school we are not so much together anymore because Guillaume go to study in Geneva, and Laurent and me study in Paris. But then Laurent is in love with Françoise and he go back to Bordeaux, and then I meet Isabelle and we decide quite quickly to get married—'

'You don't waste much time when you decide to get married, do you?'

He grinned, raised my hand to his mouth and kissed the back of it. '*Bah, ouais,* Nicole, when I see you I decide immediately I will marry this woman.' He blinked the hypnotic brown eyes slowly at me, and for a few seconds I could do nothing but blink slowly back at him.

'So, after the Three Musketeers were split asunder by perfidious women, did Guillaume also get married?'

D'Artagnan frowned. 'No. Guillaume did not find anyone he want to marry. But he have children now, with a very beautiful Swedish woman who was a model. He meet her in New York when he work there. Or maybe Milan when he work there.' He paused and smiled, an odd, slightly confused smile. 'Sometime I think that his mother is so protective of Guillaume, I think she don't approve of any woman that he want to marry.' He shrugged. 'So Guillaume, he is always looking for these young, beautiful women that maybe one day his mother approve of.'

'He's your age, Guy,' I protested. 'Surely he no longer needs his mother's approval?'

Another big shrug, this one with an accompanying big pout. 'I don't know Nicole. I don't really understand why Guillaume continue to date these young girls but – *bah*, he is my friend. I know him since I am a child. And now we are in business together, and he is clever. It is a good investment, and we are going to make a lot of money.' He was smiling again as he reached over and brushed my hair off my face 'And then you can spend all the money on making the château like you want it to be, *n'est-ce pas, mon ange?*'

'You make it sound so simple, D'Artagnan, and yet we seem to spend an awful lot of time discussing what I want to do to the château rather than just getting on with it,' I mused.

He carried on smiling tenderly, and didn't say anything. He has very selective hearing.

***

D'Artagnan was making steak and frites for Guillaume and Léa's lunch, and grilled mushrooms and salad for mine. He didn't bother to ask either of them how they'd like their steak cooked; it was served '*bleu*' (i.e. briefly waved in the direction of the vast silver-and-blue *piano de cuisson*, or range-cooker in English, a language in which music and food are rarely combined).

Apparently, it was perfectly cooked; D'Artagnan never has any qualms about congratulating himself on his culinary skills. 'Ah, tender as the inner thigh of an angel!' he proclaimed rapturously after he'd chewed and swallowed the first bloody mouthful.

'You speak with authority, *mon ami*.' Guillaume glanced slyly at him, then shifted his gaze to mine, his dark eyes lascivious. 'Are you the angel in question, Nicole?'

I blushed and looked away. 'He says that about all sorts of things he eats.'

'No, I don't.' D'Artagnan was watching me, a roguish smile on his face. 'And yes, of course Nicole is the angel in question.'

Although I tried to smile, I felt uncomfortable at the way creepy Guillaume continued to stare at me. I reached for my glass of wine and hid behind it while I took a long sip.

Léa hadn't said a word since we'd exchanged greetings, and Guillaume was ignoring her. Although she sliced her steak into small pieces, she ate almost none of them.

'Are you from Bordeaux, Léa?' I asked, trying to engage with her.

She glanced up and flashed a shy smile at me. 'No, I'm from Toulouse. But I'm studying in Bordeaux.'

'What are you studying?'

She hesitated and glanced sideways at Guillaume. He was talking to Guy again. 'Art,' she said quietly.

'Anything particular? Fine art? Contemporary art? Photography?'

Guillaume turned slowly towards her and she instantly looked down. He watched her for a second then said to me, 'She's studying photography.' He gave a weird little smile as he turned back to her and put his hand on her leg. I was sure I saw her flinch.

After that, she answered my questions in monosyllables.

The conversation moved on, although I was aware of Guillaume's very direct gaze from time to time. I made sure not to meet to it. I frowned slightly as my brain flicked through endless stored images, searching for a match: where had I seen him before? I was certain now that I'd met him somewhere unconnected with D'Artagnan. Perhaps I'd met him when I'd been the inbred sociopath's secretary?

Soon Guy and Guillaume were deep in discussion about the next phase of their joint venture, which evidently involved

Francesca joining them. Francesca is, *quelle surprise*, yet another ex-Master of the Universe.

I knew Francesca – or rather, I knew *of* Francesca even though I had never actually met her. Her reputation, as they say, preceded her. I had met D'Artagnan when I was working in the London office of a well-known American investment bank as the secretary of the aforementioned inbred sociopath. D'Artagnan, who worked for a French investment bank, quickly came to loathe my boss. Francesca was a close personal friend of D'Artagnan's and also MD of my bank's New York office, so it had been easy for her to offer the sociopath a position in the bank's New York office when D'Artagnan suggested it. This had resulted in the termination of my employment, conveniently around about the time that D'Artagnan and I were married. I found this out afterwards – D'Artagnan had never admitted his skulduggery in so many words, but he had not denied it either.

He is very talented in the art of strategy and manipulation, my musketeer.

Francesca is Spanish-French and her family is absurdly wealthy. They own a major Spanish fashion house and several smaller French and Italian ones, a fairly famous Danish furniture chain, and have significant interests in the world of contemporary art. She and D'Artagnan had worked together on many mergers and acquisitions over the years.

At the beginning of our relationship, he used to throw in her family name in an effort to impress me, presumably because of my background in fashion. He waxed lyrical about how many hundreds of gazillions of dollars or euros or pounds or whatever the deals they had worked on together had been worth, the subtext being how very important and positively godlike he was.

I had listened indulgently when he did this, stroked the back of his hand and made conciliatory noises, until it gradually dawned on him that I was taking the piss. He was quite cross at first that I was mocking him – he would pout and I would kiss him softly if he continued to sulk. If I carried on with the kisses I could always make the pout disappear. After a while he realised his omnipotence didn't impress me at all; it was not why I fell in love with him. If anything, I fell in love with D'Artagnan *despite* his terribly important position as a Master of the Universe.

Anyway, Francesca had also decided to leave the world of investment banking and now she was bored, so she was going to become a third partner in the venture with Guy and Guillaume.

D'Artagnan had started explaining all of this to me the night before, about how Francesca's family owned half of Biarritz and that the next property development was going to be there, but I had quickly become bored and started mentally decorating the bedrooms on the second floor instead. Every now and again I smiled at Guy and said, 'Really? That's brilliant!' That seemed to work.

We had dessert and I had indeed got the *fève* in the sliver of *galette des rois* that I agreed to have. It was a small porcelain owl, and it had been stuffed rather obviously in the side of my slice.

I looked quizzically at D'Artagnan when he handed me my plate and he winked at me when I extracted it. 'You are the queen, Nicole. You can wear the crown today.'

Your reward, if you survive not choking on the *fève*, is to wear a gold-paper crown for the rest of the day. I can't help but feel that risk and reward are not quite in balance.

Guillaume smirked. 'A queen *and* an angel. You are a lucky man, Guy.' He looked intently at me and, once again, I blushed, which was extremely annoying. I shoved a large forkful of galette in my mouth and studied the tiny big-eyed owl in the palm of my hand as if it were an archaeological marvel.

We did Kissies again when they left, and this time I caught a whiff of Guillaume's cologne. It had undertones of nutmeg, a smell that I hate very much. Léa made only the most fleeting eye contact with me as we kissed; that made me want to hug her very tightly and prevent her from leaving with him.

***

And then it was February. It rained, and then it rained some more. And some more. The river Charente rose, rose, rose, spilled lazily out of its bed and continued to rise. The town of Cognac, the parts of it close to the river, were gradually submerged, and the beautiful Roman town of Saintes (with my favourite restaurant that did truly excellent vegetarian food) was badly flooded. The phrase 'climate change' was very *à la mode*.

'I think we should go to Thailand, Nicole,' said the ecologically aware D'Artagnan. 'To Phuket. There is a good resort there, where the villas have private pools. We need to go there, Nicole, next week. I need some sun. We need some sun, *mon amour.*'

I frowned at him. 'I thought there was a shortage of money? I thought we were economising?'

D'Artagnan spends eye-watering sums of money on holidays, mostly because he is unaware that one can turn right on entering an aeroplane and that it is quite a bit cheaper to do so. He also hasn't realised that there are hotels that don't feature in American Express's *Departures* magazine.

He looked annoyed. 'Why are you talking about money again, Nicole? I never tell you there is a shortage of money.'

I raised my eyes to the ceiling. 'Fine, whatever. Let's just pretend we didn't spend a good hour yesterday arguing about the cost of shower trays.'

'That is different. I ask the architect how much is reasonable to pay for a shower tray and she tell me.'

I wondered how much the architect was regretting ever meeting him, let alone signing a contract, given that every time he had a thought, however small or irrelevant, about the development in Bordeaux or the renovations to the Duchess (or, indeed, a small disagreement with me) he called her to get her detailed opinion on the subject.

I sighed. 'Shower trays aside, there's still loads of stuff I need to source and order. I haven't finished working out how the bedrooms will be decorated, or what furniture I'm going to need for them.'

We were in the library again. I was sitting at the ancient green-leather topped writing desk, working on my final plans for the bathrooms. Guy was lying on the chesterfield in a T-shirt and jeans, flicking through the channels on the enormous TV he'd somehow managed to cram into the library shelves. The Muffins were in their usual spot.

'*Bah,* Nicole, *mon amour. La vie est trop courte.* We need to take a proper holiday. I am very tired of the rain and my leg is sore with all the humidity. Maybe it is time to celebrate our one-year anniversary? It was very good last year, you remember, *mon ange*? Mauritius, the sun, the sex…?' He waggled his eyebrows at me suggestively.

'We were married at the end of March. It's February now.'

'The exact date doesn't matter Nicole. We need to have a holiday in the sun.' He fixed me with the imperial brown beacons. 'I am going to reserve the hotel. The week after the next one, *mon amour*. I want this, Nicole. We *need* this, *mon ange*.' He gave me the long-lashed, sensuous blink.

'But Guy, I haven't finished—'

'Well, Nicole, you need to finish. I will help you to finish if you want me to, but we are going to the sun next week, or the week after.'

***

We went to Thailand.

D'Artagnan insisted that we should both go to a Thai cooking class with an (apparently) world-famous Thai chef. I was sitting on the double sun-lounger by our pool, sipping my first espresso of the morning. 'But I don't really do cooking,' I protested.

'*Bah, mais* Nicole, this is a very famous chef – it will be very interesting, I promise.' He leaned against the sun-lounger and slipped his hand underneath my hair, lifting it up and twirling it around his fingers gently so that I was forced to look up at him. 'Please?' All big brown drowning-puppy eyes.

So, we went to cooking class.

He surreptitiously de-veined my prawns and de-boned my fish for me, because they were an integral part of the food we were learning to cook. I only nearly cut off my fingertip with one of the razor-sharp knives that the four of us had been rather cavalierly equipped with, and I tried to ignore the fact that my spring onions were less thinly sliced and rather more pink than everyone else's. I avoided making eye-contact with the world-famous chef, who no doubt thought I was the biggest basket case he'd ever had the misfortune to teach about food.

But D'Artagnan seemed to enjoy it and that made me happy. I ate the crunchy vegetables, which were actually rather nice, and picked out all the prawns and bits of fish and transferred them to his plate, which made him roll his eyes and shake his head a little, but we shared a soft smile as he did so.

Actually, Thailand was wonderful and it was just what we needed. It was hot and humid and, although the sun was often obscured by cloud, it kissed us both and we were both tanned by the end of the first week.

I had hardly any nightmares; it seemed that they had (mostly) not travelled with me. I managed to keep the diazepam dosage to a minimum by swimming and exercising a lot. But it rained in Thailand too, and there was invariably a tropical downpour every afternoon. It arrived suddenly, big hard drops of rain, the intensity increasing rapidly until they were a torrent, as if the sky were emptying an excess of rainwater it had mopped up earlier.

It caught us once. We'd been drowsing together on the double sun-lounger after lunch and woke as the first heavy drops splattered down. Guy leaned over me as they fell and kissed my mouth softly to wake me. '*Il pleut, mon ange.*'

I smiled drowsily, welcoming the fat, warm raindrops in the thick, lethargic heat. He kissed me again, deeper this time, and I opened my mouth and kissed him back, his mouth sultry, soft like silk. I was still half asleep but I enjoyed the sensation of his hand flat on my stomach, his thigh over my thigh as the intensity of the rain increased. The raindrops bounced off my body, off his. He stopped then, gazed into my eyes and gave me that slow, sensuous blink. I blinked slowly in acquiescence and then he lowered his mouth onto mine and we kissed again, an intensely lustful kiss.

His hand slipped down between my legs, his mouth, his tongue, his teeth on my nipples, his long fingers sliding inside me, the rain heavy, hard, deafening as I strained against him, until finally he sat back and lifted my slippery body, my legs sliding over his strong shoulders as he entered me very slowly, so hard, so deep and then withdrew and thrust again, a little faster, and then again, each time increasing the momentum until my body was arched in ecstasy against his. The rain was sluicing off his shoulders and pounding my body, his dark eyes fixed on mine as we fucked until I was overcome, gasping as shockwaves of intense pleasure radiated from my core. He groaned, a great, raw groan, as he came, and the rain continued to batter us relentlessly.

We were utterly consumed in the moment; it was as if life itself had orgasmed.

***

When we came back from Thailand, it had finally stopped raining in the Charente. And Camille's horses were about to arrive.

***

Chapter Four

The day the horses arrived is forever imprinted on my mind. As the ramp of the trailer was lowered there was a primeval shriek from one of them, a raw, anxious cry. Camille entered the trailer through a door at the front and I heard her speak in a low, soothing voice to them, then the first horse slowly started to back down the ramp.

His coat was golden but his mane and tail were the same flaxen colour as Camille's hair. When he finally descended and his four feet were firmly on the ground, he gave a loud snort and pranced a little. He looked at us and then looked beyond us, lifted his head and tossed his mane. 'So this is where you little humans think I should live, huh?' he seemed to be saying.

Camille touched his cheek and he arched his golden neck so that she could whisper in one of his pricked ears, but he pranced regally as he did so as if he were irritated at having been imprisoned in the trailer and needed to move his feet.

'*Quel magnifique cheval…*' Guy said softly, his arms around my waist. I could hear the reverence in his voice, could feel it in his taut body.

Camille seemed small next to this proud, beautiful creature, but he bowed his head to her again as if they were having a private conversation. She led him easily towards the paddock, opened the gate for him and removed his halter.

The second horse was a lot more agitated. After the golden horse had descended from the trailer, the second horse started stamping his hooves in a fast, panicked dance. My heart went out to him trapped in that closed space. I felt his anguish.

Camille entered the trailer from the front again to untie him, and I heard her speaking to him in the same low, calm voice that she'd used with the golden horse. Even so, he shot backwards out of the horsebox and half-fell off the ramp so that she was dragged behind him on the end of the rope. Then, when he had all four feet on solid ground, he stopped dead. He raised his magnificent head and shouted, a furious shout in horse-speak, and pawed the ground with one of his enormous hooves. He snorted loudly once, twice, and then circled Camille on the end of the rope, eyes wild, white at the edges.

Guy took several steps back, pulling me with him until we were at a safe distance.

The horse was very dark brown, almost black, and his body was glistening with sweat even though it was a cold day. His long, black mane undulated in waves and hung thickly below his neck; he held his tail out proudly behind his compact, muscular body. His small ears were alert but he wasn't listening to Camille like the golden horse had done; he was less interested in what she had to say, much less connected.

Finally he stopped dead and stood like a statue, raised his head high and glared at us imperiously.

'*Oh-là-là-là-là-là-là-là*' Guy murmured. (Trust me, this is verbatim; French people really do say '' *Oh-là-là*'' surprisingly often.) He held me protectively against him. '*Mais, ça, c'est un cheval sauvage, dangereux!*'.

I looked at the wild horse and I thought, no, he's not dangerous, he's just angry because he's been imprisoned in that small space for so long. And I also thought: *he is the most extraordinarily beautiful creature I have ever seen in my whole life*. I was mesmerised.

***

It was wonderful having Camille's horses at the château. The golden one was called Emperador, and the dark chocolate one was called Espiritu; they were both seven years old, and they were Pure Race Espagnole.

Camille and Guy both started to explain what that meant, interrupting and contradicting each other until eventually I just Googled it. I found that it is an ancient horse breed from the Iberian Peninsula, the breed of the Spanish Conquistador, and previously the steed of choice for European nobility (before Ferraris were invented, obvs). I read and looked at pictures while Camille and Guy continued to bicker about exactly where in the Middle East the bloodline had originated.

Every morning, I looked for the horses from the upstairs window at the back of the château before descending the staircase, and D'Artagnan and I stood at the dining-hall window with our coffee, watching them.

Later that week the weather improved and there was a hint of spring. The trees were still bare, but there was the faintest breath of warmth in the morning air. We started to take our coffee across the courtyard and lean on the paddock rails. Sometimes the horses were at the very far end of the paddock and sometimes they were close by, dozing in their shelter.

The first time I saw the golden one lying down, he was flat out. The gleaming browny-black one was standing nearby like a statue, glaring at us as usual. I clutched Guy's arm, panicking. 'Oh my God, what's wrong with him? What's wrong with Emperador? Is he sick?'

He turned to look at me and snorted as if I were thick. '*Non*, Nicole. He is sleeping, he is not sick!'

I frowned at him. 'I thought they slept standing up.'

'Yes, they have a little sleep standing up, but they also have a proper sleep sometime, a deep sleep on the ground. It is normal, and it is very good that Emperador sleep like that; it means he is happy here, he know he is safe. And Espiritu is watching out for danger while he sleep.'

He took my cold hand and kissed the back of it. There was a look on his face that I can only describe as reverent, and I was quite amazed that there was another living creature that D'Artagnan considered worthy of such awe. And he looked so happy. 'They are very beautiful, aren't they, *mon amour*?'

'Very,' I agreed. I could not stop staring at Espiritu.

***

I spoke to Jules later that day. She rang to tell me that her eldest brother Pascal was having an exhibition of his art at a gallery in Bordeaux the following week, and she wanted to know if we would come. I was a kid the last time I'd seen Pascal, so my memory of him was hazy, but I remembered that he had always been kind to me.

Jules' family had lived two floors down from the apartment that Tiffany and I shared, and I spent a lot of time with them. I craved the warmth of their overcrowded apartment, the obligatory mealtimes with all five kids (six, including me) sitting around the cramped dining-room table, some arguing, some sulking, some laughing, all reaching over one another to grab this or that, the rich smell of garlic and onions cooked in butter.

The apartment that Tiffany and I shared was nothing like that. The omnipresent smell was that of stale alcohol, and the atmosphere depended on which of Tiffany's limited repertoire of moods was prevalent: indifferent and bored; drunk and violent, or hungover and contrite about the violence.

I told Jules that I was in love and she laughed down the phone. 'Still D'Artagnan? My God, Nicky, you guys are permanently stuck in the honeymoon stage, aren't you?'

'Oh no, this isn't D'Artagnan. This is Espiritu. I'm completely and utterly in love with him, Jules.'

'Who the fuck is Espiritu?' She sounded slightly worried, as if I were a bit deranged.

'Ah, sweetheart, let me describe him to you. He's the colour of dark, dark chocolate. He has a compact, muscular body and long, thick black hair – and four feet. And this incredibly powerful neck that arches... Jules, I love this horse. He's so beautiful, and I'm so scared of him and he hates me. He thinks I'm an idiot! He just glares at me. My love for him is very unrequited.'

It was so good to hear her laugh. When she finally stopped, she said, 'Nicky, you are *so* not a horse person. You know nothing about horses! And they really don't go well with Louboutins! I know about this because I live in Bucks, babe. There are lots of horses here and their environment involves a lot of mud and horseshit. How the hell have you fallen in love with a horse, darling girl?'

I told her about Emperador and Espiritu and how they had come to live with us, about how we went every day to gaze upon their beauty.

'And Guy? D'Artagnan?' Jules asked. 'He was okay with this idea, to have someone else's horses live on his land?'

'Yeah, apparently D'Artagnan really loves horses. He goes all gooey-eyed and channels Byron when he talks about them to Camille. He likes the gold horse, Emperador, but he's a bit more wary of Espiritu, the one I'm in love with. Guy says he's dangerous.'

She laughed again 'Well, yeah, I suppose he does come from that sort of family. But is the horse really dangerous?'

I shrugged 'No, I don't think so. I think he's just angry – angry and a bit scared of humans.'

A long pause then Jules said, 'So you've found your alter-ego, albeit in animal form.'

I frowned. 'I'm not angry, Jules. I'm really happy.'

'Mmm. How's the therapy going?'

'Oh, you know,' I said airily. 'It's going well. I really like the therapist. We have great chats.'

There was another long pause. 'You didn't ring the therapist, did you, Nicky?' she finally said.

I felt bad. 'No. Sorry. I didn't.'

'It's okay, babe, I'm not that surprised.' I could hear the smile in her voice and that made me feel worse.

'I did Google CBT therapy, though, and I've gone through all the steps. I've made a list, and I started recording the unproductive thoughts but then—'

Suddenly my eyes were glassy again as I gazed out of the window. I was in the salon watching the sun set behind the poplar trees that now glowed a faint spearmint green, festooned with tiny new spring shoots. Mrs Muffin was curled coquettishly around my hand as I scrumpled her tummy.

I shook my head slightly, annoyed at myself. 'But then I kinda got stuck because I don't know how to create replacement thoughts. I'm stuck on that bit.'

Jules sighed deeply. 'This is why, Nicky – this is why I said to ring her. You can't do this on your own. I know you hate asking for help, but this is why people spend so long studying psychology, so that they can help people like you who've had a traumatic childhood!'

I watched as the robin that lived in the front garden and guarded his apple-tree territory rather viciously, hopped from branch to branch. He seemed particularly sprightly.

The real problem wasn't with Tiffany and that monumental pile of shite; that could probably be resolved – it would be painful but it could be done. The problem was the Marble Villa in Hell sequence; it seemed to have won an Oscar in my twisted little brain, and it was playing relentlessly in my subconscious, sometimes with variations on its theme. Sometimes the hard-eyed masked creature thrust a long, sharp knife through

D'Artagnan's chest and then, as D'Artagnan died, the creature turned to me, his mouth curled in a cruel smile, his jewelled mask reflecting the wall lights in the marble villa in hell.

There had recently been a new addition to the sequence. The first time it flashed up, I was so shocked that I had to lay my forehead against the cool marble tiles in our bathroom and count backwards from five hundred in French to try to dislodge the image.

Above the bed in the flashback sequence, there'd been an enormous painting of a Madonna and child in gold, red and blue hues. The Madonna had been looking away, as if she couldn't bear to watch what was happening.

'I do ask for help, Jules. I've always asked you for help and you've always given it to me,' I said finally.

She sighed, and I could imagine her shaking her head. 'I just think, y'know, that—'

'Look, sweetheart, can we just drop it for the moment? I understand what you're saying and I'll have a good, hard think about contacting the therapist, okay?'

A slight pause, then she said, 'Okay.' Resignedly.

'So, where in Bordeaux is the gallery?' I asked, moving swiftly on. 'Can I invite Françoise? She lives just outside Bordeaux and she's interested in art.'

'Of course you can!' Her voice was warm again. 'The more the merrier. It's Pascal's first big exhibition in Bordeaux and he's quite excited about it. Do you remember how animated he used to get?'

I didn't; my memory of Pascal was that he was tall and had dark hair and blue eyes like Juliette's. And he had a nice smile. But I was about twelve the last time I'd seen him and he was about nineteen.

'Yeah, I remember,' I lied. 'It will be lovely to see him again. Is Mark coming? Are the lovely bears coming? I miss them so much, Jules. Every time I see them, they're just a little bit bigger – soon they won't be little bears anymore!'

Jules laughed. 'They miss their auntie too, babe. But no, they can't come for the exhibition. They have school and Mark will stay behind to look after them. I'll come on my own.'

'Well, that's cool too. We can hang out together and I can show you around my new favourite city in the whole world! Bordeaux is *so* brilliant. We'll have an excellent time together.'

I was thrilled that she was coming over the following week; Jules and her family were the only things I really missed about the UK.

***

I told D'Artagnan that we needed to go to Bordeaux for Pascal's *vernissage* – this is a specific French word that doesn't have an English equivalent. Jules had explained to me that it meant 'the first night that a new art exhibition is publicly launched'.

'*Bah*, that will be good,' Guy said. 'We take a little holiday in Bordeaux, *mon amour.*' He smiled lazily and blinked at me slowly. Sometimes I wondered if that sensuous blink was a genetic thing; was it pre-programmed, or was it engineered?

We had just finished dinner and he was sitting across the table from me, one of his bare feet on my chair between my legs. It was a surprisingly warm evening for March, and the big windows at the front of the dining hall were wide open. The promise of summer felt almost tangible.

'And it is a good idea to invite Françoise, like you say – she would like this, I think. She will be interested in an artist that you know. And after, we have a dinner – you, me, Juliette, my sister, her brother the artist, if he want. This would be good, I like this idea.' He nodded authoritatively, in full agreement with his brilliant suggestion.

That, in turn, sparked a little management moment. He has these quite often; they're his equivalent of my flashbacks, only the PTSD he suffers is the result of not having minions to manage anymore, so he tries to manage me instead.

'So Nicole, why have you not done anything about the invitations for the wedding? The list I give you last week is still there on the desk in the *bibliothèque*. It has not moved.'

I was slightly wrong-footed. I had meant to put the list in a drawer. 'Well D'Artagnan, I've been quite busy ordering and organising bathroom stuff – tiles, showers, paint for the bedrooms, bedroom furniture, beds, wardrobes… You know, ordinary things people take for granted when they come to stay in one's home, dearest heart. So I haven't had time to focus on the fu—' I stopped myself just in time. 'The fun wedding celebration, yet.'

Gabriela and Camille had ripped out the Peach Panoply while we were away in Thailand and discovered an unpleasant surprise: the Duchess had been secretly cultivating the very worst kind of mushroom in the wood beneath the vile lino floor. Dry-rot mushrooms, the kind that buckle floorboards and destroy timbers. I was a hundred percent certain that they were directly under the spot where the Duchess peed on the floor from time to time.

That discovery had required a thorough inspection of the whole château by the dry-rot treatment people which – surprise, surprise – took them a week to come and do. It took a further two weeks for them to send their report saying that fortunately there was no other sign of dry rot apart from in the bathroom. The renovations had already been delayed by three weeks.

But there had been another renovation setback; of course there had been. The company from which I'd ordered the bathroom fittings had decided they did not want my business. They had cancelled the order and, even better, decided not to tell me they'd cancelled it until I phoned them to ask why I hadn't been given a delivery date.

I spent most of the call making a conscious effort not to smash my phone repeatedly against my forehead. The woman I spoke to was very sympathetic, apologised sincerely and encouraged me not to take it personally. She explained that it was a '*berg*' that had caused the problem.

'A what?' I asked in French.

'*Un berg dans la système informatique,*' she replied.

I was none the wiser. WTF was a '*berg*'?

'Don't worry,' she continued cheerfully. 'I'll reinstate the order now, if you like.'

Faced with the choice of having to research and find an alternative supplier or throw myself on the mercy of the god of *bergs* and wait a further four weeks, I opted for the latter.

I asked D'Artagnan what '*un berg*' was.

He frowned at me. 'I don't know, Nicole.'

'She said it was *"un berg"* in the IT system. *"Un berg dans la système informatique"*, that's what she said.'
He blinked at me. '*Mais voilà*, Nicole. That is what it is, then. A *berg* in the *système informatique*. The order was not deliberately cancelled. It was a *berg*.'
I stared at him. Finally, it dawned on me. 'Oh, you mean a *bug* in the IT system!'
'*Ouais, voilà*. A *berg*.'
Who knew that Inspector Clouseau was still alive and well and living in everyday France? It made me smile for several days afterwards whenever it crossed my mind.

***

D'Artagnan's haughty gaze did not waver. '*Bah,* Nicole. You need to do these things. If the guests do not receive the invitations, there will not be a celebration. It will just be you and me. And a lot of food.' Another pause. Longer, more suspicious. 'Did you contact the *traiteu*r, the catering person that I give you the number for?'

I glared at him. 'I am aware that things need to be done, Guy. Tell you what, my busy little entrepreneur, why don't you do some of the organising?'

Deep frown. 'Men do not organise fucking weddings, Nicole. And I am busy with the development in Bordeaux.'

'Oh I *see*. I didn't know it was a gender-specific thing! Silly me! Tell me, my angel, where is it written that "men do not organise *furking* weddings, Nicole"?'

A look of intense irritation crossed his face; he gets really annoyed when I parody his accent. 'Maybe, Nicole, maybe I am going to find a wedding person, someone to organise the wedding. It does not seem that you want to do this. You do not seem very interested in doing this.' He sniffed contemptuously.

I gazed at him. 'Maybe that is actually a good idea. Because *actually*, I have rather a lot of other things to organise, in case you hadn't realised.'

He sighed a big put-upon sigh. 'Okay, *mon amour*. I find someone. I find a wedding person and I give her your details and she will contact you. But you will need to meet with her, Nicole.'

'Fine, whatever. I'll meet with her.' I liked this idea quite a lot, so much so that I didn't even bother pointing out to him that he had just committed yet another sexist *faux-pas*. It was perfectly possible that the wedding planner would be a man because men do organise *furking* weddings, actually. But I just smiled sweetly at him instead.

***

Unbeknownst to me, D'Artagnan had arranged lunch with Guillaume and Francesca when we got to Bordeaux. Jules wasn't arriving until the following day so I couldn't wriggle out of it. I started to say 'Why do I have to—' and he shot me a look.

'*Bah,* Nicole, I know it is a big, big thing for me to ask you to have a nice lunch at a Michelin restaurant in the spring sunshine in my beautiful French city. I am so sorry to ask you to do this.' The sarcastic tone was quite pronounced; normally it was more subtle.

With your ex-Masters of the Universe friends who think my function is purely decorative, I added in my head.

He blinked his dark eyes at me several times from across the room. Sorry, the suite – D'Artagnan is incapable of booking a room in a hotel. I think it's a verbal tic; he believes he's saying 'room' when he makes the booking, but in fact he's saying 'suite'. And then the verbal tic forces him to add, 'Yes, with a bottle of Champagne on ice.'

I was so looking forward to our next philosophical discussion about why mixer taps cost so much money.

'*Merde*, Nicole, is this so hard for you to do?'

I took 5mg of Valium while I did my make-up in the bathroom.

***

We ate on the terrace of the hotel where we were staying. Cream linen tablecloths flapped in the gentle breeze and the occasional clink of glasses or cutlery was audible above the low murmur of conversation. The air was warm and the sun high in the sky, obscured by carefully positioned sunshades.

Francesca and Guillaume were already at the table when we arrived. She was exactly as I had imagined her: athletically skinny, androgynously beautiful, a thick, solid-gold Cartier bracelet on one slender brown arm and an Apple watch (the truly wealthy eschew luxury Swiss bling in favour of fitness) on the other. She was super-hard, super-smart and probably spoke fourteen languages. It was clear she had never taken one microbe of shit from anyone.

I've often wondered if the graduation ceremony from D'Artagnan's elite École de Commerce à Paris involved tattooing male students' penises with the phrase: 'I AM A GOD'. (In D'Artagnan's case, the tattoo would read 'I AM GOD OF THE EARTH, THE KNOWN UNIVERSE AND EVERTHING ELSE BEYOND.') Francesca would have laughed scornfully at that: she needed no penis and certainly no tattoo. It was *obvious* that she was a god.

She took one look at me and instantly filed me under 'Arm Candy: Ignore', which was annoying but exactly what I'd expected. I leaned forward, made air-kiss noises and we exchanged '*enchantées*'. She didn't bother to make eye contact with me.

Guillaume was in full Italian mode, darkly tanned and wearing a crisp white shirt, open at the neck. As he removed his sunglasses and leaned towards me to exchange kisses, I had a sudden image of him in a white shirt with a black bowtie.

I frowned as he flashed his teeth at me and made a conscious effort not to brace myself as he once again nuzzled the side of my face as we kissed. It was far too intimate. I regretted having taken only 5mg; it didn't seem to have touched sides.

'Nicole, *ça va*? You look very lovely today. Thailand was sunny, I see.' He gave me the sort of lazy smile that D'Artagnan does but without any of D'Artagnan's warmth in his eyes.

'Thank you, Guillaume. You look well too.' I smiled brightly at him, thinking: *Fuck you, creepy git*.

He sat opposite me, smouldering behind his sunglasses, fully aware of the effect he was having on those around him. Because he *was* having an effect. There were two pretty blonde women lunching together at the table to my right and, even though they were in my peripheral vision, I was aware that one of them was staring at Guillaume most of the way through lunch. At one point she murmured something to her friend, who clumsily reached for something in her handbag so that she could turn and get a good look at him. His eyes flicked lazily over them and that nasty little sneer touched his upper lip, but other than that he showed no interest.

D'Artagnan and Francesca had immediately started gossiping in fast French after we sat down. I was conscious of Guillaume focussing on me when I asked the waiter as charmingly as I could if it would be possible to leave the (single) langoustine out of the salad I had ordered. I have learned that, in the world of French gastronomy, if one asks very politely for something that stands alone in a dish to be left out, there is a reasonable chance your wish will be granted. You have a far smaller chance of success if you ask for the sauce or the dressing or some integral ingredient to be excluded. In any event, I could always just give the giant dead sea-cockroach to D'Artagnan if it was absolutely necessary to include it.

'Your French is very good, Nicole,' Guillaume said patronisingly when the waiter left.

'Thank you, Guillaume. I'm having lessons. But restaurant French isn't exactly difficult.'

'No, you have a good accent. You don't speak French with a strong English accent. It can make the language very ugly.' He paused. 'I worry that my children already speak French with a terrible accent.'

'How old are your children?' I asked politely.

He gave a little shrug, as if it were a really boring question. 'Seven and – four or five, maybe. Two girls. They live in Sweden with their mother.'

'How ... lovely?' I offered lamely, a little shocked by his dismissive tone. How could you not know how old your kids were?

He stared at me. 'Yes, it is quite lovely. Maybe you would like to visit sometime?'

'What, Sweden?' I frowned.

'Yes, *Sweden*.' He was mocking my tone. 'It's a very beautiful country. I have a place on the islands and in the summer I have many parties. We have a lot of fun. You should come – I'm *sure* you would enjoy it.' His gaze seemed piercing, even from behind his sunglasses, and he emphasised the 'sure' very deliberately.

I was confused. Did he mean me on my own, or me and D'Artagnan? If the former, would he really come on to me so brazenly?

I asked pointedly, 'How's Léa, by the way?'

He made a very dismissive pout and gave a wave of his hand. '*Pfffff.* I don't see her anymore.'

'That's a shame.' I said, staring at him. 'She seemed nice.' About thirty years too fucking young for you, I thought, but nice. I fervently hoped she was with someone less unpleasant. Someone younger and less – evil.

He gave the faintest 'whatever' shrug. 'You should come to Sweden, Nicole.' He sat back in his chair.

D'Artagnan turned to me. He'd lit one of his rare cigarettes after Francesca's phone had buzzed and she'd broken off their conversation to take the call. 'Do you want to go to Sweden some time in the summer, *mon amour*? We can do that.' He picked up my hand and kissed the back of it, smirking a little. I wondered if he could see that I wasn't comfortable with the way Guillaume was talking to me.

I frowned at him. 'Uh, no thanks, I don't want to. Have you forgotten that someone has to organise a massive wedding celebration for the end of August?'

'Ah yes, Guy mention this to me,' interjected Guillaume. 'He must love you very much to want to marry you not once but twice! You must be a very special kind of angel.' The emphasis on the word 'angel' was drawn-out, seductive and predatory.

I took a big sip of wine and didn't say anything.

D'Artagnan touched my cheek lightly but I refused to look at him. I felt as if I were being stalked, and I didn't like it. Each time I met Guillaume, I disliked him even more – and I still couldn't place where I'd seen him before, although now I was certain that wherever it was, he'd been wearing formal black tie.

***

'Well, I don't like it! I don't like the way he is towards me, and I don't like that you think it's amusing!' I stared at Guy across the salon. I was standing in front of the French windows that were open onto the square in front of the hotel, the gauze curtains billowing into the room behind me. He was sprawled on the sofa. It was early evening and I'd had a shower and washed my hair, which was still wet.

He'd opened the Champagne and given me a glass, which probably hadn't been a good idea given that I was still angry about what had happened at lunch.

'*Bah,* Nicole, he is just flirting with you! Guillaume likes beautiful women and you are a beautiful woman. Why is this such a big problem for you?' Pouty mouth, raised eyebrow.

I carried on staring at him. 'And you, Galahad? You're okay with that?' I remembered him slamming Uncle Harry into the wall on New Year's Eve.

'Who is Galahad, Nicole?' Confused frown.

'A pure and courageous knight of the Round Table who always acted honourably and was never jealous.'

'Why do I need to be jealous? I have seen you flirt with other men, I have seen other men flirt with you. Why is Guillaume different?'

'Who have you seen me flirting with?'

'You flirt with Benoît. You flirt with the waiters.'

I was astounded. 'I don't! I have a laugh with Benoît – I tease him sometimes, if that's what you mean but I don't think I'm flirting with him! And I don't flirt with waiters, I'm just nice to them!'

'Well, maybe you don't think you are, but you are flirting with them. French people flirt all the time, *mon amour.* You have told me before that I flirt too much and I tell you it's nothing, it is just something we do naturally. We like to have a bit of that tension, that sexual tension, when we interact.'

'Well, I don't like the sexual tension when Guillaume interacts with me. It's not fun and it's not funny.'

He made a face. 'Sex is not meant to be funny, Nicole.'

I stared at him. 'Did you really just encourage me to have sex with your business partner? Really?'

He sat up, exasperated. 'No, I did not encourage you to have sex with my business partner! But I am starting to wonder – why is this a big thing for you? Why is Guillaume such a big problem? All of your life you have men look at you and want you, and now suddenly it is a problem when Guillaume flirt with you a bit?'

I thought; *there is so very much that D'Artagnan doesn't understand about me.* I leaned against the edge of the armchair and didn't say anything.

'You know what I think, Nicole?' He gazed at me steadily. 'I think the reason why you are having a problem with this is because you are attracted to Guillaume. I know he is a very attractive man, I am not stupid. And this makes you worry because you are attracted to him.'

I took a sip of my Champagne and carried on gazing at him without saying anything. D'Artagnan had already decided on the narrative, even if it was utter rubbish. I was interested to see how it played out in his head.

'But you don't need to worry, *ma chérie*. You can relax. You can flirt with Guillaume, even if you find him attractive. It's okay, because Guillaume will never touch you.'

I kept my tone level. 'Gosh, Guy, you control Guillaume too? How fascinating.'

Slightly withering look. 'Guillaume knows that nothing will ever happen between you and him, *mon ange*.'

I nodded slowly, took another sip of Champagne. 'How do you know that?'

Full Gallic shrug. 'I just know, Nicole.'

'No, I mean how do you know that he knows that?'

'It's very simple, Nicole. He knows that I will kill him if he ever touch you.'

I stared at him and he stared back at me. His brown eyes reflected the light from the window; they were very frank.

'You're not serious?' I realised I was smiling, a disbelieving half-smile, my eyes wide.

'I am completely serious.' He made wide eyes back, mocking me.

I had to look away then as incredulous laughter began rising inside me 'Oh my God, you batshit crazy, alpha French men! Can't you just live *normally*, without all the drama, without the intrigue and the overwrought emotion, the toxic masculinity? Death threats, for fuck's sake! It's not the sixteenth century, we're not living in Venice – this is real life, not a Shakespearean play!' I shook my head disbelievingly.

He watched me calmly.

'Seriously, Guy, don't you ever imagine what it would be like to live in a normal, calm, adult world where everything isn't running on super hi-octane testosterone?'

'What, *comme les Anglo-Saxons*?' He laughed scornfully. 'No, I would rather die than live like that. And you – you would not be happy with someone like this, even though you are an *Anglo-Saxon*. And don't argue about that, I don't need to hear all that bullshit about South Africa. You are descended from *les Anglo-Saxons*, you are not Latin like we are, like the French and the Italians.'

He paused 'Look at me, Nicole. I am talking to you. Don't look away. You, *les Anglo-Saxons*, you think you are in control all the time, that your world is clean, neat and organised, that you can control your passion, your jealousy, your pain. You think you can close it up in a box and pretend that everything is fine. But this is never a good way to be. It will make you sad, and you will become a sick, sad person, like that *connard* you used to work for when I met you. Sad, like you were when you leave your *Anglo-Saxon* boyfriend. Sad for all those years.'

There was a long silence. Behind me, the gauze curtains billowed languorously as I stared, mesmerised, into his eyes. I realised that I still didn't fully understand how D'Artagnan worked, either.

He sipped his Champagne, then looked at me very candidly.

'You need me, Nicole. You need all this crazy passion I have for you. It means that you can dare to let go of some control. You can dare to let go of your boundaries that say no, this is too much passion, too much intensity, too much danger, because I challenge those boundaries all the time. I don't close up any part of myself. It is why we have incredible sex, because I won't let you be *Anglo-Saxon* when I make love to you, with boundaries and rules about how much you can dare to feel. I make you let go of all of that. I have all of my emotions here, in my heart, every day.'

He thumped his chest with his fist. 'And I know them all very well. I don't try to hide them from myself. So, I don't have to be jealous when my friend flirt with my beautiful wife, I can be proud that she is so beautiful and keep that in my heart. And at the same time, I know in my heart that I will kill him if he ever touch her. And he knows this, because he is also French, he is also Latin. It's very simple.'

Our eyes were locked. I blinked first. 'My darling man, that's so wonderfully, incredibly romantic, and I agree with so much of what you've just said.'

'But?'

'But I also have two fundamental problems with what you've just said.'

He rolled his eyes and gave a big sigh. 'Of course you do, Nicole.'

He got up off the sofa and went to get the bottle of Deutz and came over to stand in front of me while he refilled our glasses. He put the bottle down on the table and reached out to touch my cheek gently with the back of his finger. 'Come, sit with me while you tell me about your problems, *mon ange*.'

He sat on the sofa and patted the seat next to him, fixing me with two beams of chocolate-coloured lust. I knew that, as far as D'Artagnan was concerned, the conversation was over and now we should have make-up sex; he wasn't particularly interested that I disagreed with his pistols-at-dawn approach to modern life.

I was determined that he was going to hear me out. I picked up a cushion and hugged it against me, then sat cross-legged on the sofa, slightly out of his reach.

'Well,' I said carefully, 'the first one is quite specific. You might enjoy the idea that your friend is flirting with your wife because you're confident it's harmless, but I really don't enjoy it. Guillaume has a way about him that isn't... It doesn't feel fun, or amusing. It feels predatory, and I don't see why I should have to deal with that. It's not as if I'm leading him on – at least, I'm pretty sure I'm not.'

Muted Gallic shrug. 'That is easy, then. Just say "Guillaume, please don't flirt with me, I don't like it".'

'And that will work?'

'Yes, I think so. He is not stupid.' He frowned at me thoughtfully. 'You know, Nicole, French women are very direct and they say what they think. If they don't like something, or don't want something, they say it. It doesn't cause offence.'

'I'm not French, Guy.'

'Yes, Nicole, I know this.' Sarcastic eyebrow at thirty degrees. 'But this is how you must learn to be with French men.

If you want them to stop doing something, you must tell them directly.'

'So if I tell him, he'll stop doing it – stop thinking about it?'

His eyes narrowed. '*Bah non,* Nicole, that is something else. You cannot stop what is in his head. If he want to think about you, you can't stop him. But that is true of everyone, of all men. Of all women, too.'

I thought about that for a minute. 'Yeah, okay. I get that.' I took a sip of Champagne. 'But the second thing is more generic. It's tied in to what you said, that you would kill him if he did anything. As bodice-rippingly romantic as that might sound to some people, it's exactly what's happening to women all over France who dare to leave their partners or who have affairs. That's really, really not acceptable.'

'I did not say I would kill *you*, only *him*.' Tight smile.

'Yes but that's such a nuclear option, my darling. It would destroy so many lives – his, yours, mine, his children's, his partner's – if he ever managed to keep one for longer than a few months. It's wildly disproportionate.'

'Are you planning to have an affair with Guillaume, *mon amour*?'

'Try and be a bit objective here, Guy. Surely you understand what I'm trying to say?'

'Are you?'

'Oh my God,' I groaned. '*No,* Guy, I am absolutely not planning to have an affair with Guillaume. It is the very last thing on my mind.'

'But it *is* on your mind?'

'Starting to get irritated with this conversation is what's on my mind, particularly because you insist on subjectifying the objective point I'm trying to make!'

'What is the point you are trying to make? As usual, Nicole, all I am hearing is you trying to tell me how I should think, that the way I feel is wrong! But it is not wrong. It just is – it is what I think. It is how I feel! And if Guillaume try to fuck you, I will kill him.'

He shook his head angrily. 'I don't understand what is so difficult for you to understand about that, and the more you talk about this subject, the more my mind is going, "Why is she talking about this? Why is she going on and on about it? Why is she trying to say I must change my mind about this? Is it because this is what she want to do?" Is this it, Nicole? Do you want to fuck Guillaume and you are just trying to see how I will react? *Putain de merde!*' He looked away from me and took a big swallow of Champagne.

There was a long silence and some very moody gazing out of the window.

Finally, I said quietly, 'If you'd listened, you'd know that I wasn't talking about Guillaume. All I was saying was that it doesn't make for a healthy society to perpetuate this myth that violence in a so-called crime of passion is in any way an acceptable and proportionate reaction.'

I wanted to say: *Because it is usually the woman who bears the brunt of that. I trust you when you say you wouldn't hurt me, but that trust wobbles a little when you make bold, violent statements like you're going to kill your friend or business partner or whatever he is, if he touches your wife. Suddenly you don't seem very rational. And if you're not rational, how can I trust what you say?*

But I thought it was probably better to stick to theory. I decided to try a different tactic. 'Let's look at it another way. You and Isabelle were married for – I don't know – how many years?'

'Twenty years.' Very sulky.

'And from what you've told me, there was minimal bloodshed when you divorced, wasn't there?'

He shrugged. 'Yes. We were not in love with each other at the end.'

'So, surely you'd agree that it is possible for a relationship to end in a calm and rational manner?'

He turned his dark eyes on me. 'Why do you think it was calm and rational?'

I had a sudden and uncontrollable urge to laugh, which wasn't at all appropriate but was impossible to ignore. Here I was, sitting next to Othello and imagining that anything to do with his love life had ever been approached in a calm and rational manner.

'Why are you laughing, Nicole?'

'So sorry, not laughing at you. Laughing at me! So stupid,' I spluttered, stuffing my face into the cushion while I howled at the ridiculousness of my supposed counterargument. When I finally stopped laughing enough to wipe my eyes, he was watching me closely. He looked faintly bemused.

'I'm so sorry, my darling.' I tried to keep my face straight. 'That was just so deadpan, the way you said that. I don't know why I've always imagined that you all played nicely together and had a calm, friendly adult divorce when you and Isabelle split up, like – you know—'

'Like *les Anglo-Saxons,* you mean?'

'Yes, I suppose I'll give you that one. That you had a nice, quiet, Anglo-Saxon end to your marriage – which I'm not laughing at, by the way. I would never laugh at that. The end of any relationship is painful and I feel awful for anyone going through it. I know how absolutely gutting it is, and I wouldn't wish it on anyone. I was laughing at myself for being so stupid as to imagine your divorce was calm and rational.'

Guy gave a subdued shrug. 'Yes, I understand this. No, it wasn't calm. It was difficult, and messy and very painful – but in the end there was nothing left. There was no passion, no love between us. It was all gone. It was very sad.'

'I'm so sorry, my darling.' I touched his shoulder gently. 'I really wasn't laughing at that.'

'I know you were not. Come here, *mon ange*, come to me. I need you, I need to hold you close, Nicole.' He reached over, pulled me onto his lap and wrapped his arms around me tightly. The faint scent of Dior, his scent, was intoxicating and I felt a surge of love for him. I leaned forward and kissed him softly; his mouth was cool and felt like satin.

He undid the tie on my bathrobe. I unbuttoned his jeans. Negotiations on appropriate levels of machismo were parked for the moment.

But later that evening, as I was brushing my teeth, I thought about it again. I thought about what he'd said about killing Guillaume, and I wondered if he really would do something crazy if I ever had an affair – not that I had any intention of doing so.

I remembered how he had chosen to say nothing when Karl had unexpectedly reappeared at the château on the day of the chainsaw demi-massacre. D'Artagnan had sat quietly on the edge of the sofa within hearing distance, blood pumping out of the deep wound in his thigh without saying a word about his injury, because he deemed it more important that I sort out the shit that Karl and I had been through when our catastrophic relationship had ended five years earlier. *That* was more important to him than the fact that he was about to – and very nearly did – haemorrhage to death.

So, I knew that Guy was capable of being abundantly, stupidly, super-alpha. That was worrying, but there didn't seem to be anything I could do about it other than – not have an affair. Which really wasn't a problem as we were almost incapable of going twenty-four hours without mind-blowing sex and, as far as I could tell, that wasn't about to change. I didn't want it to change.

***

Chapter Five

Before we went to the airport to meet Jules the following morning, we visited the renovation project in Chartrons. It was a series of interconnecting warehouses on a narrow side street, just off the semi-pedestrianised main street. The *quartier* was super-cool, super-bobo (*bourgeois-bohème*) with lots of organic restaurants, boulangeries, art galleries and antique shops.

The warehouses were covered in scaffolding. The foreman tried to get D'Artagnan to put on a hard hat but, having a head made of titanium reinforced with arrogance and coated with extreme disdain for health and safety, he ignored the request. I put one on because I'm a good girl who doesn't like making other people's jobs unpleasant, and my head is made of normal blood and bone.

There were going to be seven apartments: three smaller ones at the back of the buildings and four large ones running along the front, each with a garage at street level. Two of the three at the back were nearly finished and one of them had been temporarily designated as an office.

I wandered around the apartment while Guy took down one of the project files from the shelf in the kitchen and sat down at the desk in the open-plan area because 'I need to check something'. Presumably what kind of bog-roll holders they were going to order, with a view to future discussions that he and I might have about the cost of bog-roll holders.

Then we went to the airport and I felt a rush of joy as I spotted Jules emerging from the automatic doors. We hugged each other very tightly for a long time, her dark ringlets pressed softly against my cheek as I breathed in her familiar Chanel No. 5 scent.

When we finally stopped hugging, I held her at arms' length and we both grinned. '*Bonjour,* gorgeous girl,' I breathed. 'It's sooooo lovely to see you again!' I dived in for another hug and she laughed as we rocked from side to side.

'Ah, Nicky, it's so lovely to see you too!'

D'Artagnan gave her a big hug too, and kissed her resoundingly so that she laughed again and her cheeks flushed lightly. He took her luggage as she and I walked back out to the car park, arm in arm.

The sun was shining, the sky was blue and I was with my two favourite people in the whole world: life was good, really good, that day.

***

I remembered Pascal as soon as I saw him. He had the same sapphire-blue eyes as Jules, the same dark hair, a bit wild and very curly. He laughed delightedly when he saw me. 'Oh my God, little Nicky! I can't believe it's you after all these years!' He embraced me warmly then stood back. 'Wow, you really turned into a stunner! I remember when you were just a scrawny little thing, all big green eyes and knobbly knees!'

'Yeah, they're still knobbly,' I laughed. 'It's lovely to see you again, Pascal. I remember how kind you were to me, even though I know Jules and I were really annoying. I remember we used to steal your fags...'

'Yeah, you were thieving little brats.' He grinned and winked at me.

I turned to introduce him to D'Artagnan. They didn't do Kissies, they did hearty, manly handshakes instead, but Pascal did do Kissies with Françoise. The Kissies ritual seemed so random; how did the French know the rules, the when, the where, the who, the which side to start on, the number of kisses (because that varied as well, depending on the region)? It seemed very complicated.

The gallery was *très tendance*, very trendy, in a buzzing part of Bordeaux not far from Chartrons. There were a lot of people milling around and it wasn't easy to see Pascal's paintings, but I managed to get a look at some. One of them was amazing: a big, square canvas filled with thousands of silver-blue fish swarming in a circular shape. It was full of movement and colour. Unfortunately, I could also see that it had already been sold because there was a red dot in the top right-hand corner.

More people arrived and Pascal left us to chat with his guests. We did a circuit of the gallery with some difficulty. I only managed to stand on one person's foot, but she was very kind about it; she seemed to have quite enjoyed having her foot pierced by the heel of my shoe and waved away my horrified, grovelling apology.

I liked Pascal's art very much. We stood in front of one of his bold, almost abstract paintings depicting a brilliant blue sky and a cyclist and his shadow reflected on a vibrant pink wall. I loved the colours and the form of it. D'Artagnan seemed to like it too.

He looked at me quizzically, I nodded back enthusiastically, and he went off to reserve it – it was one of the few pictures that hadn't already been sold. Apparently, we were not economising on the art collection that evening.

Everything was sold by eight o'clock and the gallery started to empty. Quite a few people asked for Pascal's business card as they left and he looked very happy; his cheeks were pink and his eyes sparkled. He was pleased that we'd bought a painting. When we told him which one, he smiled and explained that it was inspired by the time he'd spent in South Africa. That made perfect sense to me; it was a painting that seemed to be soaked in sunshine.

As we walked to the restaurant that D'Artagnan had booked, Pascal fell into conversation with Françoise. When we arrived, they sat side by side at the table. She was laughing a lot, her pretty face lit up and her brown eyes softly creased. Pascal was laughing quite a lot, too.

I made a face at Jules and waggled my eyebrows; she made suggestive eyebrows back at me. We grinned wickedly at each other while D'Artagnan studied the seventeen-page wine list and had a deep and meaningful discussion with the sommelier which *eventually* resulted in actual wine arriving at the table.

After we'd ordered food, and the wine had been blessed by D'Artagnan (a gracious tilt of the head at the sommelier after he'd tasted it to indicate that *oui, zat would do*), Pascal turned to him. 'So, Guy, your sister tells me you're developing some property here in Bordeaux, in Chartrons. I'm thinking of moving to Bordeaux, so please tell me about it. I'm interested!'

Hundred-watt Gallic charm instantly flicked on.

Françoise had just returned from the loo as our entrée was served and she sat down as D'Artagnan explained the joint venture with Guillaume, how far along they were with the first phase and where the second phase was going to be. She frowned and interrupted him. 'Guillaume? Guillaume Martin, that you went to school with?'

Guy shifted his eyes to hers for a minute. '*Ouias*, him,' he said dismissively, then turned back to Pascal.

'You know he has a bad reputation here in Bordeaux, don't you?' Françoise's tone of voice did not change; it was still sharp. 'Are you sure you should be investing with him?'

Hooded eyes, withering pout. 'I've known Guillaume all of my life, Françoise. We went to school together.' Very slow blink. 'In fact, didn't you and he have a thing when you were teenagers? Before Laurent?'

Françoise glared at him. 'I was fourteen, Guy. It was a very, very long time ago and it wasn't for long.'

'Anyway,' said D'Artagnan, spearing a vivid purple octopus tentacle with his fork, 'what reputation? He only came back to Bordeaux two years ago. He's been in Sweden for the last eight years and before that in Italy, in America. How does he have a reputation in Bordeaux if he hasn't lived here for many years, *mon petit chou*?'

I was familiar with the trigger phrases now, the one's dripping with sarcasm and *faux* tenderness. They usually had the word '*petite*' in them; I knew that '*mon petit chou*' was particularly incendiary.

Françoise's eyes narrowed. 'You think everyone has forgotten about his sister, Guy?'

'*Pfffff!*' Epic eyeroll. 'That was more than twenty-five years ago, Françoise! Surely some other things have happened in Bordeaux since then!'

Jules glanced at me and frowned. I raised my shoulders slightly and made big 'fucked if I know' eyes at her. I didn't want Françoise to stop talking.

'What happened to his sister?' Jules loves a good mystery.

Françoise turned to her. 'Guillaume gave Colette a drug overdose and she died.'

'Really?' exclaimed Jules and I at the same time, our eyes wide. I *knew* he was a bastard.

D'Artagnan's dark eyebrows knitted furiously. 'No, Françoise, that's not true! You shouldn't say things like that. It's defamatory!'

Françoise glared across the table at him. 'We all know it's true, Guy. You weren't here in Bordeaux at the time, but everyone was talking about it. And nobody has forgotten Jean-François' death either!'

'Wait – who's Jean-François?' Jules was fascinated. D'Artagnan was looking thunderous.

'He was Guillaume and Colette's father,' said Françoise. 'He was a very well-known wine *negociant* here in Bordeaux, a lovely man.'

'What – Guillaume killed his father too?' I couldn't resist.

'No!' D'Artagnan glared at me and then at Françoise. 'He did *not* kill his father, either!'

After our 'discussion' the previous day, I was conscious that showing interest in Guillaume had the potential to create a nasty rash between us, even if that interest was only because he was apparently a fratricidal psychopath.

Françoise held Guy's glare. 'He did, you know. Indirectly.'

'*Putain de merde, Françoise!*' D'Artagnan shook his head angrily. 'I cannot believe you are saying these things aloud. I cannot believe that everyone in Bordeaux is still gossiping about something that happen twenty-five years ago. It's only because they're jealous that Guillaume inherited the business, and now the warehouses are worth a lot of money!'

'Are those the warehouses that you're developing?' asked Pascal pleasantly in an attempt to turn the angerometer down a little.

'Yes.' Tight smile, a flickered glance in Pascal's direction.

'Yes, Guillaume inherited everything when his father died of a broken heart after Colette's death,' said Françoise darkly. 'It was very – fortunate being the only remaining child.'

D'Artagnan rolled his eyes. 'His father had a heart-attack, Françoise.'

'He died of a broken heart, Guy. He was devastated.'

'What about their mother? Where was she while Guillaume was doing all this?' Jules had clearly decided that Guillaume was culpable.

D'Artagnan had finished his entrée. He frowned and started to say, 'Guillaume didn't—' but his sister interrupted him.

'*Oh-là-là-là-là-là-là-là-* the mother! *Quelle horreur!*' Françoise cried theatrically.

Jules, Pascal and I were spellbound. The waitress had to ask us to move our elbows off the table as she collected the plates. D'Artagnan was now in a foul mood but I didn't care; his sister was a brilliant narrator.

Her eyes were alight, her expressive, full-lipped mouth slightly parted. She tucked her dark hair back behind her ear; it brushed her slender shoulders and contrasted perfectly with the fuchsia silk shirt that she was wearing. She was beautiful, vivacious and positively *radiated* good health. When I glanced at Pascal, I knew he was smitten. He looked like he was drugged as he watched her, and I had to press my lips together hard so as not to smile.

'She was an Italian countess that Jean-François had the misfortune to marry – a terrible woman!' Françoise went on. 'So vain, so proud. She only ever cared about Guillaume, she didn't care about Colette at all – and she didn't care about Jean-François either. Guillaume was her little treasure. She always took him to Italy with her. When he crashed his father's car while drunk and one of his friends lost his leg, she found a lawyer to defend him and he walked away without any punishment. And when he was arrested for dealing drugs, she got the charges dropped. There was nothing that Guillaume did that she couldn't find a way to resolve.'

She paused, aware that we were all hooked. 'They say that her family is very old, very powerful, maybe even descended from the Medicis. They have a big château outside Milan full of Renaissance furniture and art. That's where she's living now.'

A shudder ran down my spine and I looked away from her, frowning deeply. D'Artagnan saw it and glanced at me. I tried to smile, but I couldn't make the frown go away.

'So did he really kill his sister?' asked Jules, eyes wide.

D'Artagnan leaned forward, waggled his long index finger back and forth and shook his head sternly at Françoise. '*Mais non*, Françoise, you can't keep repeating this. There was a police investigation and Guillaume was not charged.'

Françoise held his gaze. 'It's what everyone thinks, Guy.'

The waitress reappeared with our main courses; there was a brief hiatus while the plates were placed in front of us and our wine glasses were refilled.

'Anyway,' said D'Artagnan airily after the sommelier left, 'now that my lovely sister has told you that I'm in business with a criminal, I would like to tell you the non-Hollywood version of what actually happened.' Françoise opened her mouth. '*Non*, Françoise, it is *my* turn to speak now. Don't interrupt me!'

She rolled her eyes, but she shut her mouth.

'It's true that Guillaume was always a bit wild, we all knew this.' D'Artagnan paused for effect and gazed at each of us in turn. 'But he loved his sister and he would never have done anything to hurt her. And the car accident with Pierre – well, that was an unfortunate accident. What mother will not protect her son from going to prison when he is young and stupid?'

He took a sip of his wine. 'But people in Bordeaux were jealous. When Colette died and then their father died – of a *heart attack*—' deliberate glance at Françoise '—and Guillaume inherited the *negociant* business, suddenly they decided that everything was his fault simply because he was a bit wild when he was young. But you know, we were all a bit wild when we were young. Laurent and I did some stupid things too, it wasn't just Guillaume!'

Françoise's eyes were very narrow as she stared at her brother. 'He was the last person to visit her at the clinic before she overdosed,' she said quietly. 'You weren't here, Guy.'

'*Pffff*, it was never proved.' He paused again. 'You know, this is why I stay out of France for a long time, because I get so tired of this small-town mentality, this constant gossiping. Because the *Bordelais* never like his mother and because Guillaume has a bit of a reputation, they make up this story that he killed his sister and that her death killed his father. Françoise, we all knew that Colette had a big problem with drugs. It was not a huge surprise to anyone that she overdosed.'

His callous dismissal of the young woman's death was a bit close to the bone for me. That could have been me. D'Artagnan knew I had overcome heroin addiction in my late twenties because I'd explained it to him very clearly on our second date. He hadn't been bothered; he seemed to think that I had waltzed in and out of addiction as if it were just one room in among the many different rooms one passes through in life; pick up a heroin addiction at the entrance, discard it at the exit.

But I would never have touched heroin if it hadn't been for what happened in Milan. And I knew from the extensive group therapy I went through in rehab that most of my fellow recovering addicts had also suffered something traumatic that had kicked off their addiction. Not all of them were able to get past it. Colette hadn't been able to, and that made me sad.

Still holding his sister's gaze, D'Artagnan sat back in his chair. Françoise did a complicated Gallic movement that consisted of raising her shoulders and her eyebrows, then pursing her lips while continuing to blink sceptically.

'Actually, Guy, there is also more recent gossip about Guillaume since he's been back here in Bordeaux. About the way he treats women – that he is violent.' Her voice was very measured.

That made me think about those two blonde women on the restaurant terrace; perhaps their interest in him hadn't been because they found him attractive.

'*Merde,* Françoise! Can you just leave Guillaume alone? I have already told you that everyone in Bordeaux is *jaloux*. It's not surprising that now the warehouses are being developed they're already making up new gossip about him!'

It occurred to me that D'Artagnan was not a very good judge of character. I found Françoise' revelations perfectly believable. I remembered how Léa had seemed when she'd come to the Duchess, and the best word to describe it was *frightened*.

Françoise gave a big shrug. 'Okay. I won't say anything else. I'm just warning you – your reputation might be at risk if you go into business with Guillaume.'

'Well, *ma petite cocotte*, you can let me worry about my reputation, okay? It's a great business opportunity and it will be very profitable.' Guy had now moved into patronising smugness mode. He turned to Pascal. 'So, do you still want to buy one of the apartments now that you have the full Hollywood history?'

***

It was about a week later. I had forced myself to start practising yoga again in the mornings in an attempt to alleviate the recurrent back pain that I was struggling with, and to try to cultivate calm of the non-chemical variety.

I was halfway through my routine when D'Artagnan called me. 'Nicole! Nicole! Come here, you must come here. Come to see this, Nicole! *Now*, quickly, Nicole!'

I knew that he would not shut up unless I went to look at whatever had grabbed his attention. Last time it had been a nest of tiny baby birds under the eaves of the roof; they were sweet, but not so wildly interesting that my yoga routine needed to be interrupted.

I padded barefoot to the window at the top of the staircase where Guy was standing, the one that looked over the paddocks behind the château. He pulled me to stand in front of him. 'Look,' he said softly and pointed.

Espiritu was standing in the paddock, his muscular body shining in the bright morning sun, his thick neck relaxed and extended, his head down. He looked as if he were thoroughly enjoying the forehead rubs the tiny girl was giving him. She was talking to him, her head sometimes on one side then on the other, her other hand making expressive gestures. Emperador was standing slightly to one side watching her, flicking his tail lazily at the flies. On the one hand it was a very bucolic scene; on the other hand...

'Oh my God,' I whispered. 'Oh my God, what if he hurts her? What if he suddenly jumps and runs over her?! It's really dangerous. We need to get her out of there!'

I started to turn but Guy held me around the waist and laughed. '*Bah*, he will not hurt her Nicole! Don't be so silly. He will never hurt her – horses love children. He is very happy to have her there.' He continued watching the scene, smiling softly.

'How do you know that?' I demanded. 'You were the one who said he was dangerous! Anything could happen even if he doesn't mean to hurt her. What if he gets frightened suddenly? You've seen the way he suddenly spins and runs off—'

'*Pffff,* Nicole! He doesn't run, he gallops. You must learn the words for horses. Horses do not run!'

'This really isn't the time for a discussion about semantics, Guy!' I wriggled away from him and went back into the bedroom, pulled on my trainers then ran quickly downstairs. I was sure the little girl was Nina, the child that Marion was fostering, and I knew that I had to get her away from that potentially dangerous horse.

D'Artagnan followed me downstairs, keeping up a running commentary about how I was being stupid, that I was overreacting. He trailed behind me as I ran across the courtyard. I slowed down as I got near the paddock railings; if I were not careful, I would be the cause of exactly what I was most afraid of. Espiritu might take fright, spin around, gallop off and trample the little girl under his heavy feet.

The horse raised his head when he saw me arrive and surveyed me with his big blue-black eyes, but he still seemed relaxed, still seemed to be enjoying his forehead rubs.

Nina's slight body was turned away from me, so she hadn't seen me arrive. I called out to her in French, 'Hi there, Nina... Uh, maybe you shouldn't – er, perhaps you should—'

She snatched her hand away as soon as she heard my voice, turned towards me guiltily and hid it behind her back, her enormous eyes fearful. Espiritu didn't move; he carried on standing there behind her, watching me.

'It's okay, please don't be scared.' I smiled nervously, feeling bad that she looked so frightened.

'Do you like horses?' Guy smiled at her as he arrived next to me at the paddock rails and leaned his arms comfortably on the top one.

She shifted her gaze to him and gave an almost imperceptible nod. She looked terrified, guilty, as if she might cry.

'I like them too. That one is called Espiritu. The gold one is called Emperador. Don't worry, we are happy that you are stroking them. You can touch them, it's fine. They like you, I can see that they like you.' His voice was friendly, easy.

I turned and glared at him. It was not fine – she might get badly hurt.

Nina still looked as if she might cry. Guy climbed under the paddock rail and walked forward until he was a few metres from where they were standing. At each step, Espiritu raised his head a notch and the muscles in his neck started to tense. He eyed D'Artagnan with maximum suspicion. The horse now seemed frighteningly large, dwarfing the little girl immediately in front of him.

D'Artagnan stopped and crouched down on his haunches so that he was at eye level with Nina. I saw him wince with the pain in his bad leg. 'It's fine, you can come and visit the horses anytime you want to. They would like that. But does Madame Marion know that you are here?'

The tiniest shrug of her skinny shoulders, a slightly disdainful blink and a little shake of her head.

'Well,' he said, his voice still calm, 'you can visit the horses any time you want to but you must tell Madame Marion, okay? Would you like that?'

A little nod.

'It's Nina, isn't it?'

She nodded again and seemed to relax a bit.

'My name is Guy,' he said. '*Enchanté,* Nina. It is very nice to meet you properly, to meet someone else who loves horses too. And that—' he turned and pointed at me '—that is my wife, Nicole. She also loves the horses, and she has green eyes too, just like yours.'

He grinned at me and winked then turned back to Nina. 'She's very pretty, isn't she, my wife?'

Another little nod. Her eyes alighted briefly on mine.

'She's a princess, you know. She's a real princess and I am her prince and we live here, in this château, with the horses and our cats. We are very happy. Have you heard stories about this, about princes and princesses?'

Nina nodded again, this time more vigorously; there was even a little smile trying to creep onto her face. I wanted to laugh then, and I also wanted to cry.

'Well, Nina, why don't you come with us? We will go into the château and have a *pain au chocolat*. Would you like to come and have a *pain au chocolat* with us?'

She shrugged again, but this time she smiled properly. When she nodded, Guy stood up and she went over to him. They walked out of the paddock side by side.

Espiritu watched them go warily. Emperador was much less bothered; he had started grazing again.

***

Nina was extremely shy. She didn't say anything, but she took the *pain au chocolat* Guy offered her and climbed onto one of the chairs in the dining hall, her legs dangling while she ate it, flaky crumbs falling onto the skirt of her dress.

I sat on the table, my legs also dangling, and I chatted to her in my bad French about how I had been unhappy before I came to live in the château, and how happy I was now to be living here with my prince and the horses and our cats. I asked her if she liked cats and she nodded fervently.

She was so skinny, and one of her knees was quite badly grazed, but her eyes were enormous, so green, and her skin was the colour of milky coffee – perfect, unblemished child's skin. She was such a pretty little thing with her shoulder-length dark hair, the fringe brushing her big eyes. She didn't stop looking at me the whole time she was eating.

Guy went into the library, found Marion's number and called her. When he returned and Nina had finished her *pain au chocolat*, he stooped and murmured in my ear that we were going to walk her home.

Nina walked between us. I asked if she had a cat and she told us, hesitantly at first, about Marion's cats. I asked her how old she was and, when she said she was six, I told her that she was nearly as old as Espiritu and Emperador. She looked kind of amazed about that.

'They're very beautiful, aren't they, the horses?' I asked her.

She turned and gazed up at me with her big green eyes. 'They are the most beautiful animals in the world,' she said quietly, her gaze very grave.

I felt an overwhelming urge to cry and had to bite my lips together hard.

Marion looked harassed when she came to the door. She frowned at Nina crossly and told her to go inside and wash her hands, then started apologising profusely. She spoke fast and her accent was quite strong, so I didn't understand a lot of what she was saying.

D'Artagnan spoke soothingly to her. He said we didn't mind if Nina visited the horses, that she hadn't been bothering us, that we'd only been concerned that Marion might be worried if she didn't know where Nina was. We could hear the two boys somewhere out the back; it sounded like they were fighting. Marion went into another room and shouted something at them, and they were quiet – for a while.

Guy and I left soon afterwards and walked back towards the Duchess. He held my hand like he did when we went to the *marché*, his fingers interlaced with mine against his chest, and he told me about the horse he'd had as a child. She'd been the same colour as Emperador, a difficult horse that only he could ride. I asked what her name was and his voice caught slightly when he said it was Artemis. That made my heart ache a little.

And as we walked in the warm spring sunshine, I imagined him as a child astride a beautiful golden horse with a flowing mane and tail, his long-limbed body and sun-kissed hair, the joyful smile on his childish face. It saddened me to think that spectre was gone forever.

***

Annabelle the wedding planner was everything I'd ever imagined a wedding planner would be, and I instantly disliked her. She was one of those insincere British women who bitch constantly about France and 'the French', despite having lived in the country of her own free will for more than fifteen years.

'Do you even know what your colour scheme is going to be?' she asked when we sat down with our coffee at the dining-hall table. She'd already given me a lecture about how late I'd left it to contact her and repeatedly informed me that it was already April, which wasn't exactly news.

Overhead, the sounds of Gabriela and Camille gutting the first floor of the Duchess were quite loud. Annabelle glanced up at the ceiling as the Duchess let out a particularly deafening shriek of horror.

'Just ignore her,' I said. 'She's a real drama queen.'

She looked at me in confusion and blinked rapidly several times.

She took two sparkly folders out of her briefcase and placed them on the table in front of us. One of them had a fluffy pink unicorn on the cover, which did not bode well.

'Colour scheme ... hmm,' I mused, as if I had given it some serious thought, which I hadn't.

I'd woken at 4.30am, bathed in a film of sweat. This time I'd obviously disturbed D'Artagnan because his arm was around my shoulders and he was stroking my hair, murmuring, 'Shhh, shhh, *doucement mon ange, tout va bien.* It's okay, it's okay...' as I clawed my way out of the nightmare where the gold and blue and red Madonna and child looked away from what was happening below them.

When he fell asleep again, I took 10mg just in case the nightmare returned, noting that I only had another six tablets. A rendezvous with lovely, compliant Doctor Malin was top of my agenda. I was, therefore, still quite chilled for my first meeting with Annabelle at 10am.

Finally I said, 'I dunno. Cream?'

'Just cream?'

'Shades of cream?'

Annabelle blinked rapidly again. Her eyelashes were heavily mascaraed and she was wearing electric-green eyeliner that didn't quite work with her watery blue eyes, not least because her face was orange. There was a lot of colour going on, and none of it was harmonious. And then there was the fluffy pink unicorn.

'Normally there's another colour that the bride chooses, other than the neutrals,' she said finally.

'Oh. Okay.' I thought for a moment. The image of Nina's green eyes that morning slid into focus. 'Green.' I said.

Nina had been in the paddock with the horses again. She'd been there every morning since the Easter school holidays had started, standing in the cool morning air next to either Emperador or Espiritu, stroking them gently, chatting away to them. That morning I'd spent ages at the window at the top of the stairs watching her, watching Guy cross the courtyard and lean on the paddock rails, watching her smile at him when he spoke to her, watching her walk next to him to the house for the *pain au chocolat* we always made sure to have a stock of for her.

That morning tableau had made me feel very calm, very ... tender.

Mr Muffin suddenly jumped up on the table and Annabelle gave a little exclamation. 'Shoo!' She waved her hand at him. 'Shoo, shoo!'

Mr Muffin stared at her. No-one had ever told him to get off the table before. The table belonged to him; what on earth was this strange-smelling woman on about?

'We let them up on the table,' I said. 'He doesn't understand why you want him to get off.'

'It's not hygienic!' she protested.

'Cats are very clean, actually.'

She made a little huffy noise and turned away from him. He was eyeing up the pink unicorn on the sparkly file. Very gently, he reached out a black-and-white paw and touched its fluffy pink mane with his claws. Annabelle snatched the file away and he looked deeply offended for a moment before jumping off the table. 'What kind of green?' she asked crossly.

I frowned at her. 'The green kind.'

'No, I mean what *shade* of green!'

I wondered if I could get Nina to come inside and stare into Annabel's eyes so that she could see the exact shade of green I meant. Then I thought: *Why on earth would you want to traumatise the child?*

'Pale green. Well, not very pale – kind of spearmint green. Like the colour of the sea, but in winter. Sort of bluey-green, with the sun shining on it.'

'Pastel green,' she said.

I picked up my phone, Googled 'sea-green images' and scrolled through them until I found one that was the closest colour to Nina's eyes. I turned my phone screen towards her.

'Pastel green,' she said again.

I looked at my phone; the colour was called 'aquarelle'. 'Yeah, pastel green.' I knew that Annabelle would not understand what aquarelle meant, that it didn't mean pastel green, that it meant about a hundred different shades of green all across the blue-yellow spectrum.

'Lovely,' she said and wrote 'pastel green and cream' in big, overly loopy cursive at the top of an otherwise blank sheet of paper in the file.

She opened another sparkly folder and smiled brightly. 'Now, the invitations. Let's look through twenty-thousand almost-but-not-quite-identical ones together while your brain melts into a pool of goo and you lose the will to live, shall we?'

I chose the third one on the first page.

***

After Annabelle finally left, I stood at the window in the salon and looked out at the lawned garden in front of the Duchess. I imagined what it would be like to marry D'Artagnan for the second time, but this time in his own country under the gaze of the château that had been in his family for more than five hundred years while a hundred and twenty people, most of whom I didn't know, watched us.

I picked up my phone and made a rendezvous with Doctor Malin on the next available date, then I went outside to see what D'Artagnan and Camille were arguing about that day.

Bits, it seemed.

'But he needs to have a bit,' D'Artagnan was insisting as Camille buckled the belt on Emperador's saddle. 'If he doesn't have a bit you have no control, no direction and you can't stop him!'

Camille laughed at him scornfully. 'No, Guy, he does not need a bit! Do you really think that a piece of metal is going to control 600kgs of horse? Don't be stupid!'

Her flaxen hair, tied back in a ponytail, shimmered as she pulled down the stirrup on the side of the saddle. She went back inside one of the old stables in the outbuildings around the courtyard.

Nina was standing quietly in the paddock next to Espiritu, brushing his long, undulating mane with his hairbrush. He really did have his very own hairbrush (both he and Emperador had their own make-up and hairbrush boxes) and he'd lowered his head so that she could reach him more easily.

I'd asked Camille whether it was safe for Nina to be so close to him in the paddock. Camille had frowned at me. 'Of course it is, Nicole. Nina is very good around the horses, she's quiet and respectful.'

'No, I meant because Espiritu is a bit dangerous. Is it safe for her?'

The frown deepened. 'Why do you think Espiritu is dangerous, Nicole?'

I shrugged. 'Guy said he was dangerous when he first arrived and – well, you never ride him, do you? You only ride Emperador.'

'*Pffff,*' said Camille crossly. 'Espiritu is not dangerous. Don't listen to what Guy says!'

It was my turn to frown. 'But you never ride him,' I repeated.

She gazed at me. 'Nicole, Espiritu is not dangerous, but he had a difficult beginning in Spain. His first experiences with humans were not good, and he was very frightened and confused. Now he's somewhere safe and, when he's ready, I'll start working with him again to try to show him that not all humans are bad.'

She paused. 'But you know, I think he would be okay if someone sat on his back. Do you think you might want to do that, Nicole?' She grinned at me wickedly when I recoiled in horror.

***

D'Artagnan shook his head in exasperation and turned to me. 'She ride him without a bit, you know.' He was standing with Emperador, his fingers deep in the horse's flaxen mane. Emperador's head was low and his long-lashed, brown-gold eyes were half-closed as D'Artagnan caressed him. His coat gleamed in the sunshine.

'A bit of what?' I finally asked.

He stared at me. 'A bit. Not "of what", Nicole, just a bit.'

I stared back at him. 'None the wiser after that detailed explanation, D'Artagnan.'

He pointed to the leather halter fastened around Emperador's head and touched the reins that were attached to it. 'Look, no bit.'

I looked at Emperador's head and thought: *Nope, don't think there's a bit missing.*

'In his mouth. There is no bit of metal in his mouth that is normal so that you can control and steer him and stop him,' he said crossly.

Camille had returned outside. '*Putain*, Guy. I already told you that this is a stupid old idea, this idea that a tiny bit of metal allows you to control a horse. It is useful only if you are going to do *haute-école* dressage and you need to communicate something complicated to your horse, but not if you're riding out for fun.'

She untied the rope from the metal ring on the outside of the stable and led Emperador towards the paddock rails until he was standing parallel to them, then she put one leg on the lower rail, hopped up and turned nimbly. She put her other foot in the stirrup and sprang lightly and effortlessly into Emperador's saddle.

It fascinated me to watch her get on his back as if it were the most natural thing in the world.

Guy shook his head. 'I always rode with a bit.'

'Yes, well, things have changed now, Guy. And if you are ever going to ride my horse, you will ride him without a bit,' Camille said firmly. She picked up the reins, clicked her tongue authoritatively and they walked majestically out of the courtyard, her flaxen ponytail and his flaxen tail swishing in perfect tandem.

D'Artagnan turned to me after we'd watched them go. He was grinning. 'She's going to let me ride her horse.' His brown eyes were lit with something more than just the spring sunlight.

Chapter Six

It was a week later that my life changed. Everything changed. Fundamentally.

I was in Bordeaux for my rendezvous with Doctor Malin. We had the usual chat about his last holiday to Antarctica (not really a sun-seeker, Doctor Malin) and then he asked how D'Artagnan was and whether I was enjoying life in France. I told him about the Duchess's bad behaviour and made him laugh.

Finally he asked the reason for my visit and I asked for a repeat prescription of diazepam. He wrote it out without blinking an eyelid and I felt very relieved – even though something weird had happened two nights earlier.

I'd woken from one of the recurring nightmares involving D'Artagnan, the masked bastard, a lot of blood and the usual intense feeling of helplessness. I'd woken with the familiar hammering heart, cold sweat and breathlessness, and had automatically reached for what remained of my diazepam supply in my bedside cabinet.

But then I had paused. It was a bright night, lit with a full moon. I climbed carefully out of bed so as not to disturb the lightly snoring D'Artagnan, pulled on my kimono and my slippers. Heart still beating much too fast, I went to the back hall window to look for the horses. I could see them; they were quite close to the stable block. I watched them for a while, still aware of my racing heart. They seemed so peaceful, standing there in the moonlight, that I had a bizarre urge.

I tiptoed downstairs, across the salon, through the medieval dining hall (ignoring the musketeers and the Duchess, who were drunk as usual – I could feel the Duchess's eyes on my back as I crossed the hall) and out through the back door in the utility room.

The night air was cool, and I tightened my kimono around me as I walked across the silent courtyard, my footsteps loud on the gravel. I stopped at the paddock rails. The horses were standing side by side, head to tail, with Espiritu facing me. He swished his tail slightly from side to side as he gazed at me in the moonlight.

I don't really know how long I stood there leaning on the paddock rails. I heard the white barn owl that lived in the roof of one of the old stables screech somewhere nearby, and I heard a mouse or some other small creature investigating the grass close to the horses. Gradually I became aware that my heart had returned to its normal rhythm and I felt calm again.

I'd discovered that, for me, watching the horses worked like a non-pharmaceutical tranquiliser. I was slightly amazed: Miss Pharmaceutical-Solutions-R-Us actually finding a natural solution to her anxiety.

Nevertheless, there was no way that I was going to risk not having chemical assistance available if I needed it. Horses are really difficult to cram into one's handbag, but diazepam is really easy.

***

Unfortunately, that day Doctor Malin also told me that he was going on a year's sabbatical. Fear gripped my heart at the thought that my diazepam supply might become more difficult to source, but he waved away my concern and told me that he would make the prescription a repeat for twelve months. I smiled happily while he wrote it, and he explained all about spending his sabbatical in a yurt in Outer Mongolia. I tried hard to look as though I thought that was an entirely reasonable thing to do, though not altogether successfully.

***

As I left his office, my phone rang; it was D'Artagnan. He was in Biarritz, looking at development opportunities with Francesca. 'Nicole, *mon amour,*' he purred.

I braced; it was the seductive, coercive voice. 'Sweetheart. What do you want?'

'How are you, *mon ange*? Did you meet with Doctor Malin okay? Did you get your drugs?'

'Yeah, I did. What do you want, Guy?'

'Well, Nicole, *mon amour*, I am here in Biarritz with Francesca...'

'Yes, I know you are. What do you want?'

'*Bah, chérie*, I need some plans I leave in the office. Will you be very kind and go to get them? Because you are already in Bordeaux.'

I was almost at my car. I stopped. 'And then?'

'And then will you bring them to Biarritz, *mon ange*? It will make me so happy – it will be really helpful for me. I will love you very, very much if you do this for me.' Breathing down the phone. 'I promise, Nicole, I will make a very special time if you do this for me.' I could almost *hear* the lazy blink, the sexy raised eyebrow.

I got into my car and put my bag down on the passenger seat. 'Guy, darling, if I drive to Biarritz and back it will be an extra four hours. Do you really, *really* need them? Where's Guillaume? Can't he bring them down to you?'

'No, he cannot, Nicole. He tell me he is going to Nantes today. I really need the plans, I want to show Francesca. We are just going to have a lunch with an agent so I cannot come to get them, but if you can bring them to me I will be very happy, *mon amour*. Please?'

I sighed. I had things to do and I wanted to go home. Sometimes, though, one just has to suck it up; it's this thing called marriage, apparently. And love. Sometimes it's just love.

***

I drove to Chartrons and found a parking spot a couple of streets away in Quinconces. It was a warm, sunny day and the trees lining the streets were sun-dappled and in full leaf. My heart was light as I walked to the site.

The construction guys had left for lunch when I arrived. I pushed the main door open and took the stairs two at a time to the office on the first floor. It had a keycode entry so I entered the number that Guy had given me. The door buzzed and I went in.

The first thing I saw was Guillaume. He was sitting in the open-plan living area on one of the office chairs facing the door, his feet on the desk. I stopped dead and frowned. He looked up and smiled that lazy, cold smile.

'Guillaume,' I said. 'Guy said you were in Nantes.'

'Well, Nicole, I am not in Nantes. I am here. I go later to Nantes.'

'Oh. Okay.'

He took his feet off the desk, stood up and came over to me. '*Bah, bonjour,* Nicole.' A proprietary hand on my shoulder, his thumb stroking it for a second. He leaned in for kisses, the usual far-too-intimate nuzzling. This time, it was unmistakable that he breathed in because he murmured, 'I like your perfume, Nicole. I like it a lot.'

I shrank back from him. 'Uh, thanks. Yeah, whatever.' I looked away, tried to move past him.

He let me go but turned to watch me. 'What are you doing here, Nicole?'

'Guy asked me to get the latest architect's plans. He's in Biarritz with Francesca – but you probably know that. Anyway, he asked me to take them to him. He said they're in the file marked "Chartrons: Phase 2" on the shelf in the kitchen.'

I headed towards the L-shaped kitchen and looked at the spines of the files on the shelf, but there wasn't one with that title. I turned around. Guillaume was now standing behind me, arms folded, blocking my way out.

'Do you know where it is? I can't see it here.' I focused my eyes briefly on his; they were hard, like slate. I looked away again. I could feel my heart beating faster.

A little smirk and then a little nod. He indicated with his head that the file was on the desk where he had been sitting. He was still standing in my way.

'Well, could I get it please?' I asked. 'Could you move so that I can get it? I need to take it to Biarritz.'

A long, lazy sweep of his eyes all the way down my body and then back up again, eyes still cold and insolent when he focused them on mine. 'You are a very obedient wife to go all the way to Biarritz just because Guy ask you. Are you always so obedient?'

I frowned. 'My relationship with Guy and how it works is none of your business, Guillaume.' I took a deep breath, conscious that my heart rate was increasing even more. 'And actually, I might as well say it now – I really don't appreciate you flirting with me. I don't find it amusing, or fun, or whatever you think it is. I find it really creepy and I want you to stop. And you need to get out of my way, please, so that I can get the file.'

He gave a short, unpleasant laugh. 'I don't think that's true, Nicole. I think you do like me flirting with you.' He blinked at me slowly, lasciviously. 'I am sure you do because you always blush.'

I stared at him. 'Actually, I think I know exactly how I feel, Guillaume, and I do *not* like it at all!'

'So why do you blush, then? It's very sexy, you know, when you blush. It makes me want to fuck you.'

I shrank back against the kitchen counter. He still hadn't moved and I was still trapped. My heart was now hammering in my chest. 'If you touch me, Guillaume, Guy will kill you. You know he will. He told me that he will.' I was aware of the tremor in my voice.

He frowned angrily. 'Why are you talking to Guy about me, Nicole?'

'Because I told him I don't like you flirting with me.' I took a deep breath. 'And now I need the file and I need to go to Biarritz. Please get out of my way so that I can get it and then I'll go. I won't mention that you were here. Okay?'

He sneered and took a step back, opening the way for me to pass, but, as I did so, he grabbed my arms and shoved me against the wall. His hands were vice-like and I was suddenly aware of how strong he was. 'Don't you *dare* tell me what I can and can't do, Nicole.' His face was inches from mine, his eyes narrowed angrily.

I was completely trapped. I wanted to scream for help, but I knew there was no-one close by. The scent of nutmeg, of his aftershave, was burning my nostrils and I suddenly knew exactly where I'd seen him before. He'd been at that party in the Marble Villa in Hell on the last night of Milan Fashion Week, eleven years ago. He'd been there in a white shirt, his black bowtie loose, and I'd seen him across the crowded room staring at me. The image was as clear as day.

I tried to swallow but my throat felt blocked. I could do nothing except stare into his horrible dark eyes.

'And don't talk to your husband about me, either. There is a lot of money involved in this project, Nicole, and I don't want you to fuck it up by putting ideas in Guy's head, okay?' His voice was low, dangerous, and his eyes burned into mine.

I managed to take a breath and say it. 'If you don't let me go right now, Guillaume, I *am* going to tell Guy, and your project *is* going to be fucked up!'

He did not let me go, though I felt the tension in his body subside a little. Then he said, 'You know Nicole, you are now a bit ... ripe for me. I think this is this word in English, isn't it? I preferred you when you were ... *younger.*' He said the last word slowly and the sneer on his face was pure evil.

Then he let me go.

I moved quickly to put the desk between us. He reached over and picked up the file. 'Go then. Take the file and deliver it to your husband like the good little wife you pretend to be.' He thrust it at me, but when I tried to take it he grabbed my wrist. I stared at him, mesmerised.

'But Nicole, remember this: you don't tell me what I can and can't do, and you don't talk to Guy about me, okay?' He paused, then he reached into his back pocket and pulled out an engraved metal handle. He held it in front of my face, pressed something with his thumb and a thin, shiny blade shot out from its side. It was only a couple of centimetres from my face.

I caught my breath and tried to move back but he was still holding my wrist tightly.

'I always carry this, Nicole. Remember this before you think it is a good idea to get your husband in a jealous rage, okay?'

I nodded dumbly. I just wanted to get out of there.

'So go now, you little bitch.' He pointed towards the door.

I ran to it, fumbled it open and slammed it shut behind me, then ran down the stairs and onto the street as fast as I could.

***

Once I was in a public place where I was reasonably sure he wouldn't follow me, I scrabbled frantically in my bag for my tablets. I felt the hysteria rising when I couldn't feel the pill cannister – then bliss, I found it, managed to open it with shaking hands, shook out a tablet and then another one and shoved them in my mouth, desperately trying to accumulate enough saliva to swallow them.

But my upper lip was already tingling, twitching crazily, and the black dots were starting to bounce around in my vision because I couldn't breathe. I was walking fast, as fast as I could up the side street towards the main street, and my heart was trying to escape from my chest, bruising itself against my ribcage.

I knew I had to get to the main pedestrian street where there were people, where he couldn't follow me, couldn't touch me without attracting attention – and then I was there and there was a café on the corner. The black dots in front of my eyes had become large, fluid patches like in a lava lamp, and I flopped into a chair just as they all joined up and everything went black.

I didn't want to look at it; I couldn't bear to contemplate it, to actually look head-on at what I'd just realised. My conscious mind agreed and my subconscious mind knew; that was enough. Sitting there at the café table when I regained consciousness, my heart hammering and my breath coming in short gasps, I knew exactly what had just happened, what I'd just found out, but it was so catastrophically awful that I couldn't bear to focus on it.

The waitress was concerned when I tried to order a coffee and started crying instead. She crouched next to me, put her arm around my shoulders and made soothing noises, insisting that I come inside where she installed me in a booth and sat with me. She held my hand while my body was wracked with sobs, the dull, familiar pattern that follows all of my panic attacks.

Gradually I felt the diazepam kicking in and the sobs became less wrenching, less consuming. She asked a colleague to bring me a coffee with milk (it being Chartrons, I was required to specify whether that would be dairy, soya, oat or almond) and she insisted I put two sugars in it, even though I tried to push the bowl away because sugar is – well, I don't do sugar normally. But I did that day.

Finally, the chemical calm began to take hold. I tried to smile at her and thanked her profusely, asked for the bill and gave her a huge tip. She looked worried because I was still shaking and asked if there was someone I could call. I smiled and reassured her, lied that I didn't live far away and that someone would be home soon. And then I remembered I had to drive to Biarritz because Guy needed the file. Where was the file – oh my God, had I lost the file? I looked around wildly, but the waitress had it next to her and passed it to me. I held it tightly against my chest and tried again to calm my breathing.

I wondered how the fuck I was going to drive for two hours on the autoroute, how I was going to keep focused and not do something stupid, because I had to do this, I had to drive to

Biarritz. If I didn't take the file to Biarritz then I would have to explain why not. I would have to explain what had happened. Guy would know that something had happened, and I couldn't bear to tell him because—

And I still couldn't actually focus on it; it slid away, slithered away, this vile, vile realisation. I couldn't actually bear to admit what had just happened, what Guillaume had indirectly told me, what I had just realised.

I did some mental calculations about whether I could take another half a tablet and still be okay to drive, but I decided that it was probably a really bad idea. I'd had nothing to eat that day. I decided to take a double dose of ibuprofen instead because my back was suddenly in agony; all the muscles felt like they had gone into spasm on either side of my spine. I decided that the diazepam/ibuprofen mix was probably alright. Then I started the engine and drove to Biarritz.

***

Guy was very concerned when I arrived, but I didn't cry when he held me close against him. I was determined not to cry and I was really quite absent by then.

'But Nicole, you should not drive when you have to take a lot of ibuprofen. What did you do to your back that there is so much pain? Why did you not just call me and tell me that you cannot drive, that you are in pain, *mon amour*?'

I shrugged; it was a very languid shrug. 'You said you needed the file. I brought you the file.'

He frowned at me. 'Did you just take ibuprofen, *mon ange*? Your eyes are very dark.'

'Just ibuprofen,' I said firmly. 'Sometimes my pupils get big if I have to take a lot.'

I thought for a moment. I needed a back story. 'It was so silly and it happened so quickly. I was on the way to the car after Doctor Malin and I tripped on a pavement slab. It was uneven and I nearly fell – I think I twisted something, and now my back is all fucked-up.' I rolled my eyes theatrically. The world rolled with them rather more than I wanted it to, but I focused on the fact that it was imperative that D'Artagnan didn't find out what had really happened.

'It happens sometimes,' I continued with a brave smile. 'I think it's just a muscle or something. But it's fine. If I take ibuprofen for a while, the muscles will relax. It will get better.'

He was still frowning, his arms around my waist. 'Well, *mon ange*, I don't want you to drive any more today. It is not safe. We are going to stay here in Biarritz until you are okay to drive home tomorrow. I still have meetings with Francesca and the agent this afternoon, but you must rest. Come, I take you to the hotel. We will take a room and you can rest there until your back is better.'

I sighed tiredly. I didn't want to stay in Biarritz, I wanted to go home. I longed to be there, in our bed with Guy and the Muffins, deep under the covers. And I really didn't want to come out from under them for a very long time because the world on the other side of the covers was ... ugly. It was ugly, and complicated. More than that: it was horrific.

But I was exhausted and stoned, and I knew it would be dangerous for me to drive any longer, so I nodded. 'Thank you, darling man.'

He drove me to the hotel and booked a room. I lay down on the bed on my side, put a pillow between my knees, because that always helps the back pain, and then I passed out.

***

I woke a couple of hours later.

I woke:

– as if a stake had been hammered into my heart

– as if all the oxygen had suddenly, forcibly been sucked out of my body

– as if a thousand volts had just passed through me.

I woke, gasping for air, my heart thudding. The flashback this time was vivid, as if I were still in that blue and red and gold bedroom in the Marble Villa in Hell somewhere outside Milan, having my body, my soul, horribly violated while the Madonna and Child above the bed looked away.

For the first time, there was a new memory to add to the Milan sequence, the sequence that always went:

- someone holding my wrists tightly above my head
- the sound of male laughter, low, horrible
- my chest crushed, constricted between strong thighs

- a hideous jewelled mask with a beak, hard black eyes behind it staring down at me
- a violent slap across my face
- hands, other hands wrenching my legs apart.

And then a deep, black darkness, an intense nothingness.

Only this time my subconscious allowed another poisonous bubble to rise to the surface of my conscious mind. This time the hideous, beaked mask spoke and it said, 'Open your eyes, you little bitch. I paid for those pretty eyes.'

There wasn't the slightest doubt in my mind that I knew that voice. It was Guillaume's voice.

I scrabbled desperately on the night table for the diazepam cannister but it wasn't there. I remembered that it was in my handbag, that I hadn't taken it out because I didn't want Guy to ask questions. I knew it was in my handbag, but I didn't know where my handbag was and I still couldn't breathe and my heart and my lungs felt like they were about to explode and the black dots were getting larger...

I regained consciousness on the floor next to the bed. I took an enormous, life-saving breath of air and managed to make it to the armchair. My heart gave a little surge of joy when I saw that that my bag was there.

Once I found the bottle of life-saving diazepam inside it, I felt that I might survive – this time. I shook out a pill, then another one even though I knew it was a bad idea. I would be so wiped, so absolutely out of it, if I took another 20mg – but that was what I needed because I couldn't contemplate the giant, looming fuck-up that was the future.

After I'd swallowed both tablets, I felt a small surge of relief. I crawled back to the bed and under the covers. Clutching a pillow tightly against my body, I repeated the mantra over and over again: 'The drugs will start working. The drugs will start working. The drugs will start working,' until finally the drugs *did* start working and I passed out again.

How do you solve a conundrum like this?

Your husband, whom you love very much, has invested a lot of his money (you don't know how much but you know it is a lot) in a joint venture with two partners, one of whom drugged and raped you eleven years previously. Your husband, who is alpha-male in a kind of textbook way (actually, there's no 'kind of' about it – he is pure, unadulterated alpha-male and French to boot) has said that he will kill his business partner should you and he ever have an affair. You believe that this is not just a threat because your husband has been abundantly alpha-male stupid in the past and he very nearly died as a result.

You contemplate what he might do should he find out what you have just realised, that it was his business partner who raped you. And all *that* future seems to promise is blood and violence and police sirens and ambulance sirens, and the possibility that you will never be able to touch him again, to hold him or be held by him again because he is in prison for murder. Alternatively, your husband is dead because his business partner has killed *him* in self-defence. Your heart aches with misery at the thought.

You think how much his children will hate you for trespassing into his well-organised, successful, easy life – you, the siren, the unworthy interloper who has now chucked a giant fucking hand grenade into the middle of that successful, easy life. You think how much his sister and his nieces will hate you, and his other business partner, his brothers, his ex-wife – all of these people who were in his life before you came along and crapped all over it.

You think how much you will miss him, how much will you crave his embrace, his strong, solid body that he holds you against every night, his body that your own fits so perfectly against. How much will you ache for him?

How much do you love him?

It cannot be solved, this conundrum, so instead you decide to keep your poisonous discovery to yourself. You're not sure how, but it's not the first time you've had to keep a secret, and you're actually quite good at that. You're an expert at keeping secrets.

***

I don't know what time Guy came back to the room, but I was totally out of it. I remember him stroking my face and whispering my name. I sort of woke, my eyelids heavy, and he leaned over and kissed me softly.

'Do you want something to eat, *mon ange*?'

I shook my head a little. My eyelids were already closing again.

'Do you want to sleep some more?'

'*Ouais,*' I answered, because '*ouais*' in French, or 'yeah', is already just like a breath to me, like a soft exhalation.

'Okay, *mon amour*, I sleep with you.'

A little while later I felt his body against mine, solid and strong, and his wonderful, familiar Dior scent that was so comforting. He wrapped his arms around me and pulled my body into the curve of his. My heart felt like it was breaking just before I dived back into the velvet underworld of sleep because I loved him so much.

Chapter Seven

Happily – or rather happily but irritatingly – there were distractions back at the Duchess. The main irritation for me was bloody Annabelle.

'Only one bridesmaid? Really?' She blinked the thick black insects around her eyes at me. Today, the eyeliner was electric blue. I wondered whether Annabelle had a secret life as a disco diva and just couldn't be arsed to remove her make-up for her day job.

I nodded. 'Yup. Jules. She's my best friend.'

'And—' she looked inside the sparkly, fluffy unicorn file again '—one flower girl and one flower boy.'

I nodded again. 'Yup. Jules' kids, Katie and Josh.'

She nodded slowly. 'What will they be wearing?'

I stared at her. 'I thought that was what you did?'

Annabelle shook her head crossly. 'No, Nicole. I organise the catering and the marquee, the decoration and the seating, the flowers and the photographer, and I book the registrar and make it a very special day for you and your lovely husband!'

She had fallen hook, line and sinker for D'Artagnan. He'd wandered through the dining room earlier that morning and when they did Kissies, she went all gooey and silly-eyed. Afterwards he'd leaned down and slipped his hand underneath my jaw, tilting my mouth to his, his lips soft against mine for a moment. Then he'd gone outside.

Weirdly, Annabelle's eyeliner seemed green when I looked at her again.

I shrugged. 'Okay. I'll organise that.' I paused. 'So what else do you need me to do, apart from that?'

We were at the table in the dining hall; she'd spread out a range of table settings in various frilly guises in front of me, one of which I was required to choose.

'A bit of enthusiasm wouldn't go amiss, Nicole.'

I gazed at her tiredly and gave an apologetic shrug that made me wince; my back was in a bad way, taut with tension and searing pain. The combined diazepam/ibuprofen mix wasn't really touching it anymore.

She frowned at me. 'What's wrong with you?'

I started to shrug again but thought better of it. 'It's my back. It's a bit screwed up.'

She carried on frowning 'Well, take some painkillers for it.'

'I have. They're not working.'

The frown turned a little more thoughtful 'Is this why you're unable to make any decisions? Or respond to my emails?'

That sounded like a good excuse. 'I suppose so. I'm sorry, Annabelle, it's just been really difficult to focus on the wedding when I'm in pain. I've got a *rendezvous* for an MRI next week, so hopefully they'll find out what's wrong and fix it.'

D'Artagnan had insisted I see a specialist in Bordeaux who had booked me in for an MRI scan.

'You should get your doctor to prescribe something stronger, Nicole. The MRI isn't going to fix the problem and you need to start focusing on the wedding – it's less than three months away now!' She was cross again.

'My doctor's away on sabbatical,' I said forlornly.

Her eyes narrowed and her gaze became calculating. 'I can get you some oxycodone, if you like?'

And thus did Annabelle the wedding planner become my new drug dealer.

***

Life was significantly more serene with oxycodone, occasionally supplemented with diazepam. I found that I could mute the horror; it still existed but behind what felt like a Plexiglas divider. And oddly, now that I knew that it was Guillaume behind the beaked, jewelled mask in the Marble Villa in Hell, it somehow made it less frightening. I didn't know who the other two men were – I was pretty sure there had been three of them – because I had no visual memory of them.

So between that realisation and the marvellously serene world of oxycodone, the nightmares and the flashbacks disappeared. The horror had been muted.

Unfortunately, everything else was muted too.

D'Artagnan was not deceived. When we had sex I was elsewhere, watching us. We were very lovely to watch, but I wasn't consumed by him, consumed in the moment like I had always been.

Once I tried faking it. He sat back, still hard inside me, and held me still. 'Don't do that, Nicole. Please don't do that. Don't pretend, *mon ange.*'

'I'm sorry,' I whispered, tears pricking my eyes. 'It's just... It's the drugs, they dull everything.'

He shook his head and withdrew, then moved to lie next to me, his hand flat on my stomach. 'What drugs are you taking, Nicole? Are you taking the diazepam also?'

I sighed and looked away from his concerned gaze. 'Sometimes. It helps the pain.'

His frown deepened. 'This is not good – it cannot continue. This pain is too much. We need to get your back fixed. And you are not eating – I can see you are not eating. You are getting very thin, *mon amour,* and it is not healthy.' His eyes were concerned. I looked away from him.

'Is it just your back Nicole?' he asked softly. 'Or is it something else also? I am worried, *mon ange.* I feel, *bah...* I feel as if you are moving away from me, as if you are not really here anymore.'

A tear dislodged itself and rolled down my cheek. He kissed it away. 'Nicole? Please answer me?'

'I'm sorry, my darling. I'm so sorry that I'm all fucked up, but it *is* just my back. It's really tiring being in constant pain but it helps to take diazepam with ibuprofen. I know it turns me into a bit of a zombie, and I'm so sorry about that, my angel, but I'm sure it will get better. Once we get the results of the MRI it will be fine, it'll be better.'

He nodded slowly. 'Okay. But after we see the specialist in Bordeaux, if he cannot fix it, we go to see a specialist in Paris. I ask Isabelle – her partner is a surgeon, he will know of someone who can help you. Don't cry, *mon ange,* we will get this fixed, *ne t'inquiète pas.*'

And I wondered if perhaps surgery would be an option: a lobotomy to remove that part of my brain that stored the memory of the night in the Marble Villa in Hell. That would definitely be an option; that would definitely work.

***

'So I said to her, Jules, I said, "The menu is nothing to do with me, Annabelle. D'Artagnan is responsible for choosing the menu" and she's like "Who the hell is D'Artagnan?" and I'm like "It's Guy, Guy is D'Artagnan," and she looks at me, she gives me this look, and then she says, "I don't really need to know about your sex life, Nicole." Oh my *God*, Jules, I nearly died trying not to laugh. Then I said, all coldly, "It's part of the family name, actually, Annabelle," and I kept this total poker-face like I was really insulted. It was hilarious!'

I collapsed back onto the bed in a fit of giggles, my heart uplifted to hear Jules equally in hysterics on the other end of the phone.

When we finally stopped giggling, she said, 'Oh Nicky, I can't imagine how miserable you're making that poor woman. Does she not have a clue how subversive you are?'

'Nope.' I grinned. 'Every now and again, I muse wistfully about – I dunno – pink ribbons around little bags of pink and blue and white almonds, and she gets all excited, and then I say, "Oh, but no, that just reminds me of..." and trail off and look sad. Then she gets this cross look and she goes away. Mostly. Anyway, she wants to know what Katie and Josh are going to wear. What *are* they going to wear, Jules, do you know?'

A pause. 'We discussed this last week, Nicky. We discussed it in detail. Don't you remember?'

'Oh God, yeah, of course! Sorry, Jules, my brain is so fried at the moment and I'm so looking forward to Paris that I completely forgot!'

I had no recollection of having discussed what Katie and Josh were going to wear, but apparently that conversation had happened. I would check with Annabelle; if anyone would know, she would.

I took another sip of wine. Wine was helping the pain: wine, oxycodone and diazepam. It was a brilliant combination. I had only tripped up the stairs once, and I had a nasty bruise on my knee, but otherwise it was all good. Everything was all good, man. It was my new fave phrase.

'Me too, darling girl. I can imagine you're a bit manic – it's less than three months until your wedding! Have you and

D'Artagnan worked out what you're going to say? Are you going to do it in French?'

I did a big shrug, lay back against the pillows, took another sip of wine. Mrs Muffin jumped onto the bed, threw herself onto her back and wantonly invited me to scrumple her tummy. I accepted the invitation and she purred loudly.

'Well, he said it's up to me, but yeah, I want to do it in French. Bérengère is helping me. She's coming to the wedding, too, so you'll meet her. She's soooo cool, Jules. Have I told you about her? About Bérengère, my French teacher?'

Another pause. Then, 'Yeah, Nicky, several times. Are you okay, hon? Your mind seems a bit – selective at the moment. Are you really stressed about the wedding?'

'Oh no, I'm not stressed. It's all fine, it's all good, man.' I took another sip of wine, thought about putting on some music downstairs. I wondered where D'Artagnan was. Was he here? Or was he ... elsewhere? I thought it probably wasn't a good idea to ask Jules where he was, although she might know because I might have told her earlier.

'Anyway, darling Jules, I have to go and feed the Muffins. So, next week in Paris – I'm sooooo looking forward to it. I can't wait to see you again!'

'Er, it's this week, Nicky, on Friday night. Listen, babe, are you sure you're okay? You sound a bit – I dunno – pissed? Like a bit out of it?'

I shrugged then realised that wasn't really going down the phone. 'Y'know, I've had a glass of wine, Jules sweetheart, but I'm fine. Maybe I'm a little stressed but it's fine. It's all good, man. Jules.'

'You know Nicky,' she said slowly, 'the more you keep saying that, the more I keep thinking, it's really *not* all good, man.'

I took a deep breath. Where *was* D'Artagnan anyway? Was he here? Was he in Bordeaux? In Biarritz? I looked out of the open windows at the soft, purple sky. The air was warm as it flowed into the bedroom. 'Jules, it's fine. Maybe I *am* a bit stressed. But I'm really looking forward to seeing you at the weekend. I love you so much, sweetheart.'

'I love you too, darling girl. I'll see you on Friday night. I'll WhatsApp you from the Eurostar when I'm on it.'

'Lovely. Love you, Jules.' I pushed the off button, swigged the rest of the wine, put my glass on the bedside table and rolled over to cuddle Mrs Muffin.

***

D'Artagnan woke me gently, stroking my temple, whispering my name. He lifted me up and held me close, running his hand up and down my back, pausing occasionally against my ribcage. I could feel that he was shaking his head, but he didn't say anything. He just held me against his body – his wife, the rag doll.

***

'Fuck's sake, Nicky!' Jules stared at me. 'Have you completely given up eating?'

I had put on my preferred choice of wedding dress, a silk-satin cream mini-dress by Lanvin, completely bare backed. It fell sharply away from the halterneck, just covering my breasts, and pooled in silky folds at the base of the spine. It stayed on with two ties – one at the halterneck, the other at breast level, both in long, unfinished (vegan) rawhide.

There wasn't a hint of lace, frill or fluff in it. This was a dress that gave off only one vibe: how quickly it could – and would – fall to the ground once it was untied. It oozed ... *un je ne sais quoi*. Actually, there was no *je ne sais quoi* about it. I knew exactly what it oozed: sex. But the cut was exquisite; like all Lanvin, it was effortlessly, elegantly sexy.

I made a face. 'It's a thirty-four, Jules. It's quite normal.'

'Nicky, it doesn't fit you. It's too loose. That's like a size six in the UK...' She looked up and registered my face. 'It's fine, darling. You look absolutely gorgeous in it, but Nicky, you're too thin. I'm just a bit shocked. I don't think I've ever seen you this thin. It doesn't look – healthy.'

I did a big shrug and sighed. I was getting really tired of hearing about weight. Mine, in particular. 'So, I'll try a thirty-two,' I said to the assistant in French. I smiled as sweetly as possible considering I was one oxycodone/10mg diazepam/one glass of Champagne (they offered) into the fitting. It was 11am.

***

Bérengère didn't say anything about my weight; she just got straight to the point. 'So, Nicole, of all of the drugs that you are taking, which is your preferred one?'

We were sitting under the wisteria-draped pergola in her pretty, wild garden where my lessons were conducted now that it was summer. It was a sweltering day, the air pulsing with heat. Her dogs were lying prone on the stone paving slabs, their tongues lolling out of their mouths.

I frowned at her. 'What do you mean, Bérengère?'

'Nicole, the last three lessons it has been very obvious to me that you are high. I'm just curious. Which is your preferred drug?'

I blinked slowly. 'Well, you know, I'm having a lot of problems with my back. So I'm taking ibuprofen for that.'

She snorted. 'No, Nicole, it is not the ibuprofen I am talking about. What other drugs are you taking? Something with opioids, I think?'

I shrugged. 'Well, yeah, sometimes. When the pain is very bad I have to take oxycodone.'

She nodded slowly, sipped her tea and smiled at me. 'There is nothing wrong with your back, Nicole.'

'Yes, Bérengère, there is. I've had an MRI and I'm seeing the specialist in Bordeaux tomorrow to discuss the results,' I said crossly.

She carried on smiling, a mild, knowing smile. 'The MRI will not show any problem with your back. I can see there is no problem with your back. The problem is in here, *ma biche*.' She tapped the side of her forehead with her finger, raised an eyebrow and nodded slightly.

At first I'd been confused whenever she called me '*ma biche*' and assumed it was just a really cool French thing to do, to refer to your students as your bitches. I'd floated this idea past D'Artagnan, who had thought that was hilarious. A '*biche*' is a small deer and Bérengère was saying 'my dear' colloquially.

I did my now-perfect version of a Gallic shrug and slid my eyes away from her cool grey gaze.

'I am not judging you, Nicole.' Bérengère leaned over the table and touched the back of my hand. 'We all have difficult things at some time in our life. I just want you to know that if you want to talk about anything, I am here. I do not judge. I only want to help you if you want some help.'

I smiled. 'Thank you, Bérengère. That's very kind but everything is fine. I'm fine.'

She shrugged. 'Okay, Nicole, I just wanted you to know.' She sat up straight. 'So, let us work on the things you are going to say to your D'Artagnan at your marriage ceremony so that you say it all in perfect French!'

***

There was an upside to being permanently stoned: I spent a lot of time with Nina, because she was totally unjudgmental. She didn't care about my weight, she didn't ask questions about what drugs I was taking, and she wasn't sad and concerned about me like D'Artagnan. She was just easy to be with.

We sat together in the paddock with the horses grazing nearby, sometimes grazing right next to us. I wasn't afraid anymore; either Nina's lack of fear had rubbed off on me or the drugs had dulled it, but I was no longer frightened by the horses. Nina chatted away about all sorts of things as we sat there, about her adventures in the woods, the fairies she had seen, the birds she had talked to and, of course, about the horses and how she was going to ride them. Camille had said that soon Nina could ride Emperador and maybe one day, Espiritu. She leaned against me as she chatted and that made me so happy. I loved the feel of her skinny little body against mine.

I could touch Emperador now, approach him quietly and stroke his silky, golden body, put my nose against his neck and breathe in his intoxicating smell. I was a little more hesitant with Espiritu; I got the sensation that he didn't necessarily want me to touch him. That was fine. I was okay with that.

Nina touched him, though. She laid her forehead against his flank and he bowed his gleaming head towards her, his strong neck wrinkling as he nuzzled her hair with his soft, whiskered muzzle. Then he blew a huge raspberry and she giggled endlessly. It was so lovely to watch and hear her uncontrolled, childish giggles.

***

Bérengère was right: the MRI showed nothing wrong with my back. There was no damage to my spine, nothing touching the nerves. I was surprised; somehow, I had managed to buy into the idea that there really was something physically wrong that necessitated all the drugs I was taking. I had persuaded myself that this was the real reason I was now, once again, a fully functioning opioid addict.

The specialist peered at us over his glasses and said, 'Perhaps it is a muscular problem, or perhaps it is a psychiatric problem.'

I glared at him. 'No, it's not a psychiatric problem. The pain is real. I've had it before.'

He shrugged. 'Well, there is nothing I can do. Maybe you should see an osteopath or a chiropractor.' He said this with obvious disdain, because osteopathy and chiropody are considered alternative treatments in France, i.e. not real medicine.

'Well, Nicole, *mon amour,*' said D'Artagnan with a tired sigh as we left the office 'Maybe that is what we should do. We need to find an osteopath for you. I ask Françoise when we see her on Saturday at Emma's wedding. Unless you want to go to Paris? We can see a specialist there.'

His shoulders seemed to sag and a wave of guilt washed over me. He looked sad and resigned almost all of the time now and he'd stopped trying to make love to me. Now when we went to bed, he just held me against him, wrapped me in his arms and we went to sleep. If I hadn't already passed out.

I was conscious that this was not how things had been before, but I was also conscious that I didn't have any desire for sex. After that wave of guilt had subsided, the deep, oily waters of self-hatred remained, unperturbed.

I shook my head and squeezed his hand 'No, I don't want to go to Paris. It's okay, I'll try an osteopath. Don't worry, my darling. I'm sure it will get sorted.'

I knew that something had to give, but I wasn't sure if that something would be my sanity, my will to live or something else.

My desire to disappear was strong.

***

The only thing that made me feel calm and happy was being around Nina, or outside around the horses. D'Artagnan liked being outside around the horses too, but it did not make him feel calm. It made him argumentative.

That morning, Camille was lifting each one of Emperador's feet and scratching at the underside of them with a special scratchy tool while D'Artagnan held the halter rope and they argued.

I sat on the upper paddock rail next to Gabriela, who was on the next rail along. She was smoking a roll-up and I wondered if I could ask her for one. Then I remembered that I really shouldn't be re-developing more than one addiction at a time. 'Is Guy really annoying her?' I asked.

She narrowed her already narrow, melancholy Portuguese eyes, the ones that seemed filled with collective centuries of poverty, misery and Atlantic Ocean loss, and gave a little shake of her head. 'No,' she said firmly. 'She loves it. She's so happy that her horses are here – and Guy does actually know quite a lot about horses. But the way he thinks about them is quite... *old-school*.' She said that in English.

I looked at her. The sun was very warm and she was darkly tanned. So was I, actually; so was everyone. It had been a very sunny, very warm spring.

Nina was sitting on the lower rung of the paddock fence, leaning against one of my legs. From time to time I touched her silky dark hair, brushed it with my fingertips. She seemed to like it because she turned and smiled up at me after I did it the second time. It made me feel so happy to see her smile.

'What does that mean?' I asked. 'They seem to argue about *everything*.'

She gave a little snort. 'Nicole. You need to know this about horse people; if there are two of them together in the room, they will have at least three different opinions.'

I frowned at her and she nodded as if to say, *'Trust me; I know what I'm talking about.'*

I turned back to watch D'Artagnan and Camille. Today was the day that Camille had agreed that D'Artagnan could ride Emperador for the first time. He was acting like it wasn't a big thing, but I knew that it was.

He was wearing a black T-shirt, jeans and cowboy boots. His tanned arms were muscular and his light brown hair was flecked with sunshine; he looked rather gorgeous. 'But I can easily mount from the ground,' he said to Camille, exasperated.

'Maybe you can, Guy, but it isn't good for Emperador! It can hurt his back. You need to stand on the mounting block!'

D'Artagnan had found an old, but solid, tree stump in the small forest around the château and dragged it into the courtyard with the tractor for Camille to use as a mounting block.

'*Putain...*' He rolled his eyes but he did as he was told and led Emperador towards it. Clearly a mounting block infringed his macho sensibilities. Emperador had obviously plugged into that because he wasn't standing still, he was prancing about next to it, his hooves crunching on the gravel. He also looked rather gorgeous.

'Wait until he stops doing that. Wait until he stands still,' said Camille.

D'Artagnan ignored her, put his foot in the stirrup and swung his butt easily into the saddle. Emperador snorted and pranced forward, his golden body shimmering in the sunshine. Camille rolled her eyes.

D'Artagnan was grinning, a huge grin that split his face from ear to ear. He gathered up the reins and held them firmly in one hand so that Emperador arched his neck even further. Now he was dancing underneath D'Artagnan, who was clearly loving it because he turned and glanced at me as if to say, 'Don't I look good on this beautiful horse?'

'No!' Camille's voice was sharp. 'Don't do that! Don't shorten the reins, that just makes him think you want him to go!'

Emperador heard the sharpness in her voice and leapt across the courtyard. D'Artagnan didn't move in the saddle; it was as if he were a part of Emperador. They did a short, snorty, arch-necked circuit of the courtyard then came back to idle in front of us, Emperador's four hooves lifting alternatively off the ground as he danced on the spot.

Camille shook her head slowly. 'He thinks he's a fucking *conquistador,*' she said to no-one in particular. Then louder, to D'Artagnan, 'You are not a *conquistador,* Guy. Let go of his head – for fuck's sake, let the reins out! Don't make my horse hot!'

'*Bah,* Camille, your horse is already hot.' He grinned but he loosened the reins a bit.

Guy did look good on Emperador. He sat proudly but his body was relaxed, supple. His free hand was hanging down at his side, his legs long in the stirrups, and there was a slight, satisfied grin on his face. 'Nina!' he called. 'Do you want to come and sit up here with me on this beautiful horse?'

I felt Nina freeze against my leg. She glanced up at me and her eyes were absolutely enormous. I looked at Camille. She shrugged. I shrugged. I smiled at Nina. 'Go,' I said softly.

Nina climbed down from the rail and walked hesitantly towards D'Artagnan. 'On the mounting block, *s'il te plaît,* Nina,' he said authoritatively.

She climbed onto it, her bare legs like brown twigs under shorts that seemed too big for her.

D'Artagnan leaned back slightly in the saddle and I saw him squeeze his legs against Emperador's side. Emperador leapt forward again and they did another small, tight circuit of the courtyard before passing next to Nina on the mounting block.

He reached down effortlessly and grabbed her around the waist, lifting her easily into the saddle in front of him. He had the biggest grin on his face, and her expression as she straddled Emperador, her hands buried in his mane, was one of ... ecstasy? Can children experience ecstasy?

As I watched D'Artagnan, holding Nina with one hand around the waist, ride Emperador around the courtyard in the warm French sunshine in the grounds of the ancient château I seemed to have found myself living in, I thought: *How on earth have I ended up here?* And I also thought: *How can I hold on to all this, to these people, this world that I love so much?*

Because I never wanted to leave.

Something had to give.

Chapter Eight

It wasn't one particular thing that gave in the end, it was more of an accumulation of things.

The first thing happened at Emma's wedding. It was midsummer's day, a beautiful day straight out of an advert for *la belle France*. The weather was perfect and the leafy green vineyards surrounding the family home stretched in every direction under an endless azure sky. The stone façade of the eighteenth century *longère* was covered in glossy Virginia creeper cut back around the long run of white-shuttered windows. It made a perfect backdrop for the ceremony that took place on the back lawn.

D'Artagnan and I had only bickered once on the way down in the car. The current favourite bickering topic was what I was – or was not – eating, and it was getting tedious. I'd finally eaten the croissant he'd bought for me when we stopped at a motorway service station because it was easier to eat it than to continue refusing to eat it. At least that had shut him up for a while, and I had been left to gaze out of the window, watch the scenery flash past and enjoy the oxycodone calm.

I threw up the croissant in the toilet when we arrived at Françoise's house, rinsed my mouth with toothpaste, re-applied lipstick and adjusted my dress. It had always been one of my favourites: a pale-blue, boat-necked Chloe with a closely fitting bodice that fluted from the waist into a full-circle skirt, ending in a froth of silk just above the knee. It kept slipping off my shoulders, which was annoying.

Emma looked stunning, so young and beautiful in her understated wedding dress, her long dark hair cascading in ringlets down her back as she walked down the aisle on Guy's arm. She radiated happiness.

After a while I realised that tears were flowing freely from my eyes as I watched them. I hastily scrabbled around for a tissue in my handbag, praying that the waterproof description of my mascara was not a misrepresentation. D'Artagnan made the briefest of eye contact with me as they passed, and I saw that his cheeks were wet, too.

He hadn't told me that he would be giving Emma away until just before the ceremony started. 'I promise Laurent that I do this for his girls,' he'd whispered after he'd led me to my seat. His voice had broken as he pronounced his friend's name, then he'd kissed me gently on the forehead before disappearing.

After the ceremony there was Champagne, *apéros* and chat on the lawn. I took a glass of Champagne and held it close to my chest, taking only the tiniest, occasional sip so that none of the circulating waiting staff was tempted to refill it. I was determined that if there were any scenes at Emma and Conor's wedding, they would be nothing to do with me.

I had seen Randy-Hands Harry out of the corner of my eye and was monitoring him on my radar, but I was feeling pleasantly calm behind my enormous Chanel sunglasses. I leaned slightly against D'Artagnan, my other hand tucked under his arm as we chatted to a tall bloke with dark curly hair.

He had come over to greet us rather shyly. 'Hello, Guy. I don't know if you remember me. Xavier. I used to work with Laurent.'

'Of course I do, Xavier!' D'Artagnan smiled warmly and shook his hand. 'How are you? This is my wife, Nicole. Nicole, Xavier.' He turned to me. 'Xavier was Laurent's protégé at his law firm.'

We shook hands and exchanged greetings; apparently it was not a Kissies situation. Xavier had long, slender hands and a nice smile.

'Where are you practising now? Still at the same firm?' Guy asked.

Xavier shook his head. 'No, after Laurent—' he paused, and looked a bit furtive, as if it were wrong to mention death on such a happy occasion '—er, after Laurent passed away, I left the firm. I, er—'

He coughed; he was quite shy, poor thing. 'I decided I didn't want to practise commercial law. I decided to become a criminal lawyer instead.'

'*Mais quel dommage,*' said D'Artagnan. 'Laurent always said you were a very good lawyer. He told my wife – my ex-wife Isabelle – that she should hire you!'

'Yes, I know.' Xavier smiled. He had soft grey eyes. 'I had a lunch with Isabelle in Paris last year before I came back to Bordeaux. We were working on a case together.'

D'Artagnan tilted his head and frowned. '*Ah bon*? But Isabelle is a commercial lawyer, not a criminal lawyer. What were you working on?'

'It was a sexual harassment case. She'd referred one of her clients to me,' said Xavier.

'She must think very highly of you. Did you win the case?' Xavier nodded. 'Yes. It was very successful.'

My radar suddenly started beeping alarmingly. We were about to be hit by a very nasal Glaswegian torpedo.

'Eeeehhhhh, if it isn't young Guy and his gorrrrrrgeous young wife!' Harry jostled Xavier's hand as he barged between him and Guy holding what looked like a large glass of Cognac at a dangerous angle.

Xavier brushed off the Champagne that Harry had made him spill on his shirt.

Harry slid a stealthy, tenacious hand around my waist and pulled me sharply towards him. It was indeed Cognac in his glass, because the fumes he exhaled made my eyes water. D'Artagnan placed his hand flat on Harry's chest in an attempt to stop him mauling me, but Harry still managed to plant a big, wet-mouthed kiss on my cheek.

'Eeeehhhh, how are yae gorrrrrgeous geerrreeell?' He paused a minute then frowned. 'Yae look like yae nae aeatin' aiirnything, gerrelll!' He glanced at Guy. 'Why are ye starving this poor wee wench, y'evil young bastard?' At the same time, his hand was busy sliding down over my bum.

Guy moved me swiftly out of the way and smacked Harry's hand away hard. '*Putain,* Harry! I've warned you before!'

'Please, Guy, please don't make a fuss,' I said quietly. He paused and glanced at me, his face angry.

Xavier's brow was furrowed. Guy turned to him. 'Have you got a business card with you, Xavier?'

'Yes, of course.' He fumbled for his wallet, opened it and held one out.

'No, give it to Harry,' D'Artagnan said, motioning at Randy Harry. 'Because he's going to need a criminal lawyer very soon if he doesn't stop trying to molest my wife, *merde*!'

Harry made a face at Guy and turned away. Suddenly he saw fresh meat in the form of Amandine, Françoise's youngest daughter, and launched himself in that direction.

Xavier looked embarrassed as he stood there holding out a business card that no-one wanted. I felt sorry for him and took it. 'Thanks, Xavier. Maybe it'll come in useful if my husband does anything stupid to defend my honour.' I gave D'Artagnan a hard stare as I slipped the card into my handbag.

***

I was not thrilled when I saw the table plan for the formal dinner. 'Why can't we just sit with your children?' I murmured, my mouth against Guy's ear.

He glanced at me. 'Because I promise Françoise that we will sit with them, Nicole. I'm sorry. It is better than inflicting my *pieux* brother and sister-in-law and my stupid, racist brother on people who have never met them. We take one for the team, *mon ange*, okay?'

I gazed into his fathomless brown eyes. The second oxycodone tablet of the day was kicking in and I'd finally finished my first glass of Champagne. It was after 7pm, and everyone had gradually wandered towards the enormous barn behind the house where dinner was to be held.

Walking next to D'Artagnan, his arm around my waist and my hand hooked in the belt of his trousers, I'd felt almost carefree, happier than I could remember feeling for a while. I'd felt a surge of love for my charming, charismatic musketeer who had walked so proudly down the aisle that afternoon with his niece.

He turned to smile at me. 'Everything is okay, *mon amour*?'

'Everything is just fine, my angel.' I smiled back and squeezed his upper arm. I put my head against his shoulder and allowed myself to bathe in the luxurious feel of his body against mine. His scent was so familiar, so comforting.

***

The tables were exquisitely dressed, with sparkling glasses and silverware, big bouquets of white roses and sprays of gypsum. I wondered if our wedding in two months' time would look as elegant and that made me feel vaguely bad, but bad-behind-Plexiglass bad. I seemed to have dropped that particular glitter-filled ball.

Happily, Benoît and Viking Veronique were also at our table. Darth Vader and the Arch Bitch were cool towards me but their disapproval lacked the customary sub-arctic *froideur,* and I was reasonably certain that it wasn't just because of my Plexiglas serenity. Stephane looked even more gaunt than usual but also kind of ... untidy. And he didn't do that deeply disapproving sucking in of air when we exchanged kisses. We'd just – exchanged kisses. It was weird.

Catherine, on the other hand, was wearing *lipstick*. Very, very red lipstick. And her mousy brown hair was not really mousy brown anymore, it was *lusciously* brown.

She still hated me, though. 'Nicole,' she said, when we did Kissies. 'You look very unwell.'

'Thank you so much, Catherine. So do you.' I smiled back at her sweetly.

Because the Arch Bitch did look weirdly unwell. She looked as if she were lit inside, as if she were full of life, full of happiness. And Catherine had always disapproved deeply of happiness.

After the entrées, main course and cheese course had been served, I went to the loo and had a brief, unscheduled nap while I was sitting on it. I only woke up when I nearly fell off the seat. I was feeling very chilled and sleepy; I'd had a glass of wine with dinner (some of which I had managed to eat), and I'd made a concerted effort to make polite conversation with Antoine and his boyfriend, who were seated on my left. I steered the conversation carefully away when the subject of politics, immigration or Marine Le Pen and how brilliant she was, came up. It had been quite tiring.

As I returned to the table, I saw that Pascal had joined us. Pascal and Françoise were now a thing; they were dating. It felt nice to have indirectly been the harbinger of joy and happiness and not chaos and doom as I seemed to be usually.

I slipped back into my seat next to D'Artagnan. He was deep in conversation with Pascal but he turned to me when I placed a hand lightly on his leg. I smiled at him.

He frowned at me. Pascal, who was sitting on the other side of him, was frowning at me too. 'Why did you never tell me about the terrible childhood you have, Nicole?' D'Artagnan asked.

I glared at Pascal; he had clearly been scattering beans far and wide while I was gone. 'I did tell you, Guy.'

He shook his head. 'No, Nicole, you never tell me about your mother, that she drink all the time and that she hit you.'

'Mmm. Well, she did sometimes. But not all the time.' I reached for my glass of wine, which had been refilled during my absence. I was quite pleased about that because D'Artagnan was looking very solemn and the mood would need lightening. 'She wasn't all bad. Sometimes we went to the beach together,' I offered. Normally to bars on the beachfront so that she could drink and pick up a new surfer-boy, like she had when she'd got knocked up with me.

Pascal snorted loudly. 'My God, Nicole, your mother was terrible. Don't make excuses for her!' He fixed me with Jules' sapphire-blue eyes.

'I'm not making excuses, Pascal. I'm just saying that she wasn't *all* bad. There were bits that were okay.'

He shook his head. 'Nicole.' He gazed at me 'Even apart from the violence, your mother was a very bad mother.' He glanced at D'Artagnan. 'She caused so much worry in our family because she'd get drunk, pick up men in bars and bring them home to her apartment. We were worried that something would happen to Nicole – she was only a little kid! My father tried to contact the social services but they weren't interested. There are so many social problems in that country and hardly any public funding to deal with them.'

I glared at him. I really did not want the extremely dirty laundry of my childhood to be aired at a table full of my new, arrogant, judgemental French in-laws, whose bloodline went back to before Charlemagne (probably). Whereas mine began and ended with surfer-sperm-boy Jeff and violent, alcoholic Tiffany.

'No-one ever touched me when I was a child, Pascal.'

He gazed at me intently. 'I suppose that was partly luck, and also because you were a pretty smart kid.' He gave a wry smile. 'Do you remember that time that my father tried to insist that you come to our apartment if your mother brought a man home with her?'

I allowed my eyes to slide away from his penetrating gaze. 'Not really. Not specifically.'

His tone was thoughtful, sad. 'I remember it so well. You refused. You stood there in front of him, this skinny little kid, and you explained that you were quite safe, that you knew to lock your bedroom door when you heard her come home with someone, that you knew to put a chair under the handle, that you could hide in the wardrobe if you needed to.'

D'Artagnan had not taken his eyes off my face.

Pascal drew in a deep breath and shook his head. Then he exhaled and looked at me again. His face was pained. 'It was all wrong, Nicole, a little kid telling an adult not to worry, that you had made arrangements to make sure you were not molested!' He lowered his voice. 'Nicole, you need to accept that your mother was not just a bad mother, she was a *terrible* mother!'

I met D'Artagnan's gaze and, as I expected, it was full of sorrow. I hate sorrow. I hate people feeling sorry for me.

I gave a big shrug. 'Okay, whatever. She was a terrible mother. But I was never molested as a child.'

I looked around the table to see if any other unrequested sorrow was being expressed. To my relief, Antoine and his boyfriend were giggling at something on YouTube and ignoring us. Stephane had wandered off somewhere. Benoît was talking to someone standing slightly behind him. Catherine and Veronique were comparing their suntanned forearms. Hang on a minute ... the Arch Bitch had been in the *sun*?

'Can we change the subject please? It's not really a suitable topic for a wedding, is it?' I asked.

D'Artagnan was frowning deeply. 'Why are you so hostile about this, Nicole?'

Because I feel irritated that I'm being ambushed by things that happened thirty years ago that I can do nothing about. What the fuck is the point? I thought.

I shook my head crossly. 'Because I don't need your concern. It was a long time ago. It was a bit shitty, but a lot of kids have shitty childhoods. Like I said, I wasn't molested, so can we just drop it? Please?'

I had to admit that, until Pascal had mentioned it, I hadn't remembered the defiant, practical child that I'd been, the Nicole who had taken sensible precautions to protect herself from her mother's drunk, potentially paedophile boyfriends. I wondered where that child was now? In her place was an adult, her finger welded to the trigger of an automatic weapon filled with fear, spraying her life with an endless hail of toxic bullets, destroying everything that she loved while coolly observing herself doing so from behind a pharmaceutical mist.

I had failed that child, that practical, determined child, and I felt ashamed. And angry, angry at my adult self. I hadn't felt angry for quite a while. It was weirdly liberating.

D'Artagnan did drop it, although his eyes were still sad. He needed distracting so I put my mouth against his ear and whispered, 'Don't you think Catherine looks different tonight?'

He watched her across the table for a minute, then turned to me and said, 'Sex.'

I raised an eyebrow. 'What, right here? Right now? Surely it's a bit public, my darling?'

He grinned and the sadness in his eyes faded a little, which made me happy. 'No, I mean I think Catherine has been having sex. That's why she look different.'

I smiled at him. His eyes were rather lovely, chocolate-brown with little flecks of gold in them. 'It's not always about sex, y'know, D'Artagnan.'

He raised an artfully arched eyebrow. 'I know *that*, Nicole.' There was a pause while we both silently acknowledged that, actually, it had been a while since...

'But Catherine, she look like a woman who has ... *bah*, who *is*, enjoying sex.' His voice was low and he blinked very slowly at me.

I couldn't, even if I'd wanted to, stop the smile that spread across my face, so I looked away and reached for my wine glass.

Stephane had returned and was sitting across the table from us. He had put on his glasses and was holding one of the wine bottles and glaring furiously at the label. I wondered what it said that was making him so unhappy.

'Sex with your brother, do you think?' I asked D'Artagnan, making no attempt to hide the scepticism in my voice.

Catherine had just thrown back her head and was laughing uproariously at something Benoît had said, as if it were the most hilarious thing she'd ever heard. Her throat was exposed and flushed. I had never seen the Arch Bitch in technicolour before; she'd always been monochrome.

I wondered if Stephane was studying the label on the wine bottle so fastidiously because he was trying to find out why his wife had gone mad. Because that had been another first: Catherine had drunk several glasses of wine.

'*Mais, bien sur,* they are *catholiques,* Nicole! It is inconceivable they have sex outside of marriage.' D'Artagnan frowned, as if my scepticism were unwarranted.

'So why doesn't Stephane look like he's just rediscovered his G-spot as well?'

He looked at Stephane and shrugged. 'Maybe she buy a sex toy.'

Catherine gave a shriek of unadulterated hilarity at that point and grasped Benoît's arm so tightly that I saw him wince.

'Musta been a very big one...' I said.

And then dessert was served and I ate a little of mine, which made D'Artagnan pout approvingly. I no longer felt tired; instead, I felt strangely alive. The anger I'd felt earlier seemed to have permeated the Plexiglas, and I no longer felt quite so muted. Perhaps it was because the music had started. Music always changes my mood, and the music was excellent because Matthieu, Amandine's gorgeous, super-cool dreadlocked boyfriend, was a semi-professional DJ and had agreed to DJ for the wedding.

D'Artagnan sat back in his chair. He was holding my hand and stroking the back of it gently with his thumb. 'You seem a bit better tonight, *mon amour.* How is your back? I ask Françoise for the details of the osteopath earlier.'

'Thank you, my darling. Actually, my back feels okay. It's not bad tonight.'

'Did you take a lot of drugs for it?'

I wondered how to answer that. 'Yes. But they seem to have worn off and it still feels okay.'

He raised my hand to his mouth and brushed it softly with his lips. 'I am so sorry to learn about the terrible childhood you have, *mon ange*. I think I understand so much more now.'

I frowned. 'Please don't let's talk about that again.'

The last song was fading and gradually the opening chords of Chopin – the opening chords of *our* song – became audible. I stared at Guy and he smiled back at me, a sly smile.

'You asked Matthieu to play it?' I asked.

'Of course I ask him, Nicole. Come, *mon cœur*, come to dance with me?' He rose and held out his hand, and I gazed up at him thinking, *this man, he's always on the case, he never stops thinking about me, about us.*

I put my hand in his and we went to the dancefloor. He held me, one arm around my waist, the other with my hand firmly in his, and we danced. His body was strong and hard against mine and our eyes locked hypnotically while Pepe Raphael sang *La Soledad* in his deep, tortured baritone voice, a song about losing the love of his life. The cello swooned and the bossa-nova-beat swished. It is the most heart-wrenchingly romantic song in the world, and it is the song that made me finally throw all caution to the wind and fall in love with D'Artagnan all those aeons ago in Saint Sebastian.

I did not look away from Guy's eyes while we danced and, when he leaned forward and kissed me, I felt as if I were dissolving. I was intoxicated with love for him. The D'Artagnan Effect had kicked in.

'*Alors, te voilà de retour,* Nicole.' You've come back.

I throbbed deep inside as he gazed into my eyes; I actually felt a throb, and then we were kissing again, a sultry, lustful kiss that made me melt into his firm body. It felt insanely good, and I remembered what desire felt like. I wanted D'Artagnan again; oxycodone or not, I wanted him really badly. It seemed he felt the same.

We left the party and went to our room, the room that we always had when we stayed at Françoise's house, the room with the four-poster bed and the pale blue *toile du jour* wallpaper. He undressed me very slowly, kissing me everywhere, touching me everywhere. He slipped his fingers one by one into my mouth, his long eyelashes half-closed, and then he slid those same long, wet fingers inside me, his thumb caressing me gently, insistently, so that I strained against him, into him.

I pushed him over onto his back, and I kissed his chest, ran my tongue through the hairs in the middle of it, tasted the salt. I touched his taut stomach, the hairs that ran from his groin to his belly-button, kissed them, licked them. I moved lower and touched the scar, the raw scar on his thigh, the scar he had suffered because of me, and he flinched as I kissed it. Then I kissed his long, thick cock and took him into my mouth, caressed him with my tongue and tasted him, bitter-salty, as he groaned, '*Oh mon dieu Nicole qu'est-ce que je t'aime...*'

I worshipped this magical man who so desired and loved me, the damaged, soiled ragdoll that he had for some reason decided he wanted in his life. I wanted so much to please him, and he responded as if my touch were everything he'd ever wanted, and his pleasure was intoxicating.

When we could wait no longer, he slid his hands underneath me and gently lifted my hips. 'Is this okay, *mon ange*? Is your back okay?' and I wanted him so much I could only nod. I had no voice; I was mesmerised by his eyes. My legs wrapped around his waist as he slid slowly, deeply, inside me, as he gradually increased the rhythm, all the time holding my eyes with his, dark, liquid, insanely sensual, until finally it became unbearable. And then I was arching into him, gasping, crying out, closing on him, my core tight like a vice around him as the universe imploded, exploded...

And I heard him groan, '*Mon dieu, Nicole, je t'aime, je t'aime tellement...*' and felt him pulsing inside me. It was exquisite.

***

I loved D'Artagnan so much. I had to find a way to solve the conundrum.

Chapter Nine

Anger is a funny thing. Once that first cell had formed, the cell of anger at my adult self for avoiding rather than dealing with the conundrum, it started to replicate itself, dividing into two and then four and then eight and so on, until anger gradually replaced fear and despair.

Whenever I thought about bastard Guillaume – Satan – I no longer felt helpless and afraid. Now I felt anger, and that tight fist of burning anger didn't feel as if it existed behind Plexiglas; it existed in my solar plexus.

I was angry with myself, too, for having allowed it to happen.

By the time I was twenty-six, I knew how the world worked, and I knew what men were like. I didn't have a boyfriend and I had little desire for one: if I wanted sex with someone (and I rarely did), I had it on my terms. I was a hard bitch – or at least I thought I was. And I knew about drugs; I knew about date-rape drugs.

On the last night of Milan Fashion Week that fateful February, I was feeling good. I was on top of my game and my agent was happy because I was booked months ahead. When one of the make-up artists, a woman with a wicked sense of humour who had been making me laugh all week, suggested that I come to an after-party with her and her boyfriend, I didn't hesitate for a moment.

The image of Satan standing at the other side of the crowded room staring at me as I partied with the make-up artist and her boyfriend was very clear in my mind now. He crossed the room and chatted to the make-up artist, whom he seemed to know, and then to the make-up artist's boyfriend, who was bopping about quite wildly. The boyfriend bumped into me, I turned to push him away, and when I turned back Satan was right next to me. He was standing next to my hand, in which I was holding a glass of Champagne.

Now that my brain had decided to let me remember all that, I realised that nothing that night had happened by chance. I'd gathered from D'Artagnan that Guillaume was working for an investment bank in Milan at that time, and he'd decided to do a little shopping at Milan Fashion Week. Only he hadn't been shopping for clothes, he'd been shopping for a victim and he'd selected me from the runway catalogue.

I wondered when he'd made his selection, because now I realised that the make-up artist had been super-friendly to me for most of the week. She and her boyfriend had set me up; that was what Satan had meant when he said, 'I paid for those eyes.'

I was surprised at how furious I was at myself for only just having realised it.

***

The following week, I had the unexpected pleasure of being able to channel some of that anger.

It was a swelteringly hot summer day and I'd driven to the supermarket in Cognac to buy some essentials. Halfway across the carpark, I remembered that I'd forgotten the gas canister refill for the SodaStream machine, so I went back to my car. There was no one parked next to me, so I opened the driver's door wide and leaned in to grab the canister from where it had fallen into the passenger footwell. I was wearing shorts and sandals; not short shorts, but short-enough shorts.

Suddenly, I was horrified to feel a hand grab at my left buttock. At the same time, I heard, 'Eeeeehhhh how are yae, lovely gerrrrrrrrellll?'

I shot out of the car backwards and in one smooth motion, which I replayed pleasingly in my head several times afterwards, I grabbed Harry by the shoulders and kneed him as hard as I could in the balls. He dropped onto the tarmac as if he'd been shot, and lay in the foetal position, gasping for air. I reached back into my car, grabbed the gas canister, straightened up, slammed the car door and locked it with the remote.

'Harry,' I said, smiling brightly down at him. My voice was very loud and very clear. 'Please listen. If you ever, *ever* lay another finger on me, or if I ever see you about to lay another finger on any other woman, I swear to God that the pain you are feeling now will be only a pleasant memory in comparison to the pain you will feel then.'

And then I went shopping. I felt confident that Randy Uncle Harry and I were now on a much more comfortable footing. And it felt as if my resolution to solve the conundrum had strengthened even further.

***

It was fully formed a couple of days later.

It was Nina's summer holidays, and she and I were sitting in the paddock. The heat was intense and the grass was long and very dry; we had trampled it down in our little corner where we often sat. Flies, bastard horse-flies, butterflies, bees, wasps were all there, buzzing, fluttering, murmuring around us. The horses flicked their tails as they grazed nose-to-tail so that they could sweep one another's heads with their tails to move the flies away.

Nina was leaning against me, one of her thin little arms across my body, her silky dark head on my shoulder. She wasn't saying a lot but I had finally dared to put an arm around her slight form and it felt good, as if I were protecting her.

She drew a deep, thoughtful breath, as if she'd been thinking about something for a long time, then she said '*Princesse* Nicole, do you think you could help me to sit on Espiritu?'

I looked at Espiritu. His head was down, his thick mane almost obscuring his huge, blue-black eyes and long black eyelashes. I had been astonished at how long his eyelashes were. Espiritu was so beautiful that he belonged on a catwalk – or rather, a horsewalk. He swished his tail as I thought that, as if he were annoyed that I should dare to think there was a horsewalk capable of containing his majesty.

I shrugged slightly. 'You should really ask Camille, Nina. He's not my horse. Do you think Camille would be happy if you sat on him?'

She did her own little shrug, skinny shoulders raised up around her neck. 'I already asked her. She said if I think it is okay, it is okay.'

I knew Nina spent a lot of time with Camille; they were always chatting – I often saw them when I looked through the upstairs window in the mornings. 'Okay. Now? Do you want to get on him now?' I asked.

She nodded and stood up, brushed herself off and held out her hand to me. I took it and stood up carefully. My back had been feeling a bit better since D'Artagnan and I had resumed our extremely pleasant sex-life, but it was still capricious. Sometimes it was agony when I was trying to figure out how to resolve the conundrum, and then I'd realise that every muscle in my body was taut, poised, ready for action. Ready to *fight*.

We walked over to the horses. Nina approached Espiritu easily and talked to him in some weird child-horse French that I didn't understand. He moved his big head towards her, nudged her a little with his nose so that she staggered back on her skinny legs. She giggled and grinned at me, shook her fringe out of her eyes and said, 'He says yes, it's okay.'

She stood next to him, stretched her arms up and placed her hands on his gleaming body. I bent down and, even though I felt a twinge, I put my hands around her waist and lifted her up. She was all legs and body, like a weird, fleshy insect, and I laughed involuntarily as she wriggled and giggled. I worried for a second that Espiritu would be bothered by the inelegance of the fleshy stick-insect about to straddle him, but he ignored us and carried on grazing. I held her up while she grabbed his mane, wrapped her little hands in it as she worked a skinny leg over his back and scrambled up.

And then she was astride him. She sat up straight, imperiously, this tiny creature, with her perfect mouth, her dark fringe brushing her enormous green eyes which were brimming with delight. She looked down at me and gave me the most delighted, radiant smile.

Espiritu lifted his head. He blinked his long eyelashes and his glossy neck furrowed as he turned to look at this tiny creature astride his back. Then he gave a huge snort and went back to grazing.

As I stood next to them, I laid a hand on his warm, silky shoulder. I knew instinctively that, for the first time since he'd arrived, it was okay for me to touch him.

That morning, I had decided I wasn't going to take any more oxycodone. I knew there would be a withdrawal and that it would be horrible but I didn't care. I wanted – I *needed* – a clear head in order to resolve the conundrum.

'*Princesse* Nicole? It's enough now. I need to come down.'

Nina held her arms out to me. Before I could think about how she was going to descend from Espiritu's back, she was sliding off him with her arms outstretched. She slipped her arms around my neck as she slid off his smooth body and then suddenly, she was wrapped around me, her skinny body enveloping mine so that I was forced to clasp her to me.

And in that moment, I knew. It was blindingly clear.

I was going to get that bastard. I was going to get that bastard Satan and, if I could, I was going to get his two gargoyles as well. I was going to get those bastard men who had dared to steal the essence of me, who had violated my right to consent, my right to exist without fear, my right to be a woman. I might be physically weaker but *by fuck* I was not mentally weaker, and I'd had *enough* of being afraid. Most importantly, I was *not* going to let what had happened to me happen to Nina. I was going to channel my seven-year-old self; she was much stronger, much more determined and she was going to sort out this shit.

I twirled Nina around the paddock. I held her tightly against me and she kept her arms and her legs clasped around me and we laughed delightedly. She had sat on Espiritu for the first time; she was intoxicated with him, and I was intoxicated with the both of them.

When we finally stopped laughing and turning, she slid down my front onto the ground. I became conscious of D'Artagnan leaning on the paddock rails, his chin on his fist, watching us. He did that slow blink, that wonderful slow blink, and then he blew us both kisses, one downwards towards Nina and one directly at me. His lips moved and he blew '*je t'aime*' at me.

I blinked a slow kiss back at him as I mouthed '*je t'aime*' because *je t'aimed* him so much, in that moment. And I thought, *I can do this. I can neuter Satan. Satan isn't going to violate, hurt or rape any other women, ever again. Not on my watch.*

Even though I had to do something very, very difficult in order to succeed.

***

I had to ask for help.

I'd been thinking a lot about what Jules had said to me earlier that year about *not* asking for help. Once I'd started to accept that I would need help to neuter Satan, I was able to gaze clearly on the conundrum and start to see how I might resolve it – hopefully without losing D'Artagnan, without losing everything. There was a lot at risk, but unless I asked for help the situation could not be solved.

I felt good once I'd made the decision. I felt *incredible*: strong, determined ... and *capable*.

I was less confident about the withdrawal from the oxycodone. That was horrible.

I had agonising cramps everywhere – in my stomach, in all of my muscles. My body dripped with sweat as I shivered with cold, and the nightmares were petrifying. All of them were variations on the same theme, all of them took place in the Marble Villa in Hell. They were incredibly vivid and absolutely terrifying.

Each time I woke up trembling with fear, shuddering with waves of nausea, all I craved with every cell in my body was one, just one more, oxycodone. But I am well-versed in opioid withdrawal; once I had made the decision to stop taking the oxycodone, I'd driven to the nearest pharmacy and handed in all the remaining pills and my diazepam prescription for disposal. I knew I could not trust myself with the diazepam until I was clear of the oxycodone addiction.

I was incapable of leaving our bedroom for three days. This time there was no gentle methadone landing; this was an emergency landing, all systems on full alert, all sirens blaring, all airbags deployed.

It was very messy.

The only thing that helped was to keep repeating, over and over and over again in my head, *I'm going to get that bastard.*

D'Artagnan was very worried. '*Mon amour*, what is wrong? Why are you so sick?' He crouched beside me in the bathroom on the first night as I dry-retched agonisingly into the toilet yet again.

'Flu. It's the flu,' I gasped, trembling from head to toe, my body slick with sweat. I felt like I was dying.

He held my hair back from my face as I dry-retched yet again. Finally he carried me back to bed, I passed out and he fell asleep again. And then I woke ten minutes later, my whole body taut with pain. My head, my heart, my lungs all felt like they were being pounded with heavy, spiked mallets – and the stomach cramps, the leg cramps, were excruciating, so incredibly painful that I cried out and fell on the floor as I tried desperately to uncramp them.

D'Artagnan watched helplessly.

On the second day he wanted to call a doctor. I glared at him, big purple circles under my eyes, my hair hanging around my face like limp, greasy-brown spaghetti. 'It's flu, Guy. The doctor can't do anything. It's a *virus*. I don't need a doctor. There is *no point* in calling a doctor. I'll get over it.'

And then finally, on day four, it started to ease and I slept, blissful, beautiful, wonderful redeeming sleep. Twenty-four hours straight.

D'Artagnan brought me chamomile tea on the morning of the fifth day. I sat up in bed and smiled weakly at him. He smiled back gently at me. 'Better, *mon amour*?'

I nodded. 'Much better my angel, thank you. Thank you so much for taking such care of me.'

'*De rien*, I am just happy that you are better, *chérie*. I was very worried.'

Later that morning, after I'd showered and dried myself, I stood in front of the mirrored sliding doors in Heaven and dared to look at my body critically. I was very underweight. I resolved to start eating properly, starting with the croissants D'Artagnan brought me when he came back from cycling, click-clacking through the salon and into the dining hall in his special cycling shoes, full of statistics about how far, how fast, how big the incline on that morning's ride had been, sweaty in his logo-ed Lycra cycling outfit.

He was very pleased when I ate the croissants; he smiled benevolently as if I were a recalcitrant child that he had coerced into eating again. D'Artagnan was happy because his wife wasn't a ragdoll anymore.

He didn't suspect that she'd secretly turned into a Ninja.

I rang the wedding-dress shop and changed the order to a size 36 in the Lanvin two-second-undress wedding dress. I was determined that I was going to be back to a normal weight for our wedding ceremony. I knew I would be anxious, that there was a lot to do, and I was very nervous about how it would all pan out. I knew there would be times when I would be too anxious to eat but I was determined not to compromise my health. I had a lot to plan, a lot to set in motion.

When I told D'Artagnan that I wanted Nina to be a flower girl at our wedding, he tilted his head to one side and gave a thoughtful little smile. 'Of course, *mon amour*, I think that would be a good idea. But maybe ask Marion first if it is okay.' We'd already sent a wedding invitation to Marion and she'd accepted; when I rang her, she sounded delighted at the idea of Nina being a flower girl, a *bouquetière*.

When I asked Nina if she'd like to be a *bouquetière*, and explained that she would wear a fairy-tale dress and a little crown of flowers, her green eyes became even more enormous and she grinned a huge, delighted grin, which was actually hilarious as she had recently lost her two front baby teeth. I hoped she would grin like that in the very important photoshoot Annabelle had planned on the day.

***

Annabelle's gaze was hostile. 'It's impossible to change, Nicole. It's far too late.'

'Flowers? Really? They haven't even grown yet, Annabelle. It's—' I picked up my phone and tapped on the calendar icon '—it's the seventeenth of July and the wedding is at the end of August. How is it impossible to change the flower arrangements?'

Sulky pout. Annabelle was wearing a low-cut black blouse, and it was interesting to note that the rest of her body had caught up with the orange hue of her face. 'I don't know what you don't like about the pink roses, Nicole.'

'Well, Annabelle, it's the pinkness that's a bit of a problem. I remember we talked about colours in the beginning and I said cream and green ... but here we are and the word "pink" has somehow intruded into our colour scheme. So all I'm asking is that we remove the pink roses and replace them with something green. Any shade. Knock yourself out. I'm not going to be fussy about it.'

Nina suddenly burst through the door at the end of the dining hall. She ran towards me grinning, her purple gums fully exposed as she clutched at my arm, jumping up and down excitedly as she fixed her eyes on mine. '*Princesse* Nicole, *Princesse* Nicole, you need to come now. You need to see – Camille is going to ride Espiritu!'

I took her small hands in mine. 'Really? Today?'

She nodded enthusiastically. 'She told me. The *prince* is there and he told me to come to tell you.' She grinned again at me and then noticed Annabelle. The grin started to fade. She looked away, looked down, and her face became solemn. '*Désolée, Madame*' she said quietly.

French children are taught from a very young age to curb their enthusiasm in favour of *la politesse*.

'Bon-jew,' said Annabelle.

I turned to her. 'Nina, *je te présente*, Annabelle.'

Nina was still looking down but she muttered, '*Bonjour, Madame* Annabelle.'

I squeezed her hands and glanced at Annabelle. 'Nina is also going to be a flower girl at our wedding. Did I mention that to you?'

Instant pout. 'No, Nicole, you did not. That's going to be a big problem.' She sucked in her cheeks.

I raised an eyebrow while I gently brushed Nina's silky hair out of her eyes with my fingers. 'Why is that a problem, Annabelle? Flower girls don't take up much room, do they?'

A cross shake of the head. 'It's not that, Nicole!'

I frowned. 'What is it, then?'

'Well, I haven't organised... I haven't catered... I haven't... I mean, what's she going to *wear*?'

I thought for a minute. 'Well, perhaps she could wear a dress like Katie's? What do you think? Were you thinking of something more exotic ... something a bit more Rio Carnival, perhaps? Because we can do that, too.'

Annabelle really hated me. I could see that. 'Who's going to make the dress?' she growled.

'The same person who made Katie's dress,' I said mildly. I stood up and touched Nina's head so that she turned to gaze up at me. 'I'm quite sure it's possible to make a dress for a child in five weeks, so don't worry about it. If you could just find a way for her to carry a bouquet the same as Katie's, that would be fabulous.' I smiled as nicely as I could.

'Anyway,' I continued, 'I have to pop outside now with Nina to watch Camille ride the most beautiful horse in the world. Do you want to come with us? Or are we finished?'

Annabelle glared at me. 'I'm finished.'

***

'Bérengère, you know you said you would help me if I needed help?'

'Of course, Nicole.' We were sitting outside underneath the pergola in her garden. It was another stiflingly hot day; the shade temperature was thirty-four degrees.

'Well, I *do* need your help. I need to order some things and I can't have them delivered to the château. I wondered if I could have them delivered to your address. Is that okay?'

She raised an eyebrow and narrowed her eyes. Her brown shoulders were slightly moist with heat under her pale green camisole. She had just lit one of her thin, elegantly rolled cigarettes; she blew out a cloud of smoke and delicately removed a flake of tobacco from her tongue. She was always so cool, so chilled, even in the heat; her movements were very languid. 'Nicole, of course I will help you. What do you need to order? And why can't it be delivered to your house?'

'Some ... uh, well, some equipment. I don't want Guy to know about it. Is it important that you know what it is? It's perfectly legal – it's sold in France.'

Little pout, slight frown creasing her forehead. 'But why don't you want to tell me what you are ordering? You want me to help you, but you don't want to tell me what it is that I am helping you with?'

I sighed deeply. 'It's complicated, Bérengère.'

A big snort, a short, expressive expulsion of air as if I'd just said something ridiculous. 'Life is always complicated, Nicole. All of life is complicated. Tell me why yours is complicated.' She sat back in her chair, put one of her bare brown feet onto the chair next to me, took another drag on her cigarette. 'Tell me. It's good for your French to explain to me why this is important to you.'

I sighed. My eyes slid away from hers towards the verdant hedge that bordered her property, the vineyards that stretched up a long incline, the blue sky beyond. I felt a drop of sweat slide from my armpit down my side under my T-shirt.

I focused on her friendly, curious grey eyes as I said in English, 'I can't tell you in French. I don't have enough French to tell you why, and it's quite hard for me to tell you because I've never told anyone before. I've never spoken the words aloud in English or in French or in any language. Because it's more than just complicated – it's horrible. The full story is ugly.'

My eyes slid away from hers again. 'And I'm not sure that I have the right to inflict it on anyone else. Not yet, anyway.'

She leaned forward and put her long-fingered hand on my arm. 'Look at me, Nicole,' she commanded. 'Look at me and tell me this story. Tell me it in English. You can inflict it on me. I am a very, very strong woman.' Her gaze was intense but her smile was warm.

I took a very big breath and I told Bérengère about the Marble Villa in Hell. I didn't look at her as I spoke; I spoke to the vines, I spoke to the hills, I spoke to the sky. I told her about Satan, about Satan's gargoyles, that I thought there had been two of them but that I wasn't sure because I'd been drugged. I told her that Satan had probably seen me on the runway, had approached the make-up artist and she had set me up: *Bring this one to the party in the Marble Villa in Hell and I will pay you.*

I explained that Satan was Guy's business partner and that he had been creepy towards me from the very first time we'd met. Then, when I'd confronted him, he'd become very angry and let slip that he'd preferred me when I was 'younger'. That had made me remember events I had hidden away. And then I knew who the Masked Bastard was.

'But I think that he thinks I don't know what he meant,' I said slowly. 'I think that he thinks that I have no memory at all of that night, and that gives him a kind of sick thrill. That's why he's so creepy with me, so flirtatious.'

Bérengère had not taken her eyes off my face while I spoke, but her brow was deeply furrowed. 'But you must have known... I mean, Nicole, he must have known you would realise afterwards that you'd been raped? *Did* you realise it, the next day?'

'Oh yes, of course I realised. Bruising and blood and semen don't just spontaneously appear overnight, and it's not difficult to join the dots when you have absolutely no recollection of leaving a party and yet you've woken up in your hotel room.'

She closed her eyes tightly for a minute then reached forward and took my hand. She held it tightly. 'Oh my God, Nicole, I'm so sorry that happened to you.'

I blinked. I had not realised there were tears on my face and I wiped them away angrily with my free hand.

'But didn't you report it? Didn't you go to the police?'

I raised an eyebrow. 'And tell them what? I went to a party, I got pissed and I did quite a lot of coke, and it seems someone drugged me and that I was raped? And no, I don't have any idea who it was?' I paused. 'I didn't speak any Italian and my flight back to London was that afternoon. It seemed easier to accept that I'd been stupid and careless and that the bad thing that happens to so many women had happened to me, too.'

'You weren't "stupid and careless",' she said quietly. 'Don't try to blame yourself. You did *nothing* wrong, Nicole. You were targeted by an evil man and his evil friends. You were a victim.'

I glowered at her. 'Yeah, well, I'm tired of being a victim. And now that I know it was that bastard Guillaume, I want to bring him to justice. Not just because of what he did to me but because I know he's continuing to do it or, at the very least, he's continuing to be violent towards women.'

I told her what Françoise had said and how his too-young girlfriend Léa had looked when I'd seen them together. I said I wanted to stop him doing that to any other women.

She nodded slowly, her eyes very serious. She had not let go of my hand, and hers felt strong and warm. 'I think that is excellent, Nicole. I will do anything you ask to help you.' She paused a minute. 'Have you talked to your husband about this?'

'No, I can't. Well, I can't talk to him yet.'

I explained about D'Artagnan's inevitable alpha-male reaction and what he'd said about Guillaume, and how he'd already demonstrated his ability to be alpha-male stupid.

'So, I don't want to tell him until Guillaume is out of his reach,' I concluded.

She nodded slowly. 'Yes. I see that.' She paused and took a sip of water from her glass. I did too; my throat felt dry.

'But there are a couple of things I'm worried about before I kick this off,' I said hesitantly as I put down my glass. 'Maybe you could advise me on one of them.'

She took a deep breath. 'Of course I will try. But I think, after what you've just told me, that we both need a glass of Cognac now. Come, let's go inside where it's cooler.'

For once the dogs didn't follow us; they were all flat out underneath the table, pinned to the ground by the relentless heat. The house was wonderfully cool. Bérengère led me into the salon, which I'd never been in before. It was a fascinating room, a room I felt I could spend hours in just looking at everything. There were photographs on the walls from South America and Japan and Australia and Russia and India and what looked like Mars. There was a display cabinet full of intriguing objects, as well as other objects on the console tables and a bizarre sculpture on the stone mantelpiece above the fireplace. It was like a one-room museum of the world. The floorboards were covered with faded Kilim rugs.

Bérengère motioned me towards a vast, deep-red velvet sofa that took up most of the room while she went over to the intricate gilt-and-mirrored drinks cabinet and poured us both a large glass of Cognac. She returned to the opposite corner of the sofa and handed me a glass before tucking her feet underneath her.

I was aware that Bérengère knew D'Artagnan's family, even though she didn't know D'Artagnan. During our second lesson I'd asked her how she knew Benoît and she'd said, 'Oh, we had an affair for a while.'

I'd stared at her then started grinning, unable to stop myself. 'Before or after he was married to the Viking?'

She frowned. 'Which Viking?'

'He was married to *more* than one Viking?' I was astounded. She was still frowning. 'Who is a Viking, Nicole?'

'Oh sorry, I mean Veronique.'

She grinned. 'You have a lot of people in your head, don't you, Nicole? Your Duchess, your D'Artagnan, the cast of *Star Wars* ... and Vikings too! It must be very busy in there.'

'I had a vivid imagination as a child,' I offered.

She shook her head. 'You still do, it seems to me.'

There'd been a pause. 'So, before or after he was married to Veronique?' I asked again.

She carried on smiling. 'That, Nicole, is none of your business.' Then she'd explained that the word in French for 'vivid' wasn't '*vivide*' but '*vif*', and that was the end of that conversation.

'So, Nicole, what are these things you want me to advise you about before you put this man in prison?'

I smiled at her certainty, and explained what Françoise had said about Guillaume potentially having the power to damage Guy's reputation. 'I can cope with Guy being angry with me, but I would really hate it if everyone thought he was in some way complacent about Satan – or worse, compliant.'

'Why do you think Guy will be angry with you?'

I gave a big shrug, almost a full Gallic shrug because I pouted and raised my eyebrows while I did it. 'I just think that this happened long before I met him and... His life, well, it isn't chaotic like mine is. Was. He comes from an ancient French family, he had an excellent education, went to an elite university, became a Mast—' I corrected myself '— became an investment banker, got married to a lawyer. They have happy, well-adjusted children, who will no doubt be just as successful as their parents and—'

I paused again. 'And I'm about to throw a hand grenade in the middle of it. Deliberately. Publicly. I think that has the potential to make Guy very angry.'

Bérengère didn't say anything but her eyes narrowed as she gazed at me.

'I'm worried about how it will affect his reputation and his sister's reputation. Will she get tarnished by association? I would hate for that to happen. What do you think? How does French society feel about this sort of thing? Particularly the *Bordelais*, whom D'Artagnan seem to think spend all their time gossiping?'

She reached forward, picked up her tobacco pouch and Rizla papers and started deftly rolling herself another cigarette. She didn't say anything. I waited. When she'd finished, she put the tobacco pouch and Rizlas back on the table and the expertly rolled cigarette between her lips. Then she lit it. She inhaled and, as she exhaled, she finally looked at me again. 'Do you think your husband loves you, Nicole?'

'Yes, I think so. I mean, I love *him*. Very much, actually.' More than I've ever loved anyone, I wanted to say. More even than ethereally beautiful, extraordinarily talented Karl, something that I had never thought would be possible.

She nodded slowly. 'So why on earth are you asking whether your husband will be worrying about his reputation when he finds out what Guillaume did? He won't care about that. He'll only care about you.'

'Yes, but—'

'Forget about it, Nicole. It's not important. It doesn't matter what everyone thinks. If anything, from what you tell me, the *Bordelais* will be grateful to you for putting Guillaume in prison.'

I thought that perhaps there could be some truth in that.

She carried on studying me. 'I don't think you should be concerned. What you need to focus on is how you're going to get enough evidence to bring criminal charges against Guillaume. That will be far more difficult – and it is much more important. So tell me, how are you going to do that?'

I took a deep breath, a big sip of Cognac and I outlined my plan to Get That Bastard Satan.

***

I hadn't mentioned my other concern to Bérengère because I knew she wouldn't be able to answer it. The only person who *could* answer it would need to have a detailed understanding of both French commercial and criminal law. Thanks to Randy Uncle Harry, and D'Artagnan's macho sensibilities, I knew just the man; even better, I had his business card. Silver linings, eh? They're everywhere, if you look.

***

There are even silver linings when you end up with bruises on your butt and the back of your legs, and pain that feels as if your coccyx has been rammed repeatedly into your spinal column.

The Duchess had been plotting her revenge against me for some time. She was outraged by Gabriela and Camille's (very successful) renovations. She was scandalised by my audacity in installing not just one, but *two* new bathrooms, as well as removing her beloved seventies' Peach Panoply. In its place there was a smart, modern white bathroom suite; the floors and walls were tiled in pale, graded grey, dark at the bottom and almost white at the top of the walls.

Gabriela and Camille were in the process of redecorating the bedrooms. I was constantly chasing suppliers of the bedroom furniture that I'd ordered, and desperately trying to coax people into finishing the curtains before they departed *à la plage* for the month of August. I had rather let things slide during the oxycodone/diazepam shutdown.

One of the things I had *not* let slide was my daily replenishing of the secret stray-cat biscuit supply in the cellar. D'Artagnan was unaware that there was a hidden entrance to his beloved wine cellar, one that only I and all the stray cats in the area knew about. I made sure there was food and water for my stealthy, occasionally glimpsed feline guests and for the rather large, furtive hedgehog that I'd seen scurrying across the courtyard towards the hidden entrance at dusk. Although, even I had to admit that the smell of tom-cat pee was becoming quite pervasive down there, so D'Artagnan was likely to become suspicious sometime soon.

I was trotting down the cellar stairs in my capacity as waitress when the Duchess struck. My foot slipped on the damp, mossy cellar stairs and I bumped my way on my arse all the way down into her dank, musty depths.

I had been puzzled by the green fungus that had appeared on the cellar stairs and had asked D'Artagnan about it. 'Is this normal? I don't remember seeing it last year.'

A smug look came over his face. 'No, Nicole it is not normal. It is because of something you do that the château is not happy about.' He crouched down to examine it more closely, picked at a bit with his finger so that it flaked off onto the floor.

'Oh God, really? What *now*?' I rolled my eyes. 'The force is pretty strong in your family, isn't it? I mean, you get peeved about bathrooms and renovations, and the hereditary property does too! It's quite spectacular, really.'

'It is nothing to do with the bathrooms,' he retorted. He stood up. 'It is because you insist to have all of the windows double-glazed. Now the château can't breathe the way it was built to breathe, so the mould is now going to grow because it is more humid inside.'

I stared at him. 'What, the whole château is going to turn green? I'm sure that isn't normal. I've read magazines and looked on the internet and seen pictures of other people's châteaux, and some of them have actually managed to drag them kicking and screaming into the twenty-first century. *They* have double-glazed windows – and none of them, as I recall, are green inside.'

'*Bah* Nicole, always the sarcasm...!' Guy made an exasperated face and reached out as if to grab me around the back of the neck. I skipped nimbly out of his way.

But my nimble skipping days had come to an end, albeit temporarily I hoped. As I limped slowly and painfully back up the green stairs after I'd replenished the feline/hedgehog buffet, I was convinced I could hear the Duchess cackling.

After that, there wasn't any question that my back pain was psychological; it was *very* real.

***

'So, Nicole, I drop you at the osteo in Bordeaux on Tuesday, *mon ange*. Will that be good? I have a meeting with Francesca and Satan at the office then?' he glanced at me. (I'm paraphrasing a bit, obvs.)

We were having our coffee in bed. The Muffins had followed D'Artagnan downstairs and he'd fed them before they went out. It was pleasant not to have Mr Muffin shouting at me about how late breakfast was, how very poor the catering standards were, about the *very* bad review he was going to write on TripAdvisor if only he had opposable thumbs and a mobile phone of his own. I think he was pissed off about that, too.

'Yeah, okay...' I said hesitantly. 'But I can still drive. I don't want to get in the way of your meeting. I can take my car.' I did NOT want to have to see Satan again, not until I was good and ready.

'*Bah*, Nicole, I am going to Bordeaux anyway. I will drop you at the osteo and then after you can come to the office.'

'No. I'm not doing that.' I stopped, then continued in a slightly less vehement tone. 'I don't want to hang around waiting for you to finish your meeting. I have things to do.'

'More shopping?'

I frowned. 'Yes, my darling, more shopping. Really exciting shopping – bedlinen, bath towels, normal stuff that guests expect to find in a bedroom or bathroom when they come to stay in one's home.'

'I thought you order all that already? What is all the packages that arrive every week now, Nicole? Is all these things really necessary?'

I scowled; I am never particularly good-humoured in the morning. 'At the risk of sounding like a stuck fucking record, Guy, *yes*, all of these things *is* really necessary! Why don't you just concentrate on your projects, the ones in Bordeaux and Biarritz, and leave me to handle *my* project here at the château? I thought you had lots of things to do?'

Small pout, expulsion of air. 'My projects are quiet now it is summer. The meeting next week will be the last one until September. Francesca and Guillaume will be away for the summer, and the work on the developments will shut down for three weeks because everyone will be on holiday.'

'I thought they were coming to the wedding?'

'Yes, they are coming to the wedding. They will be back at the end of August.'

That was interesting to know. It was frustrating to hear that Satan was still planning to come to our wedding, but interesting to know that he would not be in Bordeaux for most of August. It was even more interesting to know that the development would be on hold, unoccupied.

'Oh, and Nicole, *mon amour*, I forget to tell you – *bah*, I forget to ask you this one thing. It is quite a big thing, and I am really hoping that you don't mind.'

'What thing?' I looked at him but he had picked up his phone again and was scrolling through it. He glanced at me, gave a little smile, looked back at his phone.

'Well, Nicole, it is something I agree to do some years ago with Manu. I think I tell you before that we always talk about going to Argentina one day, to do a long ride across Patagonia. And now, this year, he is ready to do this. He is taking a break in his studies. So, *mon amour*, after the wedding and after we have a little honeymoon in St Tropez, do you mind if I go to Argentina with Manu for two weeks? We are going to go here, I think.'

He turned the screen of his phone towards me and showed me a picture of prairies with horses in them and mountains in the distance, like I needed to approve the location.

I smiled at him. 'Of course I don't mind my darling! I think it's a fantastic thing to do, a real father-and-son adventure. I don't mind in the least!'

He smiled back at me and blinked his lovely eyes. '*Merci, mon amour*. That will make me very happy. But also, probably very full of pain too.' He grinned. 'To be on a horse for two weeks... I think there will be a *lot* of pain.'

'Never mind, D'Artagnan, I'm sure you'll survive. And it's such a fantastic thing to do – something you'll never forget!'

I really did think it was a wonderful thing for them to do, but it also meant the main event for Satan's downfall would be significantly easier for me to implement. Now I just had to find a way to keep D'Artagnan occupied while I set everything in motion.

But then fate intervened: glorious, happy, unexpected fate.

Chapter Ten

Darth Vader's life imploded. It transpired that Catherine had been having an affair with a member of their church congregation, a twenty-two-year-old from Cameroon. It seemed she had flipped, fallen head over heels in love, had now quit the matrimonial residence and installed her new lover in a Parisian apartment, where they were living together.

So D'Artagnan had been right. Well, partially right. It had been about sex, just not the kind that is delivered in discreet brown packaging. It was a wildly, astonishingly out-of-character thing for her to have done and D'Artagnan *loved* it. He bathed, he wallowed, he almost drowned in the *schadenfreude* of it all; he spent ages on the phone to Françoise, gossiping and laughing. He called Isabelle and told her, crying with laughter down the phone, and he even spoke to Antoine about it.

Finally, he spoke to Stephane. Afterwards, when he hung up, he looked a little sheepish. Later, when we were in the car on the way to Bordeaux, he said, 'He sound quite upset, Nicole. I feel a little, *bah*, bad now for laughing at him.'

'Well, yes, my darling, you should feel bad. It's never nice to laugh at someone else's misfortune, especially where it concerns the end of a relationship.' Much as I disliked Stephane and Catherine, I felt it was wrong that D'Artagnan was deriving so much enjoyment from the implosion of his brother's life.

'*Mais* Nicole, *merde*... You don't understand. All of my life Stephane has told me that I do everything wrong – that I should not marry Isabelle because she is not Catholic, that I should baptise my children, that I should not work for the evil banks. Then he tell me I should not divorce Isabelle, that I am not welcome to the *baptême* of his *petit-fils* because I am divorced. *Putain de merde,* Nicole, it is very, very difficult to be quiet now this happen.'

'It's still not right, even though I can understand it's very tempting. But it's not something *he's* done, and I can imagine he's devastated by what has happened.'

Small pout. Long silence. Then '*Bah ... ouais*, maybe you are right, *mon ange*. Maybe I go to Paris to see him. Maybe I go next week.'

'That would be a very kind, a very brotherly thing to do.' I stroked his arm. And it would also mean D'Artagnan would be distracted. I put my metaphorical hands together and gave thanks to the Arch Bitch for having deviated so wildly from her script.

***

It was the beginning of August. D'Artagnan dropped me close to the osteopath's office, which was, I'd noted happily when I Googled it, only two streets away from Xavier's offices. After my osteo session, I went to my first appointment with him.

I had not used my married name when I made the rendezvous. When the receptionist showed me into his office, Xavier looked up and frowned deeply. '*Bah,*' he said. Actually no, he didn't. It was more '*Baaaaaaah.*'

The receptionist closed the door behind her as she left.

I smiled nervously at him. 'Hello. Um, I don't know if you remember—'

He stood up, came around the side of his desk and held out his hand. 'Yes, I remember you. Guy's wife. Nicole, isn't it? How are you?'

'I'm well, thank you, Xavier.'

We shook hands. His were cool and slender, and the back of his thumb was stained with blue ink.

'Uh ... you gave me your business card?' I said, hoping to relieve the frown that was still creasing his forehead.

The frown deepened, then he remembered and it cleared a little. 'Ah, yes.' He let go of my hand and motioned to the chairs in front of his desk. 'Please, sit down.' He moved a pile of folders off one chair onto the next, then went back behind his desk. He sat down and moved aside a file that he'd been reading.

I took a quick glance around his office. There were folders everywhere, folders wrapped in coloured paper sleeves and bulging with paper piled high on his desk, on the floor around my chair, on the shelves to the side of his desk, on the floor behind his desk.

'So, Nicole. May I call you Nicole?'

'Yes, please do. May I call you Xavier?'

'Yes, of course.' He paused and then said in English, 'Would you like to talk in English?'

I was relieved but also slightly frustrated: was my French *really* so bad? 'Yes, please, if that's okay for you. I'm sorry, I know my French isn't very good but I *am* having lessons.'

A smile twitched briefly at the corner of his mouth. 'Your French is fine, but it is an *opportunité* for me to practise my English. If I have a problem to understand something you say, I stop you, okay?' He looked a little embarrassed. He seemed younger than he had at Emma's wedding and more dishevelled; his dark, curly hair was untidy and his glasses smudged. He had five o'clock shadow and it was only 2pm.

'That's just fine,' I said. 'Thank you. It is easier for me to speak in English.'

He leaned back in his chair with his elbows on the armrests, put his hands together in front of his mouth as if he were praying, then fixed me with his light-grey eyes. 'So Nicole, did Guy do something stupid like you worry he was going to?' He was sharp, Xavier; he hadn't forgotten.

'He's done many stupid things, Xavier, but no. That's not why I'm here.'

Another smile twitched the edge of his mouth. 'Good,' he said quietly. 'I am glad. So please, tell me why you have come to see me.'

It helped that I had already formed the words, had already spoken them aloud when I'd told Bérengère, because they weren't as difficult to say a second time. But I was still very hesitant at first and it took a while for me to be able to speak frankly.

It also helped not to look at Xavier while I talked. Instead, I looked at the blue folder on top of one of the piles on his desk and tried to work out whether the coffee-cup stain on it was the shape of a waxing or a waning moon. I looked at the pink folder to the right of the blue folder and wondered briefly if that was the colour of the pink roses for the bouquets that Annabelle had chosen because I couldn't be arsed to make a choice. Then I looked at the dust on his desk between the piles of folders and wondered if his desk was ever cleaned.

Finally, after I'd finished telling my story, I sat back in my chair and allowed my eyes to flicker briefly to his. His gaze was very direct, unwavering. 'I am very, very sorry to hear that this happen to you, Nicole.' His voice was sombre.

I nodded and looked down again. 'Thank you. For your concern, I mean.' I cleared my throat and took a deep breath. 'I was hoping you could give me a little advice. I'm concerned about Guy's investment with Guillaume in the joint venture. I'm worried that his investment is at risk if I bring criminal charges against Guillaume.'

Xavier didn't say anything for a long while; he just frowned and blinked at me. He had long black eyelashes, perhaps even longer than Guy's, though not as long as Espiritu's. I had a sudden urge to giggle as I thought of him with Espiritu's eyelashes.

'Why don't you just ask Guy this question?' he asked finally.

I stared at him. Perhaps he wasn't that sharp after all. 'Well, obviously I haven't told Guy about any of this.'

Raised eyebrow. 'Three month ago you learn that it is his business partner that rape you and you don't talk to Guy about this?'

I blinked at him a few times. 'Yes?'

He blinked back at me. 'Why not?'

'Do you remember when we met at Emma's wedding, Xavier?'

He nodded, still frowning.

'Do you remember what Guy did when Randy Hands Harry joined us?'

The frown deepened. Xavier took off his glasses and massaged the bridge of his nose; he looked younger without his glasses, maybe late thirties. 'I am sorry, Nicole. I don't understand – who is Randy...? *Bah*, what are you talking about?'

I took a deep breath. 'When Emma's uncle came over, he tried to grab my arse and D'Art— and Guy smacked his hand away and threatened him. Do you remember that?'

He shrugged. 'Yes, of course I remember that. The uncle was drunk. It was bad that he tried to touch you like that.'

'Okay, good. Well, try to extrapolate now.'

He put his glasses back on. 'Is this the same word in English as it is in French, Nicole?'

I shrugged. 'I guess.'

'What is it you want me to extrapolate? The behaviour of the uncle?'

'No! The behaviour of D'Art— oh for fuck's sake,' I muttered. 'Look Xavier, if Guy finds out what Guillaume did, he will kill him. Or he'll do his very best to kill him and, in the process, Guy might get badly hurt, or worse. And then he will go to prison. Or hospital. Or to a cemetery. And I'd rather there wasn't a risk of that happening.'

'*Ah bon*? You think this?' Xavier raised his eyebrows.

'*Ah bon* indeed. Yes, I do,' I snapped.

He carried on looking at me as he folded down the last three fingers of his hands so that only his index fingers were against his lips. 'Are you sure that is what he will do?'

'Yes. Positive,' I said with absolute certainty.

He nodded slowly. 'So this is why you don't talk to him about this?'

I resisted the urge to wink at him and say 'Bingo!'. 'Yes.'

'So how are you going to bring this criminal action against Guillaume without your husband knowing, Nicole?'

I sighed. 'Well, Xavier, I was hoping you would help me to put the case together. I'll take care of the Guy-not-knowing side of things. But first, I'd really like to know what the financial consequences could be for Guy.'

He leaned forward and stared at me. 'Why? Will it change your mind to bring the case if the consequences are damaging?'

I looked away. 'I don't know, Xavier. It depends how damaging.'

He leaned back in his chair. 'So you will make the decision to keep quiet about this if the circumstances are damaging? And never discuss any of it with Guy?'

I gave a small shrug. 'I really don't know, Xavier. Until I know the answer to the question, I don't know how I'll proceed.'

He did a very slow Gallic shrug. 'Okay,' he said finally. 'I look at this for you. It will take me maybe half a day. *Normalement,* I will have an answer to you by the end of the week, okay?'

I smiled. 'That would be brilliant, thank you.'

He asked thoughtfully, 'And you want me to be your lawyer to bring the case against Guillaume?'

My voice was hesitant. 'Would you? I mean, I remember that you said you were working on a sexual harassment case so I thought maybe ... if you're not too busy – I mean, obviously if you are then if you could refer me to someone—'

He sat forward again. 'I can act for you Nicole,' he said decisively.

I gave a relieved sigh. 'Thank you. Thank you so much, Xavier.' I gave him a little smile.

He gave me a quick smile back. 'But first, I need to tell you some things – a lot of things, actually, Nicole – about this accusation that you bring against Guillaume before anything else happen.'

I shrugged. 'Okay. Fire away, Mr Mason!' He looked blank, obviously not getting the reference.

'The first thing is that you must tell Guy about this.'

'And ... you're fired,' I said.

He blinked at me.

'Which bit of Guy going all Clint Eastwood did you not understand?' I asked angrily.

He shrugged. 'It will be almost impossible to bring this case against Guillaume without your husband knowing about it.'

'Well, let's focus on the "almost" rather than the "impossible", shall we?' Inwardly, I sighed. Xavier was another Nietzsche groupie.

***

For the most part, I am enormously fond and slightly in awe of my new French compatriots. I admire their passion for politics, for art, for literature, for food, for living well and enjoying life rather than making money, an attitude that bemuses *les Anglo-Saxons*. Why on earth would you shut the family restaurant in a seaside town for the whole month of August, the one month of the year when it is absolutely *rammed* with tourists? Why would you not take advantage of what is surely the most profitable month of the year? And the answer is: because August is the month to enjoy life with your family on the beach. I love this about France.

But this is nihilist philosophy in action which, in a nutshell, is: life is meaningless so *carpe diem*, people. I'm not being critical but, because the study of philosophy from the age of sixteen is compulsory in France, it unfortunately results in a fairly significant amount of pessimism ... about *everything*. It often means that the first answer to a question or a request is '*non*', but if you persevere and your argument, or indeed even just your determination, is robust, you can perhaps change that '*non*' into a '*oui*'.

This 'life is meaningless' philosophy is certainly the reason why D'Artagnan has no qualms about spending stupid amounts of money on holidays. 'Life is short,' he informs me when we are arguing about the cost of the tiles I've chosen for the guest en-suite bathroom and I am pointing out that they cost just a fraction of our holiday to Thailand. '*La vie est courte, mon amour*. We need to take every moment, we need to savour every moment because soon we die, old, broken, miserable.'

'And that's why we're flying first class?'

'Yes, of course.'

'But that costs a fortune, and the tiles only cost eight hundred euros?'

'It's not the same thing, Nicole!' Crossly.

Voilà: centuries of European philosophy distilled and viewed through the nihilistic prism of an ex-investment banker. A French one.

***

Xavier carried on gazing at me. Finally, he shrugged. 'Okay. We stop talking about this problem for a minute. Tell me again what happen when you go to the office and Guillaume threaten you.'

I explained in detail and he nodded slowly when I finished. 'It is going to be difficult to do this, Nicole. There is just what you say and what he will say. There is no evidence, not even a complaint that you file in Italy, nothing.'

'I'm very aware of that. But I've had an idea.' I outlined my idea to him.

He recoiled in horror, blinking his long eyelashes rapidly. '*Mais non*! You cannot do that, it is much too dangerous!'

'But my friend Bérengère won't be far away. She'll come and rescue me if it gets out of hand.'

'*Bah non*, Nicole! It is a bad idea. Guillaume is a dangerous man! And also, there is no guarantee that the evidence can be used!'

'That was another thing I was hoping you could you look into for me,' I said calmly. 'I've done quite a lot of research online, and I thought that perhaps it *could* be used.'

He gazed at me. 'It is the decision of the *juge d'instruction* if evidence can be used.'

'What are the odds?'

He frowned deeply. 'What?'

'I mean, what's the chance of him or her accepting it as evidence? Is it like, fifty–fifty, or thirty–seventy, for example?'

'It is not a game of chance, Nicole,' he said somewhat snootily. Bloody lawyers. 'It depend on the evidence, it depend on the *juge d'instruction,* and it depend if there is other evidence, if there are other *plaignants* as well.'

'What's a *plaignant*?'

'*Bah*, other women. Other women that also want to bring a case against Guillaume.'

That prompted me to mention Léa, and I also told him about what Françoise had said about Satan's reputation in Bordeaux.

He nodded more enthusiastically. 'But that is good! That is what we need to find, other *plaignants* to make your case against Guillaume more strong!'

His enthusiasm at the idea that Guillaume had multiple victims was a bit distasteful. 'I don't really know where to find Léa. I know she was living in Bordeaux, and I know she was studying – I'm not sure what – maybe film? Something artistic? I did ask her but she didn't really say a lot.'

'Well, maybe you can try to find her? There are a couple of universities here in Bordeaux where we can study art, so maybe you can try to find her there?'

It was my turn to frown. 'I suppose. Maybe.' I paused. I didn't say that I wouldn't necessarily have loads of time or suitable excuses to spend time hanging around outside universities in Bordeaux. 'If I did find her and she was helpful, is there a better chance that the evidence I get will be accepted?'

He gave an annoying eye roll. '*Mais non, pas forcément, Nicole*! I already tell you, this is at the discretion of the *juge d'instruction*. And it is too dangerous, what you are proposing to do. You must not do this.'

I stared at him. He stared back.

'I cannot act for you if you do this, Nicole. I cannot allow my client to put herself in danger like this.'

I blinked at him. He blinked back, of course.

'But, hypothetically speaking, Xavier, if there were evidence where Guillaume admitted that he'd raped me and it was allowed by the *juge d'instruction*, would that make the case against him stronger? Enough to have him arrested and held in custody until the trial?'

He gave me a hard stare.

'Just theoretically,' I said again.

Finally he shrugged. Without taking his serious grey eyes off mine, he said, 'Maybe.'

Maybe was good enough for me.

***

Afterwards, I walked towards the home-furnishing shop that was to be my alibi. I swung my bag in my hand as I walked, enjoying the feel of the hot summer sun on my skin. I felt capable, confident and determined. I could do this thing: I could neuter Satan.

I bought some bath towels, a soap dispenser and a toothbrush holder for the new bathroom on the second floor so that D'Artagnan would not become suspicious about where I'd been for the rest of the morning. I met him at the restaurant as arranged and I sipped my glass of delicious white wine from Françoise's vineyard and enjoyed the gentle summer breeze while Guy explained that I really ought to have gone to a different home-furnishings shop, because his one was much better. I smiled vaguely at him and thought about my first meeting with Xavier and how it had gone rather well, all things considered.

***

D'Artagnan went to Paris the day after we returned from Bordeaux to see how Darth Vader was coping. Not well, it seemed, when we spoke on the phone.

'*Mais* Nicole, I am shocked. He is so – depressed. He is always wearing these terrible sweatpants, and a sweater that smell. I have to tell him to take a shower and I don't think he always listen to me. He seem like he is not completely aware of what is going on. He is a bit like you, *mon ange*, when you have the very bad back pain.'

I heard him take a drag on his cigarette and exhale, and I heard traffic noise, a siren in the distance. I thought how unusual those sounds had become to me. *Chez nous* it is always peaceful. We hear the lush, silvery-green leaves of the tall poplars rustling in the wind, and sometimes we hear the tractors working in the vines. In high summer, the sharp whistles of the squadrons of swifts as they chase their insect prey in the hot afternoons can be ear-piercing, but it is always delightful to watch their airborne dexterity, and at dusk we often hear the scratchy screech of the barn owls that live in the stable roof as they swoop into the forest on their wide, silent white wings.

I was standing at the paddock rails watching my other love, Espiritu, while we talked. It was dusk, the magic hour, and it was still 30° Celsius. The breeze was warm. D'Artagnan had been in Paris for three days and I was missing him, and I was missing Nina, too, although I'd only walked her home an hour earlier. My heart still felt bruised after hugging and kissing her goodnight.

I didn't tell him that Nina had stayed with me the previous night. We'd spent the last two days together and they'd felt like two of the best days of my life. Nina and I had decided to go the beach the day before and left early in order to avoid getting caught in the August holiday traffic as it was sucked towards the coast, an inland wave of shimmering metal and glass reflecting the relentless summer sun as it crashed onto the Atlantic coast.

We'd parked just outside of the pretty little town of Saint-Palais-sur-Mer and walked hand in hand to the beach. We'd laid our towels on the sand and positioned the cooler box underneath the sunshade, then spent the whole day there on the butter-coloured sand.

At lunchtime we went up to the restaurant overlooking the beach, where I'd had a salad and Nina had fish and chips, and we'd giggled about the man who looked like he'd swallowed a deflated beach-ball and then inflated it inside his stomach. Nina rolled her sparkly green eyes at me when a toddler on the promenade threw an epically noisy fit about not being allowed to ride his tricycle into other people. Because she'd insisted, I'd tasted her extraordinarily lavish ice-cream sundae, which radiated a hundred-percent sugar in its psychedelic swirls of raspberry and blueberry syrup. Its appearance did not deceive. I'd had a coffee.

We'd swum quite far out in the sea in the afternoon and we'd dived under the waves together. When she was tired, I'd held her on my hip, her skinny brown arms around my shoulders and her legs around me as I walked out of the water. Then we lay on our towels and breathed in the sun, the warmth, the joy of being alive.

On the way back home in the car, however, she'd become quiet and withdrawn. 'Are you very tired, Nina?' I asked, glancing at her in the rear-view mirror.

She shook her head. Her little arms were folded and she was looking away from me, her eyes down.

'What's the matter then?' I asked gently.

She gave a little shrug but she didn't speak.

'We'll have some iced tea when we get back, okay? Before you go home.'

She muttered something.

'What did you say?' I asked.

She turned to me and her eyes in the rear-view mirror were shiny. 'I don't want to go home. I want to stay with you.'

I had to blink several times and wipe my eyes as I drove. I didn't want her to go home either, so I phoned Marion when we arrived back at the Duchess and I asked if it would be alright if Nina stayed the night with me.

Marion didn't say anything for a while, then, 'Yes, okay. I think that will be alright. Do you need to come and get her toothbrush and her pyjamas?'

I said that I had a spare toothbrush and Nina could wear one of my long T-shirts to sleep in. That seemed to satisfy her.

When I told Nina that she didn't have to go home that evening, she grinned her gap-toothed grin at me and threw her arms around my waist. I felt as if my heart were being ripped in two as I held her against me, one half ecstatically happy and the other in terrible pain.

I made her cheese on toast for supper (the beginning and end of my cooking repertoire) and we lay together on the cracked leather chesterfield in the library and watched *Ice Age 1*, *2* and *3*. Mr Muffin brought us a dead mouse, which made both of us sad, so we went outside and dug a little grave under the rosebushes that I'd planted early in spring and buried it.

I didn't tell D'Artagnan about any of that. We had had the conversation about children right at the beginning of our relationship. 'I cannot give you children, Nicole,' he'd said.

And I'd said, 'That's okay. I can't have children, so we're all good on that front.' Or something similar.

But there'd been no Nina then.

***

'Well, my darling, Stephane is depressed,' I said sympathetically. 'He's obviously really depressed and that's understandable. His whole life has imploded. His wife of however many years has run off with someone else. How long were they married?'

I could *hear* Guy doing the Gallic shrug. '*Bah...* A long time before I was married, so maybe thirty, thirty-five years?'

'Well, that's a big chunk of his life, isn't it? He's still in shock, poor man.'

Espiritu and Emperador were standing together; Espiritu was nibbling Emperador's mane at the base of his neck and Emperador was nibbling Espiritu's neck in the same spot. This seemed to be something pleasant for them both; they were thoroughly absorbed.

'*Bah, ouais, mon amour.* It is a long time.' Another exhalation.

'What about the tribe of pious Catholic children? Where are they on all of this?'

He snorted down the phone. '*Merde*, you know, Nicole, I ask Françoise about this and she tell me all kind of things I do not know before. Most of the children don't care about their parents. Only one child, one of the children in the middle, care about her parents. The oldest child is gay. He is no longer talking with his parents because they cannot accept that he is living in Berlin with his lover. And one of the girls, not the youngest – I don't know how old she is – she become pregnant when she was very young, so now she already have two babies and she is living with a drug dealer in St Denis, a bad part of Paris. Nicole, the children are not very *pieux* at all. I know this now.'

I nodded slowly. It wasn't that surprising. I thought about what Bérengère had said. 'Life is complicated. Maybe the children didn't respond well to being raised so strictly.'

'*Ouais, c'est vrai*. But you know, Nicole, when Isabelle and I decide we need to divorce, I worry about my children. Stephane, when I tell him we are going to divorce, he said this will be terrible for my children, that they will be completely *traumatisés* – but they cope fine when we tell them. *Bien sûr*, it was not easy for them, but they are good people. They are great children, they never do anything to make me worry for them.' I heard him drag on his cigarette again, exhale.

'But now I see that Stephane, he did not have a good relation with his children – his children don't care about their father. Some of them don't even speak to their parents now, and that make me sad. I am sad, Nicole.' Exhalation. And then, more softly, 'And when I am sad, it make me miss you more. I miss you so much, *mon ange*. I miss not to hold you against me. Please, Nicole, can you come to Paris? I need you, my angel.'

His voice was so seductive down the phone, the word 'angel' especially tender. A little frisson zinged down my spine. If life had been a teeny-tiny bit less complicated, I would already have been on the TGV and heading towards Paris.

'I can't, my darling man. I've got too much to do.' I sighed. 'But listen, why don't you bring Stephane back here with you? It would probably do him good to get away from Paris, and almost all of the work on the first floor is finished. I just have to get one or two more things and then it's all done. I'd reserved that room for them for the wedding anyway, so it's only a case of him coming to stay a couple of weeks earlier.'

Big inhalation. Exhalation. 'I don't know, *mon ange*. It's our château now. I don't know that I want my older brother there for some weeks.' A pause. Some deep breathing; I swear I heard the slow blink. Then, with a sly smile in his voice, 'What if we need to fuck in the dining room again?'

I smirked into the phone. 'Well, my darling, I think we could probably make it upstairs to the bedroom if we really needed to. I think we could wait that long, don't you?'

Heavy breathing. Then more urgently, decisively, 'I need to come home Nicole. I talk to Stephane in the morning. *Je t'aime, mon ange, tu me manques. Gros, gros bisous, plein d'amour.*' End of phone call.

***

Stephane came back with D'Artagnan at the beginning of the following week. I paused for a minute in the Duchess's ancient, uneven, black-and-cream tiled hallway to listen, to see if she had clocked that I, the *gauche* foreign meddler, had orchestrated the return of one of her adored, semi-blue-blooded ancestors. There was no acknowledgement, but I knew she was aware of what I had done.

We installed Stephane in the newly refurbished guest room at the far end of the corridor from ours. Previously it had been a large, shabby room with faded, floral wallpaper peeling around the edges, one of the broken window panes patched over with cardboard and masking tape, and a large brown water stain across half of the ceiling. It had been furnished in a *very* eclectic fashion, including a vibrantly pink synthetic rug peppered with blue and yellow flowers, something one could imagine being the missing sandwich from the picnic that finally tipped Van Gogh over the edge if he'd ever have had the misfortune to set eyes on it.

Now it was beautiful. The oak floorboards had been polished and the walls papered with the palest cream and blue stripes. The smart new windows were framed by pale cream shot-silk curtains. An antique Louis-Philippe cherrywood carved bed floated on a thick, pastel-blue wool rug, with an armoire and chest of drawers in the same style in front of the new plasterboard wall. The small but perfectly designed ensuite shower room (with the *outrageously* expensive tiles – duh, of course I bought them!) had been installed. Gabriela and Camille had, as always, done an absolutely brilliant job.

I was shocked at the state of Stephane when he and Guy arrived in the usual spray of gravel that is D'Artagnan's trademark Paris–Dakar–Cognac handbrake halt. He looked significantly more gaunt than he had at Emma and Conor's wedding; his shoulders sloped defeatedly and there were enormous bags under his sad, drooping brown eyes. He looked as if he were in a state of bemused shock, and I could see it wasn't just because of D'Artagnan's cavalier approach to speed limits.

'*Bonjour,* Stephane.' I leaned in to exchange kisses. His eyes were unfocussed and they flitted away from mine.

'*Bonjour,* Nicole. I hope that you are well.' He kissed me, but it was an automatic movement. His body was limp. Even so, I was kind of thrilled that he remembered my name, particularly as I'd never actually heard him say it before.

D'Artagnan smiled his lazy, sexy smile and wrapped his arms around me, moulding me against his body. He kissed me hard on the mouth while gazing into my eyes and then, his mouth sliding onto my ear, whispered, 'Nicole, *mon amour,* I missed you so much... I *need* you, *mon ange.*'

That was so lovely to hear.

***

They arrived at lunchtime. I had bought crusty bread and vegetarian quiche from our excellent boulangerie, freshly made gazpacho from my favourite organic shop in Cognac, and I'd laid out a selection of cheese, nuts, grapes and a crisp green salad on the table. There were fresh raspberries, blueberries and blackberries with crème fraîche for dessert. I had even remembered to open a bottle of St Estèphe an hour beforehand to let it breathe. Some of D'Artagnan's culinary training was obviously starting to sink in.

Midway through lunch, I won the bet I'd had with myself when D'Artagnan went and poked around in the fridge until he found the saucisson I'd also bought but had not put on the table. I'd wanted to see if he could manage to eat a meal not involving dead animal but, as usual, he could not. After he'd finished a bowl of gazpacho, a healthy slice of quiche and most of a baguette with some cheese, he proceeded to cut and eat large slices of saucisson off the back of his special saucisson-cutting knife (it's France; there are special knives for *everything*) while sipping his wine, occasionally fixing me across the table with a very direct, smouldering gaze from under his eyelashes.

Stephane refused any wine and sipped water, ate a small piece of bread, a piece of cheese, had a couple of mouthfuls of gazpacho and then sat back and gazed around the dining hall. 'I remember,' he said, his eyes mournful. 'I remember when we were children, eating in this room. Do you remember, Guy, how noisy we were, how *Mamie* Charente used to shout at us to all stop talking at once?'

Guy smiled. 'Yes, I remember. Antoine was the noisiest, always whining about something. Do you remember that time she told us to take our lunch outside even though it was raining because we were fighting? We were being too noisy.' He paused, his smile nostalgic. 'But she was never really angry. She loved us very much.'

Stephane nodded wistfully. 'Yes, she did. We always loved to come here in the holidays.' His voice was thick with reminiscence. He gave a long sigh. 'I think I am going to go upstairs to my room for a while.' He unfolded himself from his chair and stood up effortfully. 'Thank you, Nicole, for lunch. It was most kind of you to prepare it for us.'

I stared at him. I had never heard him say so many coherent words strung together in a sentence; normally he just breathed heavily and moved his lips a fraction whenever he was forced to interact with me.

'It was my pleasure, Stephane. Are you sure you've had enough to eat? Won't you have some coffee or tea?'

He shook his head. 'No, thank you.' And then he turned and left the room, a tall, angular, tragic figure. My heart ached for him in that moment.

D'Artagnan waited until he was out of earshot, then he fixed me with that dark gaze. A sly smile curved the edge of his mouth. 'So, *mon ange*, do you think we can wait to go upstairs, or shall we just fuck on the table now?'

He's such a sensitive little soul, D'Artagnan.

***

The stuff I'd ordered arrived at Bérengère's house. We unpacked it together, read the manuals diligently, compared notes in English and in French, and we did lots of experimenting.

She insisted we discuss it all in French. 'I am your accomplice, Nicole, there is no question of that. But I am also your French teacher, so we continue to talk in French.'

I rolled my eyes. 'But it's very ... technical French, Bérengère. Technical French is really difficult!'

She shrugged. 'So, try, Nicole. I will correct you if you are very wrong. But I want you to try, *ma biche*. Just try!'

So while I learned about electronic stuff I had previously known nothing about in any language, my French language skills were also improving.

Bérengère smoked one of her thin, hand-rolled cigarettes – or maybe it was a joint because it did smell a bit odd – occasionally spitting away (expertly) the odd stray tobacco flake. Her long grey hair was piled on top of her head and secured with various grips, strands escaping and sticking to her elegant neck in the endless, febrile heat that had persisted throughout that summer.

A part of me really wanted to ask how old she was, but another part of me knew it was irrelevant. Bérengère was ageless because she was completely comfortable in herself at whatever age she happened to be. Her confidence added to her attractiveness.

I still wondered about her love life, though, and that day I dared to ask her about it. 'So Bérengère, aside from Benoît, what's happening in your love life? You never talk about it.'

She gave a little shrug. 'You never ask me, Nicole. What do you want to know?'

Well, everything of course! I thought. 'Do you have a boyfriend?' I immediately wanted to slap myself for such a pathetic, juvenile question.

She shrugged again. 'Sometimes.'

'That's revealing,' I said sarcastically. 'Thanks for sharing that with me. After I've divulged my most terrible, awful secrets to you, you reward me with "sometimes I have a boyfriend".'

She grinned. 'And sometimes, Nicole, I have a girlfriend instead.'

I started to laugh, inhaled saliva the wrong way and then started coughing and spluttering. She pushed my glass of water closer to me and I took a sip of it.

'Are you very shocked, Nicole?' She was still grinning.

I shook my head as I finally stopped spluttering. '*No*, of course I'm not! It's just the way you said it, it was very ... funny. Perfect timing.'

She took a languid drag of her cigarette.

'So, you're bisexual,' I said.
A little moue of the mouth. 'If that's what you want to call it.'
'Well, isn't that what it is? A lot of the women I worked with in fashion were bisexual, or gay. It's not unusual.'
Another Gallic shrug, quite pronounced this time, followed by a stretch of her arms up and out behind her. It was a very big stretch and I could see her ribs and her nipples under her thin camisole. It was also very clear that she didn't believe in razors, wax or anything similar.
'Sometimes, Nicole, I get bored with this idea that there are only two genders in our human race. I like to think that there are many more interesting kinds of sexuality in our world. I don't like labels.' She finished stretching and folded her arms across her slim chest, took another long drag on her cigarette then leaned forward and stubbed it out in the ashtray. She gave me a very direct, all-knowing look from her dove-grey eyes.
What *is* it about the French? How are they just so damn – sexy? Obvs not all of them (generalisations are so lazy) but, despite their incestuously close history and the very narrow stretch of water that separates the UK and France, the French are fundamentally different to *les Anglo-Saxons*.
Recently I had been standing in the supermarket queue behind a couple of women in their early thirties, earwigging their conversation about their *Anglo-Saxon* neighbours. It was fascinating, not so much what they were saying because I couldn't follow all of it, but the fact that the phrase '*les Anglo-Saxons*' seemed to be normal terminology. I'd thought it was a phrase peculiar to D'Artagnan's archaic *grandes écoles* education and it was intriguing to learn that it wasn't.
Perhaps I'm just particularly susceptible to *les Français*. Perhaps I had been seduced as a child by those pouts, those expressive facial expressions, the lazy blinks, the knowing looks, the hand motions that indicate importance, ambivalence, irrelevance. Perhaps I had absorbed this unwittingly when I was a child from Jules' family, from their reactions with one another as I sat at the dining table with them eating *moules marinières et frites*, unaware that I was being subconsciously seduced by *les Français*.

D'Artagnan was the natural culmination of that – and Bérengère, because they had clearly been weaned on the same viscous, libidinous waters, both raised on the same luscious, exotic French fruit (and *fruits de mer*).

So Bérengère and I plotted. We planned, we discussed, we flirted gently with one another, she and I. We had been to Bordeaux while D'Artagnan was in Paris, where we tested the logistics out for Satan's downfall. We tested a number of scenarios and we went on testing until we were absolutely certain that it would all work as planned.

Afterwards, in the car on the way back home, I felt strong. I felt like Espiritu when he stood in the field with his whole body taut, his neck proud, his head raised, his ears pricked. I was *ready*.

Chapter Eleven

It was only a few days before our wedding when Jules, Mark and the kids arrived. I had reserved the second floor for them. The brand-new shower room was finished, and the two bedrooms adjoining it were spacious and elegantly furnished. I had even had the antique daybed that I'd found up there re-upholstered in beautiful pale mustard-gold with tiny pink flowers.

I hugged Jules tightly when she arrived and she hugged me back equally tightly. I was so happy, so relieved to know that she would be at my side throughout the ceremony. I hugged Mark tightly, too, even though he said, 'Steady on, Nicky,' in an embarrassed voice and patted my back awkwardly.

Then I crouched down and enveloped Katie and Josh in my arms, covering their beautiful little faces with enthusiastic kisses until Josh squirmed and wriggled away from me. Katie didn't though; she carried on hugging me, her arms tightly around my neck. I stroked her soft, dark ringlets and, when I finally stood up, she gazed at me with her sapphire-blue eyes, her mother's, her grandfather's eyes. She gave me a huge grin and I laughed out loud delightedly because she had toothless gums that matched Nina's *exactly*. I was thrilled that *both* of my gorgeous flower girls were going to be perfectly symmetrical, that they would bare their perfect little gums in all of the photos, that they would be unmistakable in all of the terribly important wedding photographs that Annabelle had planned.

I knew I would have to take diazepam on the day – I had refilled my prescription after I knew that my body was clear of oxycodone – but I only took 5mg in the morning. It was enough to take the edge off, nothing more.

Jules did my hair. She pinned it up with three sparkling hairgrips and curled it so that it tumbled in graceful tendrils around my neck. It looked very elegant, as opposed to very wildly 'just been…'. I did her hair in the same style, only hers looked better than mine; her natural, glossy ringlets fell perfectly around her shoulders.

I did my makeup quickly and then I did hers. I applied eyeshadow and lengthened her long eyelashes with mascara, painted her small, perfect mouth with a pale pink lipstick and brushed her cheekbones with just the right colour to accentuate her heart-shaped face.

Afterwards, she admired herself in Heaven's mirrors. 'Ooh, babe, I look – fab!' She hugged me. 'We should have a glass of Champagne, Nicky.'

I grimaced a little. 'Er ... I have a confession to make, Jules. I had to take 5mg this morning so I'm not sure I should add Champagne.' I made an apologetic face.

She shrugged. 'Duh, Nicky, you and probably every other bride-to-be! I reckon they'd take more than 5mg if they were lucky enough to get their hands on it. Don't sweat it, sweetheart! You can still have a glass of Champagne, it'll be fine.'

I trust Jules with my life, and I trust her judgment, so I WhatsApp'ed D'Artagnan and asked if he could bring two glasses of Champagne up to Heaven. He brought a bottle (of course he did) in an ice bucket together with two glasses.

Jules prevented him from coming into the room. '*Mais non, Guy, tu ne peux pas entrer.* It's girls only!' she said firmly, taking the ice bucket and the glasses from him and shutting the door in his face.

I heard his dismissive '*pffff*', though, and it made me smile.

Katie and Nina became instant friends the moment they set eyes on each other. They ran around the château hand in hand, explored the secret cupboard in the library, descended warily into the cellar, skipped across the dining hall and ran down to the paddocks, climbed up on the rails and hung their little bodies over them, chatting excitedly about the horses. Language didn't seem to be an issue.

Jules was amazed. 'It's really weird – Katie's actually answering her in French. I don't understand how! I mean, she's doing French at school but it's almost like she's fluent, as if she's just absorbed all the French she's ever heard me speak!'

'That's probably exactly what's happened. Don't you remember, I used to speak French with your family and I had no French at all before I met you! I can't explain it – it was easy, it felt natural. Kids' brains are giant sponges. Nina sometimes speaks to me half in English, half in French now.'

Jules smiled at me. 'She does seem very close to you. Does your neighbour mind that she's over here with you all the time?'

I shook my head, then turned to watch the two little girls. 'No, Marion doesn't mind at all. She's got the two boys and she has to keep a close eye on them now it's the summer holidays. She knows that Nina is safe here with us, and she knows how much she loves the horses.' I shrugged. 'I think she's quite relieved. Nina seems much happier now. She was quite withdrawn before, very shy.'

'And longer term? You said Marion was only fostering her.'

I looked away. 'I try not to think about longer term at the moment,' I said quietly.

Not thinking about Nina was using up a lot of my mental energy – not thinking that Nina might be taken from my life at any moment. She spent almost every day with us and I missed her on the days when she wasn't there. I suspected D'Artagnan missed her too, but I could never find the right words to ask him, to ask if, when he'd said we couldn't have children, perhaps he hadn't meant...

***

Jules and I made a management decision to risk dressing Katie and Nina in their flower-girl dresses before we dressed ourselves. We explained that they had to be very careful once they were dressed not to run about in the dusty paddock, or roll on the lawn, or tip blackcurrant juice over their heads, or eat *anything*. They were already overexcited and they wanted to put on their dresses, but they sort of listened to us and sort of agreed that they would make their very best efforts not to turn up at the crucial moment having colourfully customised their cream satin dresses.

Nina struggled to stand still in front of me. She jiggled about, talking to me in fast French, a lot of which I couldn't understand what with the added gummy impediment.

Jules understood her perfectly, though, and replied to her questions when I was at a loss. Nina chatted unselfconsciously with Jules but she stayed close to me. She placed her little hand firmly on my shoulder as she stood in front of me in her knickers and watched me intently as I sat on the chaise longue and unwrapped the tissue paper from her dress that was nestling in a rectangular pink box.

I took the dress out of the box and slipped it over her head and her small, perfect body. She stood still once it was on and she was suddenly quiet. I asked her to turn around while I tied the pale-green satin bow at the back, then touched her shoulder to turn her back to face me. She looked down and smoothed the creamy fabric, gazed at the full skirt flowing out from under the wide waistband, and then she raised her big, sparkling green eyes to mine and grinned the biggest, gummiest grin. She slipped her skinny arms around my neck and I hugged her against me. It felt as if my heart might break in that moment.

When I looked up Jules was watching us, her eyes shiny with tears. 'Don't!' I instructed her, through my own tears 'Do *not* cry Jules. Mascara, babe. Think of the mascara!'

She laughed at me then, and I grinned back at her and blinked away my own tears.

When Jules went upstairs to help Mark and Josh get dressed, Katie and Nina followed her, holding hands and clattering along the hall in their cream satin shoes, their voices high and excited.

I went over to the window and moved the voile curtain aside slightly to spy on what was happening out front. I looked at my watch. It was twenty past three; most of our guests seemed to have arrived and were milling about on the lawn sipping Champagne and eating canapés. Our wedding ceremony was scheduled for four o'clock.

I spotted Bérengère, resplendent in a long, flowing blue-green dress, sewn in places with silvery sequins that sparkled and winked in the sunshine. She was chatting to Benoît, Veronique and Stephane, and the latter was leaning back slightly and looking down his nose at her in that familiar, disapproving manner of his. It was true that the spaghetti-straps of her low-cut dress left no doubt in anyone's mind that a bra was not an integral part of Bérengère's wardrobe. Perhaps that was why he was frowning so deeply (he probably hadn't seen that much cleavage for, like, ever). But I thought that she looked pretty bloody fabulous, her long, grey hair held back off her face on either side with two clasps. The large silvery-blue crystal on a black velvet ribbon around her slender neck flattered her delicately boned, suntanned shoulders.

Benoît seemed to be in agreement with my analysis; he was gazing at her slightly open-mouthed, mesmerised. As I watched, Viking Veronique – super-chic in a crisp white shirt and tailored, navy blue trousers – turned and glared at him.

I spotted Françoise arm in arm with Pascal. She looked elegant in a simple dark-blue, boat-cut dress, and her pretty face lit up as she turned to gaze up at Pascal. He was laughing at something Conor had said and Emma was laughing too, her dark hair glinting in the sunshine as she leaned against her husband. Conor was holding baby Rose in a sling against his body. She'd put her tiny fist around my finger at her baptism in early June and I'd been surprised at the strength of her grip. She was the most perfect little creature, and I'd held her blue-eyed gaze with mine until Emma had gently disengaged her fist.

And Satan was there; of course he was there, smirking in his poisonous manner from behind his sunglasses, his hand proprietarily on the arm of yet another pretty, too-young, too-skinny victim, this one blonde. I watched him from one of Heaven's windows, willing a biblical bolt of lightning to strike him down, to vaporise, erase, destroy him. It didn't happen. Of course it didn't happen; he was Satan, after all – he simply deflected lightning bolts with a flick of his claw.

I straightened my shoulders, took a deep breath and moved away from the window. I had been doing a lot of thinking about how to play it with Guillaume. Once I had accepted that I couldn't stop him coming to our wedding without arousing all seventy-nine million of D'Artagnan's inquisitive antenna, I had decided that I would play dumb. When I revisited that comment he'd made, that *seismic* comment when he'd said he'd preferred me when I was younger, I examined my reaction closely. I finally concluded that I hadn't given anything away; I hadn't said anything that suggested that I knew what he was talking about. It was perfectly feasible that I would not have known what he had meant.

Not everyone who has been drugged with Rohypnol, or whatever Satan had used to drug me, has any memory of it. Happily for them, not everyone experiences the vivid, extraordinarily frightening and debilitating flashbacks that I did. But a lot of victims do, and the flashbacks could start many years after the event; in some ways that's even more frightening. You know it's not a dream because it has more immediacy than a dream, but you don't know why your brain has flashed up these horrific scenes on the screen in full technicolour, sometimes with Dolby sound. And that's *incredibly* frightening because it's as if your brain has suddenly gone mad.

I had done a lot of online research after I'd decided that I was going to Get That Bastard Satan. The results had made me even more resolute, even more angry, more determined.

I would pretend that I hadn't known what he meant. What I wasn't sure about was whether I could stop myself hitting, kicking or punching him, or at the very least spitting in his face when he touched me as part of the Kissies ritual. Even if I could restrain myself, I was sure that my skin would shrivel wherever he touched me, that it would shrink away, would do everything in its power to evade his touch.

There were going to be a few challenges on our wedding day.

After she'd dressed, Jules helped me to dress. Actually, I just slipped the Lanvin dress over my head and felt it envelop my body as I tied the rawhide tie behind my neck. All Jules had to do was tie the rawhide length in the middle of my back.

I sat on the chaise longue while I laced the long ties of the gold Louboutin (no surprises there!) stiletto sandals around my calves, then stood up carefully. Jules stood behind me, effortlessly elegant in the deep-blue, thigh-split Valentino (we had argued but I had insisted that I was paying, that it was non-negotiable). She looked bloody gorgeous – the dress suited her dark ringlets and her olive skin perfectly, as I had known it would when I had suggested it to her. Clothes are my thing after all, my only real expertise.

I grimaced at my reflection in the mirror. I was shocked. 'Oh my *God*, I look like a hooker, Jules! It's too much. I shouldn't have chosen this dress, I wasn't – in my right mind when I chose it, for fuck's sake!!'

I had decided not to tell Juliette about Guillaume and the associated meltdown. She had already retrieved me from the dismal puddle of drugs, heartbreak and despair that was the end of my twenties and my early thirties; she had done it three times. Besides, Jules had a busy life; she worked long hours and she struggled to spend enough time with her family. She worried about her mother, who was not in good health and lived with her older sister near Nice. Jules' plate was full and she did not need me to add Satan and his pile of excrement to it. I had Bérengère to help me with that.

'Nonsense, Nicky!! You look absolutely *gorgeous*!! It's *so* much better now that you've got more weight on. D'Artagnan is going to absolutely die with lust when he sees you!'

'You don't think it's too much? Too ... out there?'

'Nu-uh!' She shook her head vehemently, reached for the Champagne bottle and poured us both another glass, draining the last of the bottle into mine before plunging it back into the ice-bucket. She grinned. 'I bet it will take him a max of three seconds to get that dress off you afterwards.'

I raised my glass, raised an eyebrow too. 'Two, I reckon.'

We clinked glasses, giggled at each other like schoolgirls.

***

And then it was our time. Guy and I stood in front of all of those people, most of whom I'd never met. We stood in front of the Duchess with her new, beautiful, almost-original-but-better (my words, not hers) double-glazed, latticed eyes. My gorgeous D'Artagnan held both my hands against his chest, our bodies almost touching. I gazed into his fathomless brown eyes, and he gazed into mine, and he told me that I was the love of his life; he told me how he could not live without me. He told me that I was everything to him.

And I told him that I couldn't live without him, either, that my life had been empty before he had come into it and that it was now so full, so full of love for him. I told him in French without any cuteness, any irony, how happy he made me, how he had changed my life and how much I loved him.

I didn't care about anyone else. I didn't care that we were the main act. I just gazed into my D'Artagnan's eyes and told him how I really felt about him.

He blinked slowly when I'd finished and his eyes were so sensuous, so tender, his gaze so intense. We exchanged the bracelets I'd designed and he'd had made; three hearts in yellow, pink and white gold inside a platinum circle on a black leather cord. He fastened the clasp of mine and kissed the inside of my wrist softly. I fastened the clasp around his wrist, leaned in and kissed his mouth, gazed into his eyes as he gazed into mine. He slipped his arms around my back, held my naked waist firmly in his strong hands beneath the two-second-undress dress, held me against his body and we kissed as if we were completely alone – because in that moment we were. It was just us. The French registrar smiled indulgently and wasn't at all embarrassed by the intensity of that kiss. Probably. I don't know – I was entirely consumed by D'Artagnan.

***

We went to St Tropez on our second honeymoon.

I wore the two-second-undress wedding dress on our first night – he insisted and I complied. He streamed HVOB from the en-suite sound system – I insisted, he complied. I was *obsessed* with HVOB, floored, blown away, *bouleversée* by them, by her.

D'Artagnan knelt in front of me as I sat naked on the edge of the bed, sipping a glass of Champagne. He slipped my feet into the gold Louboutins, crossed the thin leather ties and bound them around my ankles, my calves, tying them tightly at the back. His eyes were heavy as he lifted each foot and pressed his mouth against my instep, then gradually worked his way up, his lips against my ankles, my calves. I leaned back, *Cool Melt* pulsing through the speakers. He was so fucking gorgeous. I wanted him very badly.

He smiled back at me, blinked that languid blink and gave a little shake of his head. 'Not yet, *mon cœur*. First, we go out, we celebrate our wedding. Come, I dress you now. You wear the dress made from every sin in the world.' This is what he called the Lanvin dress.

It seemed I had known after all, even in my oxycodone/diazepam stupor, that it was the right dress.

I took another sip of Champagne as I watched him take the sinful dress out of the wardrobe, stand up so that he could slip it over my head, watched him while he watched it settle over my naked body, pooling at the builder's-crack base of my spine. I turned and lifted my hair so that he could tie it at the back. He kissed the nape of my neck before he tied the first tie and the kisses continued, his mouth firm, warm, all the way down to the second tie. His fingers lightly, deliberately, brushed my nipples as he took the rawhide ties at the sides and tied them firmly across my back – and then a firm bite at the base of my spine, his hands now holding my hips. I felt hot, liquid, as if I had melted inside.

'So, *mon amour*, now we go out.' He stood up and turned me around, slipped his hands around my naked waist.

'Uh – knickers?' I raised an eyebrow.

He shook his head. '*Non*, no knicker tonight, *mon ange*.' Very lusty eyes. 'Tonight, I want to think about this when we go out. I want to think about you naked under this dress.'

And that was *insanely* arousing, it was like an entire evening of foreplay. Cocktails in the rooftop bar, sitting side by side as the dusk gradually devoured the light over the Mediterranean. We sipped our cocktails and he blinked very slowly at me, increased the pressure of his fingertips on the inside of my thigh until my toes tensed involuntarily, rose against the straps of the sandals, and I felt like my eyelids were being weighed down, as if I were blinking under water. I sipped my cocktail and I blinked slowly back at him, tight inside with anticipation.

At dinner, we sat opposite one another. I put one of the gorgeous shoes between his legs, against his groin. His fingers fastened tightly around my ankle. I smiled at him, a little edge of mouth smile, and he pulled my foot hard against the bulge in his jeans and held it there, his fingers strong, curved around the arch of my foot. Then he smiled the laziest smile at me, did that slow, luxurious blink.

And afterwards in the nightclub in the basement of the hotel, locked into each other to *Capture Casa*. As the bass kicked in it was too, too much – it had become unbearable. He groaned into my ear, welded against me, hard like iron against my stomach. '*Mon dieu, mon ange*, I can't wait any more, I need to fuck you now, *now*, Nicole. I can't wait. Come, we go now,' and we did.

We went to the women's toilets, stumbled there, blind with lust, and we were blessed with serendipity. There was no queue and we went straight into a booth, slammed the door shut. He lifted me up, my legs wrapped around his waist, desperate, absolutely desperate for him ... and then finally, that exquisite sensation when he was fully, deeply, hard inside me. We both groaned with ecstasy, muted ecstasy, our mouths locked together. It was ferociously, insanely fantastic. So good. Meteor good: if a meteor had struck the Earth, had blasted it into the next galaxy, we would not have noticed.

***

Of course, when we came out, there was a queue.

'Typical French bloke, too cheap to pay for a room to shag his girlfriend in...' a woman muttered to her friend as we brushed past her.

D'Artagnan stopped dead in his tracks, so abruptly that I bumped into his shoulder. I decided to keep my forehead against it with my eyes closed, because I knew, sure as the sun rose in the east and set in the west, that there was going to be a D'Artagnan moment.

A pause. 'That is not a nice thing for a pretty girl to say, is it?'

I could hear he was smiling; I could hear that it was the lazy, sexy smile.

'What is your name, pretty girl?' He waited. I sighed.

'Nicky,' she said sullenly after a while.

'*Mais c'est merveilleux*! The same name as my wife! Nicole, look! This pretty little English girl she have the same name as you!' He put his finger under my chin, raised my face to his. I opened my eyes, rolled them *bigly* at him. I was tired, very tired and marvellously sated. I just wanted to go to sleep.

He turned back to her. 'Nicky, pretty Nicky.' Another pause. She had dared to look at him now and had immediately been mesmerised by the cobra-taming eyes. 'Nicky, I am so sorry. We are so sorry. Of course we have a room – we have one here in the hotel. *En fait*, we have a suite – but, you know, my wife here, my Nicole...' He stopped and gave me a soft kiss on the forehead then turned back to young Nicky. 'My wife, she is so fucking ... beautiful, so sexy, that sometime it is just too far away, the suite, and I need to fuck her right now, and she need me to fuck her now and so we have to use one of the ladies' toilets. I hope you can understand this, I hope you can forgive us for...' he smiled again, did the slow, sexy blink at young Nicky '...making you wait a little bit longer before you can *pi-pi*.' Pause. 'Is that okay, Nicky?'

She blushed bright pink and looked down – she didn't know where to look, poor thing. I touched her arm lightly and she glanced at me. 'I'm so sorry,' I said, quietly 'He's just ... he's always like this.' I rolled my eyes a little. 'He's, y'know, French.'

D'Artagnan gave me a wicked wink, then leaned in and kissed me hard on the mouth. Then we left. 'I'm tired now, Nicole. Shall we go back to the suite, *mon amour*?' He squeezed my hand as we walked back towards the music.

'Did you have to do that?' I shook my head, still embarrassed.

He stopped and turned to me, gave me the full imperial stare. '*Mais bien sûr*, Nicole, of course I had to do that! She make assumptions about French men! She insult me, she insult my nation and she do it in *my* country – of course I have to say something! It is important, it is diplomatic! It is essential that I say something!'

I started to laugh. 'It's also possible that she just needed a pee, D'Artagnan. It wasn't actually a major diplomatic incident.'

He frowned at me. '*Mais non*, Nicole. It is diplomatic, it is a diplomatic conquest. I conquer her. I change her life.'

He smiled, slipped his hands around the base of my skull, tilted my face towards his. 'Little Nicky, she is a pretty girl and now she is never, ever going to be happy until she have a French lover. I make her understand what passion is.' Another slow, sensuous kiss. 'So, I make another conquest for *la France ce soir, mon amour* ... and I have the most unforgettable night with you, my angel. A night I never, ever, forget.'

I shook my head a little. D'Artagnan, never off the case. I leaned into him. 'Me neither, darling man.' I pressed my mouth against his.

We took the lift to the top floor to the stupidly expensive suite, and I fell asleep in D'Artagnan's arms to the sound of the gentle Mediterranean tide sighing in and out on the shore far below, through the French doors that opened onto the terrace.

Chapter Twelve

There were only a few days after we arrived back at the Duchess before D'Artagnan left for Patagonia with Emmanuel. They were flying from Paris and he warned me that he would not be in phone contact for much of the time. 'We will be in the middle of nowhere, Nicole. I don't think there is much phone signal at all, so I will not be able to call you, to talk to you, *mon ange*. Is this okay?'

'Well, call me when you get to Buenos Aires. I'm sure they'll have a phone signal there.'

He frowned then nodded. 'I try. But it will be the middle of the night for you when the flight land and the technology is not very good there. If I can't call you, I send you a text, okay? But I will be thinking of you all of the time, *mon cœur*. I never stop thinking about you.' He put his hand over his heart. 'You are always here, with me.'

We were standing in front of the Duchess and his eyes were light brown in the morning sun. His bag was packed and his car was on the gravel forecourt.

The gravel forecourt: we'd only recently had an argument about the gravel forecourt. He wanted to put a swimming pool smack bang in the middle of it and move the drive to go around the side of the château. I thought it would look shit; it would spoil the classical façade of the Duchess to put a modern swimming pool (unsurprisingly, we were not aligned on the shape of the swimming pool either) smack bang in front of her. After a brief, very pouty discussion, we had agreed to park the subject for a while, at least until he was back from Argentina.

And now the day he was leaving had arrived so quickly. I was suddenly gripped with fear, almost a kind of grief at the thought that D'Artagnan was going to be so far away from me while I had to do the most difficult, bravest and possibly most stupid thing I'd ever done in my life.

I closed my eyes and summoned the image of Nina grinning up at us with her toothy gums at our wedding, her cream flower-girl dress stained on the back with – what? Who knew? Apricots?

Something very orange, anyway, orange and very, very stainy. I thought about how much I'd loved her in that moment, how I'd knelt down and hugged her against me, Nina with her perfect (toothless) little mouth, her skinny, brown arms around my neck, her fringe in her green eyes. And I thought: *I am never going to let what happened to me, happen to Nina. Somehow.*

I drew on that memory, summoned that image and that feeling, and I thought: *I can be this strong person even if D'Artagnan isn't here. I can do this.*

I wrapped my arms around D'Artagnan's neck and he held me tightly and we kissed, a long, slow, sensuous kiss. Then he climbed into his car, blew me a kiss and drove off with the usual wheelspin so that I coughed a bit on the cloud of dust from the twenty-first century equivalent of his exit on horseback.

***

All contact with Xavier was filtered through Bérengère. I had explained this to Xavier and given him Bérengère's mobile number and email address. He'd contacted me a few days after our initial meeting to talk about the financial implications for D'Artagnan if I were to bring charges against Satan, and I was grateful when Bérengère said she would join me on the video call with him.

'I look at the public documents for the company they make,' said Xavier. The light from the window behind him made his hair seem even more dishevelled, and there was a stain on the breast pocket of his white shirt. 'You did not tell me there are three investors, Nicole.'

I frowned. 'Didn't I? Well yes, there are now. Francesca joined them earlier this year, but I don't know how much she's invested.'

He glanced down at the file on his desk, and his black-rimmed glasses slid down his nose. He pushed them back up again. 'She is connected to this very wealthy family?' He mentioned Francesca's family name.

'Yup,' I said. 'More than connected. That is her family.'

He raised an eyebrow and did a little pout. 'How does she come to invest with Guy and Guillaume?'

'They all used to be Masters of—' I stopped. 'They all used to be investment bankers. Guy and Guillaume went to school together, and Guy went to university in Paris with Francesca. He's known her a long time.'

He nodded again. 'This is a family that is very discreet, Nicole. She will not be happy to have her family name associated with Guillaume after this.'

My heart contracted a little but I shrugged. 'I can't really help that. I don't want anyone's reputation to be tarnished, but that's not a good enough reason for me to keep quiet, is it?'

He shook his head. 'No, that is true. But I feel you should be aware of this.'

I started to feel discouraged. Bérengère squeezed my shoulder and said quietly, 'Forget about this, Nicole. It isn't important.'

I gave her a little smile and turned back to my phone screen. 'What about the financial implications, Xavier?'

He leaned forward, ran both his hands through his hair and drew a deep breath. 'I cannot be sure, Nicole, but I think it will be okay. Any amount of money the court order Guillaume to pay will be limited to the amount that he invest only.'

'But he didn't invest any actual money. His investment is the warehouses that he inherited. When both developments in Bordeaux are finished and sold, they're going to use the money to fund a new development in Biarritz.'

He frowned. 'Yes, but the liability is limited to the amount that belong to Guillaume only, Nicole.'

'Are you sure?'

He nodded. 'Yes. *Normalement*.'

I suppressed a little scream. '*Normalement*' is one of those opaque French words that is used to qualify all sorts of things that otherwise would be certainties. Example: 'The plumber is coming tomorrow, isn't he?' to the receptionist.

'*Oui, normalement*.' Which means yes, probably – if the wind is blowing from the right direction, Mars is aligned with Saturn, it is a Tuesday and it is raining.

Trying to pin down *normalement* is impossible; it's like arguing with Mr Muffin about why the new food he was served yesterday for breakfast was the best thing he had *ever* eaten and the following day it was poisonous. In other words, pointless.

I blinked tiredly. 'Okay, assuming that *normalement* neither Guy nor Francesca will be financially impacted, even if there's a chance their reputations might be tarnished by association, I think I now need to focus on getting evidence against Guillaume. Bérengère is going to help me do that.'

Xavier's eyes narrowed and he glared at Bérengère. 'I hope very much that you tell Nicole her idea to get evidence is a very bad one, a very dangerous one!' he said crossly.

'Nicole is a strong woman,' Bérengère said mildly. I had warned her about Xavier's reaction to my plan.

'It is a terrible idea! And it is very possible that the *juge d'instruction* will not accept it, so it will be dangerous for no reason! You must not do this, Nicole. It is much better that you try to find Guillaume's girlfriend, that we try to find other *plaignants*! Already I am making some enquiry. You must be patient.' He leaned forward and stared into the camera on his laptop. 'Please, Nicole, don't do this. Tell me you will not do this.'

I stared back at him. I felt sorry for him so I said, 'Okay.' Under my breath I said *'normalement'*, but he didn't hear that.

***

And then GTBS Day dawned: Get That Bastard Satan Day. It was sunny and warm and I sat on the edge of the bed and stared out of the window at the poplar trees at the end of the lawn as they painted the soft blue sky with their elegant, elongated tips. I stroked Mrs Muffin gently when she put her two front feet on my thigh and she purred richly as she fixed her big green eyes on mine. I felt calm. I was going to war and I was ready.

***

Bérengère pressed the intercom button on the outer door. The development was almost complete and most of the scaffolding had been removed. There were only two or three workmen on the remaining scaffolding at the far end of the street, way out of hearing. I pushed that thought away.

The calm I'd felt first thing that morning had diminished in direct proportion to the diminishing kilometres between the Duchess and Bordeaux. I took 5mg when we were twenty kilometres away.

'Take more – 5mg is not enough!' Bérengère urged when she asked me how much I'd taken.

'No. I just want to take the edge off. I need to be able to access anger, Bérengère. I can't be detached!'

She said softly, 'Nicole, you don't have to do this, you know. Xavier is right. You can try to make the case without doing this.'

I shook my head. 'No. I'm going to do this. I've decided.'

I stayed out of sight with my back against the wall where there were no cameras, and I summoned all of the latent anger I'd felt for the last eleven years. The anger at the knowledge that my life had been okay before Milan – chaotic, sure, but okay. But after that night, everything had changed.

It was out of character for me to fall so heavily for Karl, ethereally beautiful and serially unfaithful, and it was out of character for me to follow him into the depths of heroin addiction. I had always been wary of dangerous drugs but, after Milan, I desperately needed to bury the feeling that an essential part of me was broken. How much had the years of substance abuse affected my body? Was that one of the reasons why I'd miscarried all those times? It was certainly the reason why I'd medicated myself to the very edge of my desire to exist in order to block out the terrifying panic attacks. And all because of Satan. I hated him so much.

The intercom phone clicked as Guillaume picked it up. '*Oui, bonjour? Vous êtes Madame Martin?*' His low purr was unmistakeable.

'*Oui, bonjour. Je peux entrer?*' Bérengère asked.

'*Bien sûr.*' The door buzzed and Bérengère pushed it open. The intercom clicked off.

She held the door open for me. She put her hand on my shoulder; she looked very solemn. 'I am right here, Nicole. You only need to shout,' she whispered.

I took a deep breath and nodded.

As I walked up the stairs towards the office, I took all the anger I'd summoned, distilled it until it was a hundred-percent proof and let it flow freely into my veins.

Guillaume's eyes widened when he opened the door and saw me standing there. He scowled but he didn't say anything.

'Guillaume,' I said coldly. 'May I come in?'

His upper lip curled. 'What the fuck are you doing here, Nicole?' He looked behind me furtively. 'Where is Madame Martin?'

'Madame Martin doesn't exist.' Bérengère had contacted him and told him she was an agent looking for property for a wealthy Parisian investor. 'That was a friend of mine. She's gone now. I want to come in. I want to talk to you.'

I propelled myself forward into the apartment and heard the door slam shut. My heart was beating hard as I turned back towards him.

His face was tight with anger. 'Are you so stupid that you don't remember what I tell you before, Nicole?'

'What did you tell me, Guillaume?'

He paused and his already narrowed eyes narrowed even further. He strode across the room and, in one swift movement, grabbed me by the throat with one hand. His fingers were tight underneath my ears. He ripped open my shirt with the other hand and the buttons bounced across the newly tiled floor.

His eyes widened then narrowed again, furious when he saw the tiny microphone that Bérengère and I had so painstakingly attached between my breasts, just above my bra. It was connected to the thin wire that we had sellotaped to my stomach which, in turn, led to the small transmitting device on my side.

Guillaume grabbed the device and ripped it away. He flung it onto the floor and slammed his heel several times onto it, crushing it completely. He ran his hand over my body, over my front, my back, up and under my skirt. It wasn't sexual: he was checking for more devices. He slapped my hands away as I tried to stop him but he did it easily, as if he were used to subduing women. And he was strong. I could feel that he was strong and I started to struggle to breathe because his hand was so tight on my throat.

When he was sure there were no more wires, he let me go. He yanked my handbag off my shoulder and pushed me away so hard that I staggered back against the wall. The handle of the hall cupboard door hit me in the back and winded me.

He didn't speak a word.

I stayed against the door, clutching my torn shirt, shaking from head to toe and crying; yes, I was crying. Even though it was going exactly as I'd imagined it, I was still terrified. I was very aware that Satan had the power to do something horrible. I tried hard not to think about that as I tried to stop crying.

Guillaume tipped my handbag upside down and scattered the contents on the floor. He picked up my phone, saw that it was recording. He looked at me – *snarled* a look at me – and threw it hard onto the floor. It smashed and he stamped on it repeatedly, crushing it into tiny little pieces.

After he'd satisfied himself that it was well and truly destroyed, he bent down and rummaged through the other things that had been in the bag: a powder compact, a tampon, lipstick, a purse with a credit card and some coins, a twenty-euro note. He seemed satisfied that there was nothing in there that should worry him, scooped it all up and dumped it back in my handbag.

Finally he breathed out, a long, angry breath, and stood up. He threw the bag at me, and I caught it. His sneer was so pronounced that his top lip had pulled back to reveal a predatory white flash of his teeth.

When he spoke, his voice dripped venom. 'Why did you come here, little Nicole, all covered in wires and recording devices, when I tell you not to bother me anymore?' He stepped forward and grabbed my wrists tightly. 'Don't you remember what I tell you before?'

The smell of nutmeg was omnipresent. I stared into his loathsome eyes, into the depths of hell, and drew in a deep, shaky breath. And then I spoke, and I made sure I spoke loudly and clearly.

'I'm here because I want you to tell me why you drugged and raped me in a villa outside Milan eleven years ago. You and your friends. I know it was you and I need to know who else was involved because it's been *fucking* up my life since then. I need to know what you meant when you said – I remember you saying very clearly that night – you said, "I paid for your pretty eyes." I remember that, Guillaume, and I want to know who you paid. Who set me up?'

He gave a little laugh, half a laugh, and a horrible grin appeared on his face. That grin was pure evil. '*Bah* Nicole, I should have given you a bigger dose. You were not supposed to remember anything.'

He yanked one of my arms behind my back so hard that pain tore through my shoulder and I gasped. He leaned hard into me, his mouth against my ear. 'Maybe this is what you really want, this is why you come here to me when your husband is far away. Maybe what you really want is—' He yanked up my skirt and rammed his hand between my legs, his breath hot on my face.

'My friend is outside Guillaume,' I gasped. 'She'll call the police if I'm not out in ten minutes.'

He laughed. 'But Nicole, I can fuck you in less than that if you don't struggle too much.' His hand was inside my knickers now.

I opened my mouth to scream and he slammed his mouth onto mine.

And then we both heard it: Bérengère hammering on the door, shouting, 'I'm calling the police now, I'm going to call the police!!'

He stepped back and let me go, his face contorted with fury. 'Go then, *pute*,' he snarled, standing back and motioning towards the door.

As I stepped towards it, he grabbed me by the hair and yanked my head back. Suddenly the flick-knife blade was at my throat. 'But if you ever try to trap me again, or if you talk to your husband about this, I will kill you. Okay?' His voice was dripping with menace.

I tried to nod. 'Okay,' I whispered.

He twirled me around and slapped me hard, twice, across the face. My ears rang with the force of it.

'Don't fuck with me, bitch,' he said quietly. 'I am much, much more powerful than you.' Then he opened the door, shoved me back through it and slammed it behind me.

***

We went to a bar in the Saint Pierre quartier. It was one of my favourites because the staff were always super-chilled, super-friendly and usually super-stoned. The music was always excellent and they did fantastic cocktails.

Bérengère ordered a vanilla martini; I ordered three double whiskies. We sat at the bar, she and I, her arm around my shoulders. I'd tied my shirt in a knot underneath my bra. The all-body trembling that was entirely out of my control finally began to subside after I'd necked the second whisky.

I turned to look at her, biting my lips hard together as I raised the third whisky glass to her. My eyes were full of tears as I finally allowed myself the smile that had been waiting so long to curve onto my mouth. 'We did it, Bérengère,' I said quietly.

She smiled back at me. Her eyes were also brimming with tears as she raised her martini glass and clinked it gently against mine. 'We did, Nicole. I am so proud of you.'

She learned forward and kissed me, on the mouth. And actually, it was rather nice.

***

The body wire, the microphone, the transmitter, the phone that was recording – they were all decoys. The real camera, the super-high-tech, super-listening, super-all-seeing camera, with its various little techie babies in strategic positions – that was already there. We'd installed it neatly and discreetly in the office in August, when the development site was empty. You would have needed to be fully 007-trained to spot it.

It had worked perfectly that day. Satan hadn't said a lot, but what he *had* said and what he had *done* were there in high-tech sound and vision. When we watched the video that Bérengère emailed to my phone, the quality was crystal clear.

And Satan's anger, his violence and, most importantly, his guilt – those were crystal clear, too.

***

Xavier was furious. 'I tell you not to do this, Nicole!'

'Yes but have you watched it? Did you hear what he says? He admits that he drugged me! He admits that he raped me!'

He glared at me. 'But it is very possible that the *juge d'instruction* will not accept it, Nicole!'

I gave an enormous shrug. 'Well, Xavier, why don't we leave that up to the *juge d'instruction* to decide?'

He shook his head. 'Is this how you want us to work together, Nicole? I tell you what I believe, and you don't listen to anything I say?'

I held his stare as I shook my head. 'No, I will listen to you. From now on, I'll defer to you on all questions of evidence. But on this ... no. I needed to do this. He's wrecked my life, and I needed him to admit that on video.'

Xavier sat back in his chair. 'I know he do a terrible thing, but how can you say that your life is a wreck, Nicole? You live in a château with a rich man who love you very much? Your life is not terrible.'

I looked away from him. 'I'm not saying my life is terrible *now*, but it could have been different. I could have had a different life if that hadn't happened.'

'Are you not happy with your life?' he asked curiously.

'I have never been happier, Xavier,' I said with absolute certainty. 'I love Guy very much, and I'm fully aware that I have a wonderful life. But when Guillaume raped me, everything changed. I looked at myself differently, I looked at the world differently. I became afraid – and I hate being afraid.'

I leaned forward and gazed at him. 'And now that Guillaume has admitted what he did, I'm not afraid anymore. Now I'm just fucking angry!' I paused. 'And that feels good. I intend to do everything in my power to make sure I bring that bastard in front of a criminal court and have him locked up, so that he can *never* do what he did to me, or what he's probably still doing to other women, again. Can you understand that?'

Xavier ran his hand through his untidy dark curls and gave a very big Gallic shrug, all raised eyebrows and pout, but he finally said, 'Yes, I can understand, Nicole.'

I smiled. 'Thank you, Xavier.'

He smiled back. It seemed that Xavier and I had finally arrived on the same page.

He then started the interminable process of quizzing me in minute detail about every single thing that had happened before, during and after that horrible night in the Marble Villa in Hell. He took detailed notes and asked me questions that I didn't want to answer, that I struggled to find the words to answer and struggled even harder to articulate.

It was horrible and I shredded a number of snotty tissues, but I told him all that I could remember, so that he could prepare my formal statement to submit to the *juge d'instruction* to bring charges against Satan.

After I'd finished, we had another round of 'You Need To Tell Guy'.

I told him my position on that had not changed. I would tell Guy when Satan was safely out of his reach.

'There is no guarantee that Guillaume will be held in custody even if he is arrested,' Xavier objected.

'But rape is a felony.' I frowned. 'And, as I understand it, a felony in France means the accused is held in custody until his trial.'

Xavier shook his head. 'Not always. It is for the *juge d'instruction* to decide this. And I have started to find out about Guillaume *très discrètement*, very quietly, and he is always in the past, very good at not being ... *bah*, prosecuted. He always have very good legal representation. His lawyer will try to negotiate no custody for him at the beginning, too.'

I suddenly felt very tired. Sensing my disappointment, he leaned forward. 'But I also find out one good thing while I do some research.'

Gosh, is Nietzsche really having a day off? I thought.

'Uhuh. How good?'

'I talk to some people I know in Paris. A friend who is a *policière*. She look on the computer for me and ... she find a complaint against Guillaume.'

My heart leapt. 'Really? Recently? That's brilliant!'

He gave a quick shake of his head. 'No, not recent. Some years ago.' Frowning, he flicked through his notes. His glasses gradually slid down his nose and almost fell off before he pushed them back up again. I wondered briefly why he didn't just get glasses that fitted properly.

'Five years ago, a woman allege that he rape her in Paris. She say that they are working together, that he come from Sweden and that she is in Paris, and they are working on a business transaction, and that he rape her in his hotel room.'

'And? Did she bring a case against him?'

He shook his head. 'No. Nothing. Just this. She file a complaint, and then nothing.'

'What do you mean "nothing"? What happened to her? Did she just disappear?'

He glanced at his notes again. 'My colleague tell me that the record say that she no longer want to be contacted. She no longer want to talk about this.'

'She withdrew charges?'

'No, Nicole, she never bring charges. She just contact the police and make a statement, nothing more.'

I frowned at him tiredly. 'So how is that good, Xavier?'

He smiled at me. Annoyingly, he appeared rather perky. 'This is good, Nicole, because now I am going to try to find this woman and to talk to her about what happen with Guillaume. To tell her about what you try to do, about the case you want to make against him.'

He blinked a few times. 'Like I tell you in the beginning, Nicole, we build a case against Guillaume. We don't go and make a danger for ourself by going to his office and making a video!'

I took a deep breath. 'We've been over this, Xavier. You have to admit that the video is excellent! You're just jealous that you didn't suggest it yourself.'

He started laughing despite himself; he looked quite young when he laughed.

I grinned back at him. 'Anyway, Mr Mason, will you keep me posted via Bérengère?' I glanced at my watch. 'I really have to go. Unfortunately, Darth Vader is beaming himself back into our life later today, and I really should be there when he does.'

Xavier looked deeply puzzled. 'I don't understand anything you just say, Nicole.'

'Never mind.' I stood up and held out my hand. 'Thank you for meeting with me today. Please tell Bérengère anything that you find out about this woman in Paris, and please email the draft statement to her when it's finished.'

He took my hand. 'I will. It was good to meet with you again, Nicole.' He smiled. I realised for the first time that if Xavier got some non-NHS glasses and perhaps invested in a shirt that wasn't stained with ink, or gravy, or wine and had frayed cuffs, he would be quite attractive.

Chapter Thirteen

Back at the Duchess, Darth Vader had light-sabred his way back into residence. He had briefly returned to Paris after our wedding celebration to meet with his lawyer and put the family home up for sale. He informed D'Artagnan that he would be returning to stay with us while he looked for a suitable property to buy in our region because Paris no longer appealed to him.

We were both thrilled (not) by the news. I was making a concerted effort to try to be kind to Stephane, to be sympathetic, but it was testing my patience. He had now moved into Grief, Stage Two: Anger, which did not make it easy. He was also starting to exhibit some of D'Artagnan's imperial traits, which was *really* annoying because he had none of D'Artagnan's saving graces.

'Your French teacher, Nicole,' he sniffed the next morning as we sipped our coffee 'She is a bit of an 'ippy. Does my brother know she smoke marijuana?'

I sipped my coffee, breathed out, channelled serenity and calm. 'Yes, Stephane, he does know and he's fully on board with it. As am I. Please don't worry about Bérengère. She's just fine. And she's my friend – a *very* good friend.' I stared at him, hard.

'Hmmmm'. He hummed darkly. 'I would not let my wife...' He stopped. His nostrils flared, his thin lips tightened. '*Bah*, my *ex-wife—*' spat out venomously, 'have a lesson with somebody who smoke marijuana. A lesson in the *French* language.'

'Well,' I said, 'isn't it fortunate that you won't have to worry about that sort of thing in the future, Stephane?'

I was missing D'Artagnan a lot. He'd been away nearly ten days and, although I'd had another text message on day six, we still hadn't spoken. He'd written that the riding was hard, that he was sore but he was enjoying it. He'd said how much he loved me, how much he missed me. He was due back in Paris on Monday and I was aching to see him again. I'd done so much, so many difficult, scary things in the time that he'd been gone that I was exhausted. I just wanted to hold him and be held by him.

Stephane breathed in deeply. 'You are not very ... *respectueuse*, Nicole. This is the problem that I have with some – with a lot of my children. They are not *respectueux*. This is Catherine's fault, she never discipline the children properly!' He pushed his chair away from the table, stood up abruptly and went into the kitchen.

I contemplated explaining that I wasn't one of his children, even though I was only two years older than his eldest offspring. Françoise had imparted this little nugget to me; it had not made me feel good.

Then my heart lifted because I heard the sound I had been waiting for. It was Wednesday so there was no school in the afternoon, and I could hear Nina's footsteps in the pantry. She burst through the doorway into the dining hall, a grin lighting up her little face as she ran to me, flung herself into my lap and almost knocked my coffee cup flying. '*Princesse* Nicole, *Princesse* Nicole, today I am going to ride Emperador – Camille said I can ride Emperador! I am so, *so* excited!'

She clambered onto my chair and into my lap. Her new teeth had just started to grow, little white stumps in her pink gums, her eyes wide and sparkling with excitement.

'Oh, that's wonderful, Nina. I'm so pleased! You must be so happy!' I put my cup down, hugged her against me hard, kissed her soft dark head. Her enthusiasm was infectious. And also she was just – Nina. Being around her always made me happy.

Stephane came back into the room. I heard him inhale, heard the cold death rattle.

Nina heard it too. She sat back, shrank away from me and looked up at him from under her eyelashes. Her eyes were suddenly wary. I hated him in that moment.

I lifted her off my lap and stood her in front of me as I got to my feet, my back still turned to Stephane. I continued to squeeze her hands and fixed her eyes with mine. 'Should we go out and see him? He must be so pleased to know you are going to ride him today.'

She immediately forgot about Darth Vader. The grin came back and she said, '*Yes*, he is very, very pleased! Come with me, come and see him, come with me.' She pulled my hand as she turned to run out of the dining hall. I followed her willingly; I would have followed Nina anywhere and I think she knew that. I liked that she knew that.

Camille and Gabriela were outside with the horses, Gabriela sitting on one of the lower paddock rails, leaning forward and rolling a cigarette, while Camille brushed Emperador. Nina let go of my hand, went to get a brush out of the grooming kit and skipped over to the other side of Emperador. She started brushing his head carefully, chatting with him quietly in her child horse-French.

It was a crisp, clear morning in late September and autumn was auditioning for its forthcoming principal role. Espiritu was standing at the paddock gate watching us all; lately he had seemed more curious about human beings, as if he were thinking, 'Hmm, perhaps they're not all arseholes. Maybe they are an interesting species.'

I exchanged Kissies with Camille and Gabriela then went over to my other love. I stood in front of him, offered him a lint-ridden peppermint that I'd dug out of my pocket. His nostrils flared as he sniffed it then he snorted loudly as he always did, as if I'd offered him something *outrageously* inappropriate. It always made me laugh, because Emperador loved peppermints but Espiritu thought they were the devil's *bonbons*.

I put my hand on his forehead underneath his black mane and gave him a good, long scratch, which he always seemed to enjoy. His eyes closed halfway and he looked kinda... goofy. My nails were filthy afterwards but I didn't care. Manicures were no longer high on my list of necessities.

'How long have you been doing that with him, Nicole?' Camille called out to me. She was brushing out Emperador's tail with his hairbrush; it fell almost to the ground in shimmering, flaxen-gold waves when she let go, so it clearly merited a proper hairbrush.

I shrugged. 'A little while now. Maybe a month.'

Her black eyes were fixed on me. 'He likes you. Espiritu, he is comfortable with you.' She turned back to Emperador and carried on brushing out his tail.

Gabriela took a drag on her cigarette, raised an eyebrow at me as I turned back to Espiritu and gave me a little wink. I was filled with a moment of pure *bonheur*, pure joy. I smiled at her as I turned back to my blue-and-black-eyed love. 'I am comfortable with you too, Espiritu,' I whispered to him.

His big eyes gave nothing away. He moved his head up and down to tell me he wanted more scratches, so I put my nails back against his forehead and scratched him and he was happy. His eyes were half-closed and his compact, muscular body gleamed in the autumn sun.

Emperador was ready. His elegant brown saddle sat perfectly on the red saddle pad, the girth had been tightened and the silver stirrups flashed in the sun. Yes, I had learned some horse tack words now, in English *and* in French.

It was Nina's moment. She was wearing her jodhpurs, of course; she always wore her jodhpurs now when she was *chez nous*. We'd been to Decathlon to buy her several pairs, a riding hat and riding boots. She'd frowned when I'd said that no, I would not be buying jodhpurs for myself because I could never ride a horse.

'But of course you can ride a horse, *Princesse* Nicole. You just need to try.' Her face was very serious and a frown creased her forehead as she gazed up at me.

I smiled and ruffled her hair. 'Well, we'll see, Nina. Who knows? Maybe one day.' Even though I didn't believe what I was saying, it seemed to appease her.

We'd also bought two bags of carrot-and-apple flavoured treats for the horses, though we didn't tell Camille. We agreed that if we only gave them each two treats a day, we didn't need to tell her. She was very strict about their diet and they weren't allowed unlimited carrots or apples. My bad. I didn't tell her that I still sneakily gave them a carrot each at dusk, their soft lips snuffling the palm of my hand. I loved the sound of them crunching the carrots between their back teeth, a look of intense concentration on their faces.

Nina looked up at Emperador when he was ready. She raised her shoulders high and grinned delightedly at me and then at Camille.

'So, Nina, are you very excited?' Camille asked.

Nina nodded, her eyes wide with anticipation.

'So now you must be calm,' Camille said. 'You need to be calmer, Nina. Emperador, he is a horse who likes very much to be excited but this is not always a good thing. You need to take some deep breaths and you need to think, "I am calm. I am going to ride on the back of this wonderful animal and I am not going to be excited, I am going to just ... *bah*, be happy – but quietly happy." Okay?' Her eyes were fixed very intently on Nina's.

Nina took a deep breath. It was much more than those quick breaths that children take when you say 'breathe in!'; it was a deep, slow filling of her lungs and then a very long, calm breath out again. She had listened to what Camille had said; more than that, she had *understood*.

When Camille smiled at her again, her eyes were moist like mine. 'You are ready?'

Nina nodded, then stood at Emperador's side and bent her left leg at the knee. Camille clasped it easily in one hand and in unison they counted '*un, deux, trois*'. Then Nina was up in the saddle on Emperador's back. The stirrups had been shortened as much as possible and her small, booted feet fitted into them easily.

Camille handed her the reins. 'So Nina, ask him to walk him around the courtyard and make a circle back to us.'

Suddenly I was nervous; surely Camille was going to lead him around the courtyard? Surely she wouldn't let Emperador walk off on his own? Nina was so small up there on his back... What if he just galloped away?!

But Nina took the reins attached to the simple, three-string halter in her hands, she clicked her tongue expertly and squeezed her legs against his sides, and Emperador walked calmly away from us. They made a large, uneven circle in the courtyard and came back to us. Then they did another circuit, this one larger; Nina seemed to concentrate more on this one. When she passed us a third time, the expression on her face was intent but also so, so full of joy.

***

'Who is that child? Who does she belong to?' Stephane asked with another imperial sniff the following Sunday after Nina had spent all of the previous day with me and the horses.

I glared at him. I had run out of sympathy for him and his miserable, narrow view of the world, a view rigidly obscured by custom and society and religion. 'Her name is Nina. And she belongs to—'

I desperately wanted to say that she belonged to me, but she didn't. She could be taken from me at any moment and that thought made me shrivel up, made me die a little inside. It was too horrible to contemplate.

'She's our neighbour's foster child and her name is Nina. She loves coming here, and we love her coming here.' *So shut the fuck up*, I added silently.

Stephane gave a long, disdainful sniff. 'She is very, *bah*, noisy. Undisciplined. Why is she allowed to run into your house whenever she want to?'

'Because I like it that she runs into our house whenever she wants to!' I glared at him.

Gallic pout. 'Does my brother know that she behave like this, that she run in and out of his house uncontrolled like this?'

'Yes, Stephane, Guy is very aware that Nina "behave like this, that she run in and out of the house like this" and he really doesn't seem bothered by it. But he'll be back tomorrow, so you can ask him yourself. Okay?'

He gave me the full Du Beauchamp gaze, the imperial gaze. His mouth wrinkled in a tight, displeased pout. 'You are not, Nicole, a very *courtoise* person, I think.'

Ya fucking THINK? I wanted to say. But I didn't; instead, I just thought about how much I missed D'Artagnan.

***

And then he was back. I was in the salon as the Audi skidded to a halt on the forecourt. He was barely out of the car before I threw my arms around his neck. He lifted me up and I wrapped my legs around him. He held me so tightly against him and he felt so *good*, so strong, so familiar. The scent of him was intoxicating. We clung to each other as he buried his face in the curve of my neck, breathing in deeply. Finally he let me slide down the length of his body and we kissed, his mouth intense, sensuous.

'*Oh mon dieu, Nicole mon ange, tu m'as tellement, tellement manqué,*' he murmured, and did that slow, sexy blink. I wondered in that moment if one could actually die of love, of lust, of anticipation? Was that possible? Was it a genuine medical possibility?

I also saw out of the corner of my eye – although I didn't want to because I didn't want it to intrude on our moment – the curtain twitch in Stephane's bedroom. He was watching us.

I shrugged mentally, then I leaned into my gorgeous D'Artagnan as hard as I could. My lips against his ear, I whispered, 'I need you, my angel. I need you and I want you very, very badly.'

His arms tightened around me. '*Bah*, Nicole, *mon ange*, that is exactly what I am thinking.'

***

Darth Vader disappeared for the rest of that day. Maybe he spent it doing a two-million-piece jigsaw puzzle, maybe one of the Last Supper or something. Whatever. I didn't know what he was doing and I didn't care because D'Artagnan and I were otherwise occupied; *very* occupied.

And even though it was clear that two weeks of horse riding had left him in pain, he was still capable of turning me into a droopy-eyed, imbecilic, grinning idiot by the time we finally descended to search for sustenance some seven hours later.

***

'So Nicole, *mon trésor,* you are spending a lot of time with your friend Bérengère. I think I should meet her. I think I will make a lunch for her, for us. We will invite Benoît and Veronique as well.'

The haughty gaze softened a little and a hint of mischief crept in. 'And Stephane. My brother—' (my '*brozzair*': there were still moments when that frisson of *amusex*, amusement at his sexy accent, would zing through me) '—is very annoyed by her. I think this would be good for him. And it would be fun for us.' He gave me a wicked little smile over his coffee cup.

We were sitting in the dining hall sipping our second morning coffee. Two cups were allowed, though I usually had at least two more at some point. That invariably caused comment that, strangely, was even less audible to me than the traffic on the motorway thirty kilometres away.

Stephane had gone off early to meet with an estate agent nearer to Bordeaux. He had not liked any property he'd been shown close to us. He told us this accusingly, as if we'd orchestrated it, his mouth in the usual disapproving, upside-down crescent shape. It had been difficult to internalise my fist punch and 'Yesssss!'

I frowned a little. 'But you have met Bérengère. She was at our wedding. I introduced you.'

'Yes, Nicole, I remember you introduce her to me but I did not get some time to talk to her, and I will like to know her better. I don't know why we could not meet to have a lunch when you go to Bordeaux with her last week.'

The haughtiness was back. He was still miffed that I had refused his offer to take us both to lunch, but the meeting with Xavier had been at 11am and I'd had no idea how long it would last. Bérengère had come with me, both to meet Xavier and to provide me with an alibi for leaving the château.

I sighed. I hated having to lie to Guy, but I would hate the consequences of not lying to him a lot more.

'Sweetheart, I've told you several times. Sometimes it's nice to spend some time with a girlfriend, do some shopping, wander around. Bérengère doesn't go to Bordeaux often and it would have broken the mood if we'd had to be somewhere at a specific time to have lunch with you. It wasn't personal.'

***

The meeting the previous week was arranged after Xavier had prepared the first draft of the statement and sent it to Bérengère. He'd asked me to come to his office and discuss it when I'd finished reviewing it; he also said he had some news about the woman in Paris who had gone to the police and accused Guillaume of raping her.

When I introduced them, I realised that Xavier and Bérengère had the same colour eyes. He came out of his burrow into the reception area when we arrived. There was a porridge stain on his shirt – at least, I think that's what it was. I wondered briefly if French people ate porridge or, indeed, if they knew what porridge was.

I noted that his aftershave was Bleu de Chanel.

Xavier and I had progressed to Kissies now, but he was very formal towards Bérengère as if he knew not to mess with her. I noted that, too.

We followed him into his office and he moved the pile of folders off the second chair so that Bérengère could sit down. 'Thank you for coming to see me today. It is nice to meet you properly, Bérengère,' he said politely.

'It's good to meet you too, Xavier.' She smiled languidly at him and he blinked his long eyelashes at her. Stubble shadow was negligible today, but glasses-smudge was medium to high.

'So, Xavier,' I said. 'What news of Paris?' He frowned at me. 'The woman in Paris, the one that accused Satan of raping her. What news?'

The puzzled look that I was getting accustomed to crossed his face. 'Guillaume,' I sighed. 'You know who I mean.'

I saw him glance at Bérengère. While I didn't quite catch her eyeroll, I was pretty sure she did one.

Xavier pressed his lips together to stop himself smiling, then his face became serious again. 'It is not good news, Nicole.'

My heart sank.

He drew a deep breath. 'I find this woman. She work in La Defense in Paris for a big bank. She tell me she does not want to talk to me about this, that it is in the past. Then she put the phone down.'

'Did you call her back?'

He nodded. 'Yes. I start to tell her that you are bringing this case against Guillaume, that she can join the case, that she need not be on her own. But she tell me she does not want to. When I try to convince her, she tell me that Guillaume is a dangerous man, that I must tell *you* that he is a dangerous man.'

'Well obviously I know that he's a dangerous man,' I snapped, frustrated. 'Otherwise I wouldn't be bringing charges against him, would I?'

Xavier's face was very serious. He said quietly, 'She tell me that after she go to the police, she have a bad accident.'

I frowned at him, confused. 'And? What's that supposed to mean?'

He took a deep breath and bit his lips. 'Nicole, she tell me that she is hit by a car. That she have a broken leg, broken ribs, that she is in hospital for many weeks. And this car, it never stop. The police never find the driver. She think this is Guillaume that do this, or that it is someone Guillaume pay to do this.'

I stared at him, conscious that my heart was beating faster. When I finally spoke, my mouth felt dry. 'Do you think that's what happened?'

He shrugged. 'I don't know. It is possible that it is nothing to do with Guillaume. This thing can happen to anyone in Paris. It happen not very often, but of course it happen.' He paused. 'But this woman, she is *convaincue* ... *bah*, what is this word in English?' He glanced at Bérengère.

'Convinced,' said Bérengère.

'*Oui*, she is convince that this is something Guillaume do. So this is why she do not want to talk to me, Nicole. And I must respect her decision.'

My voice faltered. 'So we just have to let it go?'

'Yes.' His voice was firm.

I felt dejected and afraid. Would Guillaume really have done that, have tried to kill one of his victims? He had threatened me, but I had refused to believe it was any more than a threat. The thought that he was capable of attempted murder...

I put that thought out of my head. I was *not* going to let him intimidate me. 'What about the video?' I asked. 'Have you spoken to the *juge d'instruction* about whether that's going to be admitted as evidence yet?'

He frowned at me. '*Non*, Nicole. I already explain to you that first we submit the dossier to the *procureur*, and then the *procureur* refer it to the *juge d'instruction*. So first we must get the *procureur* to allow us to submit the video as evidence. And because you obtain this evidence without the *juge* ordering that it can be obtained, this is why it is quite possible that the *juge* reject it.'

Suddenly I was exhausted. There was no way the French courts would let me bring a criminal action against Guillaume when the only evidence was me asserting that he had raped me in Italy eleven years ago.

Bérengère put her hand and on my arm. 'Don't give up, Nicole,' she said quietly. 'You must believe that you can do this. Just believe. That's all that matters.'

'Bérengère is right, Nicole,' Xavier said. 'It is very early in this case. We are going to find more evidence. I start to make more enquiries here in Bordeaux, and tomorrow I have a lunch with a *procureur* that is retired. He seem to know a lot of things about the family of Guillaume.'

'Thank you, Xavier.'

His gaze was sympathetic for a moment, and then it was back to business. 'So now, we go over the statement I prepare for you in detail again. Then I make some changes, and then I send it to you for it to be final, okay?'

***

When we left his office, Bérengère and I went to a bar. I'd had two glasses of wine to try to blunt the toxic memories, and on the way home in her car we shared a joint. Consequently, I'd been r-e-a-l-l-y c-h-i-l-l-e-d by the time she dropped me off at the Duchess. D'Artagnan arrived home more than an hour later, but I was still very mellow and I think he could tell.

Perhaps that was why he was now so keen to invite Bérengère to lunch. He wanted to get to know the woman with whom his wife was getting stoned.

'Well,' I said doubtfully, 'I'm not sure it would be much fun for Bérengère, would it? Having to put up with Stephane's disapproval all the way through lunch?'

'So, we invite Françoise and Pascal too, we make a dilution. We have a lunch for La Toussaint. Stephane will approve of this. It is a good Catholic thing to do.'

'What's La Toussaint? And why on earth are we suddenly celebrating Catholic things just because Stephane is staying? I'm not sure Bérengère will want to come to a Catholic thing.' I frowned at him.

'Nonsense! La Toussaint is just a day when everyone are all together. We eat a big meal, we remember the dead in our family, our dead friends, and we maybe drink too much while we remember, then everyone drive home. In Mexico, the Day of the Dead. In France, the day of drunk driving.' He paused. 'It is the first day of November, the day after 'Alloween. You know, Nicole, the American spooky day.' He made spooky hands at me and went 'woooooh'.

I raised an eyebrow. 'Authentic. I'm impressed.'

He leaned over and poked me in the ribs, making me squirm. He knows exactly where I'm ticklish.

He grinned. 'Anyway, Nicole, I want to meet your friend, Bérengère, the one that Stephane tell me smoke marijuana and is teaching you to be *irrespectueuse*. I want to know this woman who can teach my wife to be even more *irrespectueuse* than she already are.'

He leaned over again and slid an arm around my neck, holding me in place while he tickled me so that I couldn't wriggle away, could only try to smack his hands away as I giggled and squirmed. 'Okay, *mon amour*? You ask your friend for lunch on *La Toussaint*? Otherwise, I won't stop...'

I finally managed to slide out from under his hands. 'Okay, okay! I'll ask her! Though I can't imagine why she'd agree to come!' I moved out of his reach and picked up my coffee cup.

'But you know, Guy, Stephane was really giving her the evil eye at the wedding – he was positively glaring at her! What is it with your brother? He seems to be obsessed with women being controlled! And yet – I don't get the impression that he ever really had any control over Catherine. She always seemed to be in control. Is that why she left him, do you think? Do you think she got bored with controlling him?'

He sniffed dismissively. 'No. It was the sex.' The lazy smile. 'Because, Nicole, it is not possible when you look at Stephane to imagine—'

I put a hand up. 'Stop! Stop right there. I do *not* want to imagine your brother having sex with the Arch Bitch, thank you.' I shook my head to try and dislodge the image that was forming in the periphery of my mind. 'Besides, it isn't all about sex, D'Artagnan. Not everything that goes wrong in a marriage is about sex.'

'*Pffff.*' He shrugged. 'I think that one was. I think after the *sixième* children, *bah*, that was it. No more sex. And that was twenty-five year ago. So, a long time with no sex.' Another shrug.

Then, because D'Artagnan's musings – particularly on sex – always extrapolate, he got up from the table, gave a big stretch and followed me into the kitchen. 'So Nicole, I am thinking, *mon amour*, that we need to take a holiday soon.' He slipped his arms around me from behind as I closed the dishwasher.

'I think we should take some time in the sun, somewhere warm, *mon amour*, maybe at the end of the month. For my birthday, yes? This year, no more hospital, no more pain, no more physio. We take some time to celebrate my birthday, okay?'

He was going to be fifty-one in early December; fifty had caused a lot of navel-gazing and melodrama about getting old and dying (hello again, Nietzsche!) but was mostly overshadowed by the physical pain of having nearly chain-sawed off his leg. Like I said, there are silver linings everywhere if one looks for them.

I turned towards him thinking: *Shit. I didn't factor D'Artagnan's appetite for sunshine and holidays into the GTBS timetable.*

'You don't like this idea?' Seeing my consternation, he frowned.

And then I thought: *Actually yes, let's do that. It might be the last chance we get to chill before all hell breaks loose.*

'I think it's a wonderful idea, darling man.' I kissed him slightly more intently than was warranted on a cold Tuesday morning in October. I slipped my arms around his neck, closed my eyes and thought about how sensual his mouth was. It tasted of coffee and felt like satin. And when we broke off, he held me tightly, enveloped me in his arms, buried his face in my hair and murmured, '*Mon dieu, Nicole, qu'est-ce que je t'aime.*'

***

I asked Bérengère if she could possibly endure lunch on La Toussaint with Darth Vader and D'Artagnan. Did she have the mental stamina to survive a meal served with thick, rich *Sauce à l'Arrogance Extrême*, garnished with croutons of Deep-Fried Disapproval?

She smiled her slow, easy smile. 'Sure, Nicole, that will be lovely. I will look forward to that.'

***

Gabriela and Camille had spent some time that autumn creating a large round paddock in the courtyard with posts and rails. D'Artagnan had helped them – actually helped as opposed to interfered.

Aside from the occasional day when she rode out on Emperador, Camille tried to come once or twice a week to work with Espiritu in this new paddock. On Saturdays, if the weather was clear, Gabriela often came too. She sat on one of the lower paddock rails watching Camille, smoking her ubiquitous roll-ups. I sat on an adjacent rail and mostly we didn't speak, we just watched.

I tried to keep the shivering to a minimum, despite my wool-lined Wellington boots, jeans, three layers of jumpers and the shearling-lined, hooded duffle coat that D'Artagnan had brought back from Argentina that quite clearly said 'Made in France' on the label immediately under the word 'Hermès'. He'd grinned a little sheepishly when I'd raised an eyebrow and he made a comment about not having had time to shop in Argentina. Anyway, French stuff good; everything else shit. I hadn't complained; the jacket was marvellously warm and beautifully made.

He'd bought one for Nina, too, only hers was a dusty pink and mine was powder blue. She had run her little fingers over the prancing carriage-horse logo when she'd unwrapped it, lifted her green eyes to him and given him a huge, half-toothed grin. Her front teeth were finally growing in. Katie's were slightly later and Jules and I exchanged weekly photos of their progress. Nina was pleased that hers were growing faster than Katie's.

It was a gloriously sunny Saturday marred only by a vicious north-easterly breeze. Nina was outside by the horses in her jodhpurs and boots and smart duffle coat, leaning against D'Artagnan who had a hand on her shoulder. His dark brown hair (albeit receding at the temples ... did I mention he was nearly fifty-one? *Quelle horreur!*), slightly too long as always, was brushed back. His beard was all salt-and-pepper around that expressive mouth. His eyes were slightly narrowed against the sunshine and he had one leg bent at the knee where his foot was hooked over the lower paddock rail. He'd effortlessly nailed the urban-cowboy look and he looked bloody gorgeous.

What made him even more gorgeous was the way that Nina was gazing up at him. This time I allowed myself to think the thought that I would normally have banished: *Is it possible that he feels about Nina the way that I feel?*

When I reached them, he slipped his other arm around my shoulders and kissed my forehead. I put my hand on Nina's shoulder and she turned and gave me the Halloween grin. I smiled back at her, then we all went back to watching Camille and the most beautiful horse in the world.

The wind was icy and I shivered. D'Artagnan made a face, pulled me closer. '*Bah*, Nicole, I can't believe you are still cold in that coat. You are always cold, *mon amour*. You know, it's like I always tell you, if you eat some meat you won't be cold.' Soooo repetitive.

He squeezed Nina's shoulder. 'Are you cold too, little Nina?' She made a face 'No! I'm not cold!'

He ruffled her hair. 'It is only *Princesse* Nicole that is always cold – it is because she won't eat meat.' He nodded at her knowingly, one eyebrow raised to indicate that he *knew* things, he *knew* this.

Nina frowned up at him. 'No, that's not true. I also don't eat meat and I am not cold. *Princesse* Nicole is just ... well, she is a *princesse*. It is normal for her to be cold when she is not in her warm château.'

Guy turned to look at me and asked mildly, in English, 'Nina is vegetarian too? Is this something you do, Nicole?'

I rolled my eyes at him. 'No, D'Artagnan.' I leaned into his ear and whispered, 'She's a very liberal vegetarian. She thinks chicken isn't meat so she eats chicken, and she eats fish. But don't tell her that.'

He grinned, kissed my mouth, and smiled down at Nina again, who was still frowning up at us. 'Yes, Nina, *Princesse* Nicole is very ... *fragile*. You are right, she is always cold when she is not in her warm château.' Slightly raised eyebrow, little pout at me.

Nina smiled up at him. I raised an eyebrow and smirked at him.

That day Camille was going to ride Espiritu. He was a little enervated by the cold wind and moved his hooves as he stood beside the mounting stump, as if he were doing a little dance – one, two, three, four, like a tap-dance sequence. The wind blew his tail to the side and lifted his mane.

Camille stood quietly beside him, holding the reins of his halter while he danced, and after a while he paused, calmed by her quiet presence. She climbed onto the mounting block and paused again when he tossed his head and moved his feet a little, waiting until he was standing still once more. Only then did she put her foot in the stirrup and swing herself gently into the saddle. Espiritu continued to stand proudly, his small ears pricked, his thick neck slightly arched, the wind lifting his long, silky mane.

Camille sat for a while, completely relaxed, then picked up the reins loosely in both hands. She made an opening movement with her left hand, moving it away from his neck, gave a slight squeeze of her legs and then we heard her say authoritatively, '*Marche.*'

Espiritu walked off to the left around the arena and they did a full circuit. Then Camille made a noise like a long, disappointed '*ohhhhh*' and sat up straight. Espiritu stopped and she scratched the base of his neck underneath his mane. They stood for a minute, his tail blowing in the cold wind, then she picked up the reins again and this time moved her right hand away from his neck. She increased the pressure in her left leg, repeated the instruction '*marche*', and Espiritu walked off in the opposite direction.

When they finished their circuit, Camille made the disappointed '*ohhhhh*' sound again and he stopped. She scratched his neck again for a while, and then I saw her squeeze her leg against his side. After two or three strides, Espiritu broke into the prettiest trot; his muscular body curved under her as she rose effortlessly in the stirrups to match his pace. It was so beautiful to watch that I realised I was holding my breath. D'Artagnan squeezed my shoulders.

After they'd completed several more circuits of the paddock in both directions, Camille stopped close to us. She shifted her weight, leaned forward and caressed Espiritu's neck gently before slipping off his back and landing lightly on the ground beside him. She scratched his neck again and praised him quietly.

Finally, she looked at us. 'So, Nicole, would you like to try that?' She gave a wicked little smile.

I stared at her, horrified. 'No, thank you!'

She shrugged and turned to Nina. 'Nina – do you want to ride Espiritu?'

Nina's little shoulders rose up around her neck as if she had just heard the most wonderful thing ever and she nodded her head really fast.

I could feel the tension in her body under my hand on her shoulder, and I thought once again: *these French people, this nation – WTF?! Were they always so reckless?!* Only six months ago, Espiritu had been a wild, dangerous horse that even Camille was wary about riding, and now she was going to allow six-year-old Nina to get up on his back on her own?

But I swallowed the slight panic I felt and held Nina's shoulder firmly. 'Breathe, Nina,' I said quietly, *'N'oublié pas, Nina, de respirer...'*

She took a slow, deep breath and her shoulders descended. She turned and smiled at me then started walking towards Espiritu.

'Don't forget your hat. *Ton casque,* Nina,' I called and she returned, all serious now, She lifted her riding hat off the top of the post and buckled it under her chin, then she walked to the paddock and climbed between the tape.

Guy smiled tenderly, his eyes moist. 'You talk to Nina in French and in English now, *mon amour,* and she listen to you. She understand you perfectly.'

I looked away from him, my eyes also soft, also moist. 'Yeah, well, we get each other, Nina and I. She's very... Guy, she's – '

I couldn't say any more; it was too much to ask, too much to want, to expect. He continued to gaze at me until finally he blinked and hugged me hard against him.

We turned back to watch skinny little Nina in her jodhpurs and her new, pristine dusty-pink Hermès shearling jacket (that was almost certainly not going to remain pristine) ride Espiritu, the most beautiful horse in the world around the paddock.

It is a moment that is forever imprinted on my mind.

Chapter Fourteen

We hosted the *La Toussaint* lunch, D'Artagnan and I.

'Is it a dressy thing?' I asked him hesitantly that morning, standing in my underwear in Heaven and gazing upon my fabric armoury. I was very unsure about the dress code; on the one hand, it was a day of mourning and solemn remembrance; on the other, Day of the Dead, French style. Death and Sex. What was the protocol?

'*Bah, ouais* Nicole, *bien sûr*, it is *très très* dressy. You should wear the dress made from all of the sin in the world *mon amour.*' A wicked smile as he slipped his arms around me from behind.

I frowned. 'It's November, Guy, so no, I'm not going to wear almost nothing. I'll die of hypothermia before the main course!'

A big shrug, his mouth on the curve of my neck, eyes watching me in the mirror.

'Seriously, what should I wear?' I asked. 'Is it a serious occasion, very respectful, or is it a bit more ... I dunno, chilled?'

'*Pfffft*, Nicole, it is an important day so you should wear something a bit, *bah,* not jeans, *mon amour.* A nice dress. But it is your friend and some of my family, their partners. We drink some wine, we eat some good food, we remember our friends and our family who are not with us any more. We cry a bit, we laugh a bit and then...' a slow, very purposeful bite on the trigger spot '...and then we fuck a lot. Okay? Very simple. But sexy, too. Wear whatever you want to wear, *mon ange.* You always look so beautiful, it doesn't matter what you wear.'

D'Artagnan; normally never short of an opinion but a bit rubbish, really, on the subject of clothes.

I opted for mildly subversive from 2009, Dolce & Gabbana, black-velvet ribbon around the throat, exquisite ivory lace to the fitted silk bodice that then flowed from the waist to the ankles, fitted lace sleeves to the elbow. Another band of black velvet ribbon followed by a froth of ivory lace. I put up my hair, secured it with a velvet clasp in a first-time perfect 'just been...', fastened my birthday solitaire earrings and the wedding bracelet on my wrist, slipped on the Roger Vivier cream stilettos that I'd worn at our first marriage ceremony in London, and bound the ribbons around my ankles. And then I stood up to survey the overall outfit in Heaven's mirrored doors.

It was good. It was demure, and it was also sexy. Very D&G. I smiled at my reflection, turned and went downstairs.

Françoise and Pascal arrived first, Françoise in a deep-red silk dress that hugged her slender body with a plunging V-neck that accentuated the delicate bones in her throat. She looked so happy, and her dark eyes were sparkling. Pascal wore a collarless cream shirt and smart black jeans, and his wild black curls made his blue eyes seem even more vibrant than usual. He gazed often at Françoise, always with the same smile; he was clearly very much in love, and it was entirely reciprocated. Every time I looked at his eyes I was reminded of Jules and my heart ached a little. I missed her.

We did Kissies and I handed them each an ancient, heavy, crystal glass of Champagne. As we stood together in the salon, Stephane was in full Darth Vader mode. He breathed disapprovingly as he sipped the water he'd insisted on having out of a Champagne glass. I wondered if he was even more disapproving than usual because I'd just made a massive breach of protocol: in France, one does not serve *any* drinks until *everyone* has arrived.

I had found this rule utterly absurd when D'Artagnan first explained it to me. 'What if someone who's been invited can't make it?'

He looked confused. 'But they will have said if they cannot be there.'

'But what if something totally bizarre happens – they get hit by a meteor on the way, for example? It's not inconceivable that something unexpected might happen and someone can't make it. What happens then?'

I had a vision of Miss Havisham-style salons in abandoned châteaux the length and breadth of France, cluttered with the skeletons of guests who had died of thirst or starvation because one of the invited guests had failed to make it.

'*Bah*... Finally, I suppose, the host will serve the guests, even if one is missing. But it has never happened to me.' An imperial sniff, as if I were being unnecessarily picky about French protocol.

I had decided that particular protocol was going straight into the 'to be ignored' box. People need a drink when they arrive, FFS; it breaks the ice.

Benoît and Veronique arrived. Veronique was rocking Viking Wet Dream (rather than just Viking) in pale-pink satin edged with black lace. Her dress plunged between her creamy breasts, offering them up for delectation, and then slunk away in panels to just above her knees. Knee-high black stiletto boots expertly complemented the sex-kitten look. With her perfectly coiffured blonde bob and pretty blue eyes, she looked gorgeous.

I resisted the urge to say, 'Whoa, girl!' when I helped her take her coat off. It was clear she had come in full battle dress; she knew that Bérengère was coming, and she'd packed the full arsenal. She was fully armed – or at least fully breasted.

Benoît's eyes widened as Veronique walked back into the salon. It seemed he hadn't fully appreciated his wife's outfit until that moment, and he seemed to like it a lot. He smiled a big, goofy smile at her from the D'Artagnan family eyes, slipped a hand under her arm and passed her a glass of Champagne, all the time trying not to stare her cleavage.

Bérengère arrived, late of course.

Stephane gave a big sniff. 'Very impolite,' he murmured, as she rapped the door knocker.

We embraced and I took her coat. I looked at her, she looked at me, and we embraced again, a big tight hug. She smelled of musk and of roses, deep-red roses. Her silver hair was pinned up in an untidy chignon, secured with a silver and green clasp that glinted in the light. She wore a pale green dress that swept the floor and left her slender shoulders bare. The lace sleeves ended just above her delicate wrists; it suited her perfectly. She wore no make-up other than a little gloss on her lips, and her olive skin glowed. Her sensuous grey eyes were slightly hooded as usual. She looked beautiful.

Stephane just stared.

When they did Kissies, I noticed that he looked quite terrified. I turned away to hide my face.

When D'Artagnan did Kissies with her I watched them out of the corner of my eye as I chatted with Veronique. Two alphas, one male, one female, two French masters in the art of seduction. How was that going to play out?

It was fascinating, because they both knew instantly that they had met their gender opposite. They smiled that knowing, lazy smile at each other and it took everything in my power not to grin as I watched them.

After Champagne, canapés and chit-chat, we went through to the dining hall, to the table which I'd decorated only slightly less extravagantly than I had at Christmas the year before, and we sat down to eat.

And finally, *finally*, Stephane accepted a glass of wine because it was a glass of Françoise' award-winning white wine, her château's *Pessac-Léognan cru classé*. We toasted her and her talent and her wonderful wine. She blushed a little, her eyes glittering.

Then we ate some of D'Artagnan's heavenly garlic *cèpes* on toasted, walnut-infused bread, and everyone else had *foie gras*. Duh ... France, big family meal. It's *obligatoire* that there is *foie gras*.

Stephane allowed his wine glass to be refilled and kept glancing furtively at Bérengère across the table, who was seated next to D'Artagnan. I thought, *hmmmm, interesting*, and raised a mental Poirot eyebrow at that.

I helped D'Artagnan clear the plates and bring in the next course: sweet potatoes sliced and baked in a cream sauce, wilting green spinach, rich, truffle-flavoured Jerusalem artichokes and three different species of dead animal (for them), and sublimely delicious red wine from the Medoc, 2010 St Julien.

By the time the cheese course arrived the wine was flowing freely, as was the conversation. Bérengère and Stephane were engaged in an argument about seventeenth-century Italian art and the representation of the female form (French dinner party conversations are *never* about house prices). The discussion was surprisingly heated. Before he had taken retirement the year before, Stephane had been on the board of directors of a prestigious Parisian auction house and he clearly felt he was more than qualified to express *the* definitive opinion on the subject. Bérengère unsurprisingly, disagreed.

While they argued, I caught a glimpse of D'Artagnan's charisma in Stephane, just a hint of it in those normally sad, disappointed eyes. He didn't look so old as he argued across the table with Bérengère; he didn't seem so grey in complexion and in demeanour.

After the cheese came dessert; a *magnifique tarte tatin*, D'Artagnan's *pièce-de-résistance*, served with thick, rich forty-percent-fat crème fraiche (how is it that the French are not all the size of small planets?). And dessert wine from Sauternes, that sainted, blessed region just south of Bordeaux, where wine is seemingly pressed from spring meadow-flowers; sweet, yes, but also rich, subtle, complex, a wine that would have pleased the Greek gods.

It was probably around 7pm – I couldn't be sure but the sun had long gone and the wine had flowed abundantly – when we toasted absent friends: D'Artagnan's mum, his dad (his voice cracked and his eyes were moist when he said '*à mon papa*') and Laurent. There were tears, not just from Guy and Françoise, but Stephane too. He had reached across the table when he'd seen Françoise's tears, grasped her hand and held it tightly and she had smiled at him, a really heartfelt smile.

D'Artagnan, now sitting next to me with his arm loosely around my neck, looked across the table at Bérengère, that lazy, sexy look, that little smile on his mouth, and said, 'So Bérengère, do you maybe have a little treat for us, to ... *bah*, smoke with our *digestif?*'

Bérengère replicated the look right back at him and then at me. She did a little shrug, blinked languidly. 'Of course,' she said, and she rolled a big joint and lit it. We passed it around, and we all got really, really, stoned – including Stephane.

The music came on. D'Artagnan turned off the lights in the dining hall and we danced to French music that I didn't know but that they knew all the words to *off by heart*. They sang along whole-heartedly to it, and then to iconic British music – the Beatles, the Stones, and even Blur and Suede – and for a while I felt very nostalgic for the UK.

I'd prepared a room for Françoise and Pascal, who were staying overnight. I tried to insist that Bérengère stay too but she retrieved her coat and said, 'No, Nicole. I go home to my dogs and cats, to my animals. They need me. No, I have not drunk too much, I am safe to drive. Do not worry, my lovely, brave Nicole.' She kissed me on the mouth and embraced me tightly.

She left after she'd done Kissies with everyone else. Stephane stood in the doorway between the salon and the dining hall after she'd gone, looking bereft.

Benoît and Veronique went soon afterwards, Veronique looking very triumphant, flushed and happy. She had been very careful about everything she'd consumed, had refused Bérengère's joint (of course, Benoît had not). Although she'd caught Benoît gazing wistfully at Bérengère a couple of times, she was clearly reassured that currently there was nothing more than wistfulness on his part. So they left, one happy and reassured that her marriage was intact, the other happy and stoned.

When D'Artagnan and I finally went to bed, we tried to have sex. He kissed me all over, which was lovely, but we were both too drunk and too stoned, and he kept stopping mid-way and saying in an astounded voice 'But, my *brozzair*, he smoke a joint!' We both collapsed in fits of giggles, which made the Muffins stare at us, disconcerted. And then we passed out.

It had been the most perfect day. (Apart from the sex, obvs.)
***

It was mid-November and we were leaving at the end of the following week for the Maldives. I told D'Artagnan that I had an osteopathy appointment in Bordeaux on the morning of the fifteenth, and he immediately said, 'Okay, we have a lunch afterward. There is a new Sicilian restaurant that you will like very much, *mon amour*. We meet for lunch there, okay?'

My osteo appointment was a Xavier appointment, of course.

I had read the final draft of my statement. Xavier had provided a formal English translation of the French text and Bérengère and I had read both statements thoroughly and discussed points that I felt weren't clear. And I had added one other thing I'd remembered from the party in the Marble Villa in Hell.

There had been waiters and waitresses circulating with trays of Champagne and canapés. When I'd stopped on the way back from the loo to take a glass from one of them, the waiter had touched my elbow and stared hard into my eyes. He'd said something in Italian; when he saw that I didn't understand, he'd said in broken English, 'Be careful, bad men here.' Then he'd continued smoothly on his way. I'd watched him go, but I hadn't really taken any notice. As far as I was concerned there were bad men *everywhere* – it wasn't exactly news.

As I told Bérengère this, I started to get angry at myself again for having ignored him, for not having been more careful. She pulled me up sharply. 'No, Nicole, it was *not* your fault. It was *never* your fault. You must not doubt yourself.'

That helped. I took a deep breath and banished the thought from my mind.

After we'd finished making all the necessary changes, I put the statement in an envelope addressed to Xavier and stopped at the post office on the way home to post it.

The meeting at Xavier's office that morning was to sign off on the final form of the statement. It was twenty-eight pages long and very thorough, detailing everything that happened in Milan, as well as the flashbacks and panic attacks I'd suffered intermittently throughout the next eleven years and the medication I was prescribed to deal with them. It described my meeting and marrying Guy, his joint venture with Guillaume, the way Guillaume behaved towards me, and that revelatory day when I finally realised who he was. It explained my decision to confront him, and the recording Bérengère and I had made in order to get him to admit what he had done. It was very thorough and I was quite proud of it, proud that the full story was all there in black and white. Finally, I would be rid of the endless, internalised poison; it had been bled from me, exposed to the elements. I felt ... relieved.

Which was stupid really, as we were only at the beginning of what was going to be a psychological gore-fest of epic proportions.

Xavier was in a gloomy mood and decided to elaborate on just how bad the gore-fest was going to be, assuming that I ever had my day in court. 'I have a lunch with my friend, the *procureur* who is retired, last Friday,' he informed me miserably.

He paused. He appeared to have sat on his glasses; one of the lenses was cracked and there was a bit of Sellotape around it. I wondered if criminal lawyers were very badly paid. Today, the five o'clock shadow was at 7pm, even though it was only 11am, and it looked as if it had been some time since he'd last run a comb through his hair.

I smiled sympathetically. 'Never mind,' I said soothingly.

He frowned. 'Never mind what?'

'Well, it obviously wasn't a very good lunch.'

He took off his glasses and moved the smudges around with the end of his untucked shirt. He looked much younger without his glasses, even though he was practically glaring at me.

'The lunch was fine, Nicole,' he snapped. He put his glasses back on, careful not to dislodge the cracked lens. 'It is what my friend tell me about Guillaume and his family that cause me to worry.'

I took a deep breath and then exhaled in a close approximation of a Gallic pout. 'Don't tell me. He murdered his sister and killed his father and it was all premeditated?'

He looked surprised. 'You know all this?'

I nodded. 'Yup. Françoise told us about it. D'Artagnan dismissed it as gossip.'

More blinking, then, tiredly, 'Who *ze furck* is D'Artagnan, Nicole?'

I smiled at that. His '*furck*' was richer, longer off the tongue than D'Artagnan's. There was more '*uurrck*' in it. 'It's Guy.'

Pause. 'Your husband?'

I nodded.

'Why—' he started to ask. '*Non*, don't worry. I don't want to know.' He looked a bit embarrassed.

I laughed involuntarily and felt my cheeks colour. 'Oh God, no! It's not a sex thing, it's not like we dress up and—'

At least I had made him smile. He shook his head and grinned, raised his eyes to the ceiling. His cheeks had coloured, too. I opened my mouth to explain further, then decided not to. 'Anyway, your friend. What did he say?'

He widened his eyes. 'This is a bad family, Nicole. Not the French side, but the Italian side. They are a very old Italian family, and Guillaume is very ... *bah*, protected by his family, by his mother.'

I nodded. 'Yes, I know all that. But we're in France and I'm bringing the case against him in France. He is a French citizen, isn't he?'

He nodded slowly. 'Yes, he is. But you must know, Nicole, that this is a man who, all his life, he do whatever he want to do and he is never punished. Even while he live in France.'

I shrugged. 'Well, Xavier, let's you and me change that.'

He frowned. 'You are very positive today, Nicole.'

'One of us has to be, Xavier.'

He sat back in his chair and made pyramid-praying hands in front of his face. 'You know, Nicole, I worry very much that you do not understand how much this action against Guillaume is going to ... *bouleverser* your life. Guy's life. The family of the other investor. I am very worried that you don't understand this.'

I took a deep breath then shrugged. 'Maybe I haven't fully absorbed it yet, no. But that doesn't mean I'm any less determined.'

He nodded slowly then said quietly, 'I just think that you need to talk to Guy about this. This worry me a lot, that we will submit this statement to the *procureur* and that Guy will know nothing about it.' He paused again. 'Is it not possible that you can tell him about this?'

I glared. 'Good God, Xavier, please let's not go over this *yet again*. No! It isn't possible! If Guy finds out about this – if he sees the video, he'll absolutely flip! Out will come the sword, the suit of armour, he'll be galloping down the A10 in full avenger mode!'

He frowned at me, though there was a smile around the edge of his mouth. 'I thought you say there is no dressing up, Nicole?'

I started laughing despite myself. 'It's a purely metaphorical image, Xavier.' I stopped laughing just as quickly. 'But no, it's not possible to tell him now. When Guillaume is in custody then yes, I'll tell Guy. He can't do anything stupid then.'

Xavier put the pyramid hands back in front of his face and his shoulders sagged a little. 'I need to be honest with you, Nicole. I am worried that the case we have is not very strong. If the *procureur* do not accept the video ... *bah*, there is almost no case, just what you say. Guillaume is very good at evading justice.'

He paused again. 'Maybe you can just bring this case in private, ask for some money. Because I think this is what he do when there is a problem – he pay some money, or his family pay some money.'

I stared at him; I could feel my heart rate increasing, feel my lungs filling. 'This isn't about *money*, Xavier!' I spat out the word. 'I don't want fucking money! I want Guillaume in prison! I want him off the streets, I want him to not be able to touch any more women, to abuse any more women, to destroy their lives and make them afraid! What the fuck have you not understood about that?'

He leaned back in his chair, his eyes very wide. The pyramid-hands now became supplicating, making a gently downward, soothing motion. 'Okay, okay. I understand this Nicole. I just want *you* to understand that it is very possible that the case will not ... *bah*, proceed. How will you feel if this happen, if the *procureur* does not accept to refer the case to the *juge d'instruction*?'

I looked away from him and stared out of the window at the remaining leaves on the horse-chestnut tree in the parking lot at the back of the office, at the chalky-grey sky above it. How would I feel if that really were the case? Everything I'd done since that fateful day in May had been about finding a way to Get Satan while still holding on to everything I loved, about solving the conundrum without losing D'Artagnan, without putting D'Artagnan at risk.

I turned back to Xavier. 'I think the anger I will feel will probably gradually poison me if I have to internalise it. Not necessarily in the short term, but in the long term.' I took a deep breath. 'So we really, really need to find a way to get the *procureur* to watch and then accept the video. Please.'

He looked very solemn but he nodded. 'I do everything I can, Nicole, I promise.'

***

I told Xavier we were going away for two weeks holiday, that it was D'Artagnan's birthday and that the previous year he had spent it shouting at the physiotherapist about why his leg wasn't healing quicker (four and a half weeks after three blood transfusions...). We wanted to celebrate his next birthday in a less stressful environment.

Xavier smiled warmly and wished me *bonnes vacances* when we exchanged goodbye Kissies.

I left his office to walk to my lunch date with D'Artagnan, feeling melancholy. As I started down Rue Sainte-Catherine, the endless pedestrianised shopping street with itinerant drug dealers at one end and Louis Vuitton at the other, I was feeling a lot less positive than I had before our meeting.

It was when I was very near the Grand Theatre that I saw her. Her head was slightly bowed as she walked towards me but I recognised her immediately, her almost waist length straight brown hair, her pretty face and her skinny, long-limbed body.

I didn't hesitate. I moved diagonally across the pedestrian traffic, nearly tripping someone behind me as I stepped directly into her path, and touched her arm gently. 'Hi, Léa. How are you?'

She stopped abruptly and stared at me, wide-eyed, startled. Frightened.

'I'm sorry, I don't mean to startle you. It's Nicole – do you remember me? You came to lunch with Guillaume at our château outside Cognac earlier this year.'

She shrank back, as if I'd said something horrible, scary, then she tried to brush past me and walk away.

In that instant, I knew. I clasped her arm and said, very quietly, 'Please don't go, Léa. I really need to speak to you. It's very important that I speak to you. Please.' The last word really was a plea: an urgent, desperate plea.

I think she heard that in my voice because she raised her eyes to mine and asked hesitantly, 'What do you want, Nicole? Why do you need to speak to me?'

'I need to speak to you about Guillaume.' That frightened flicker appeared in her eyes again. I continued speaking quickly but calmly. 'Léa, many years ago Guillaume raped me. I know he has raped other women, too, and I'm bringing criminal charges against him. I want to speak to you about whether he was ever violent towards you.'

What happened then was awful. Her face crumpled and her beautiful brown eyes filled with tears. She put her hands over her face, her shoulders hunched over and she started sobbing. Her thin body was wracked with sobs.

I put my arms around her and hugged her tightly, rubbed her back soothingly. I was trying really hard not to cry, too, but at the same time I was also absolutely *furious*. I hadn't thought it possible I could be even more furious than I already was with that *bastard* Satan, but I was.

We went around the corner to a café and I ordered us coffee. We sat close together and I held her hand as I told her what Guillaume had done to me all those years ago, and that I was certain that he had done the same thing to other women.

She cried while she told me what he had done to her, had forced her to do, and I felt sick to my stomach. I stroked her hand, passed her several tissues to wipe away the tears and then, when she'd finished telling me, I hugged her again. And I thought: *fuck you, you bastard, you are going straight to hell, where you belong.*

While we sipped our coffee, I explained about the criminal action and told her about Xavier, who was going to help me get Satan locked away once and for all. She didn't say a word while I was speaking. I took Xavier's card out of my wallet and held it out.

'Please, Léa, I cannot tell you how important this is, but please go and see Xavier. He is very understanding, and he can help us to put Guillaume in prison so that he never does this to anyone else.'

She pressed her lips together and blinked her watery, red eyes. She looked at the card, then she looked at me again.

'Léa, you have to do this,' I begged. 'Not for my sake but for your own sake and for the sake of other young women that he might abuse in the future. You *have* to speak to Xavier because it's the only way we can stop Guillaume. Tell me you will go and speak to him, today. I'll call him now and tell him you're coming. It's *so* important, Léa, it's the most important thing you will *ever* do in your life.'

Finally, she reached out and took the card. Her fingers were shaking, but she lifted her eyes and she nodded. 'Okay. I will.'

'Today? Now?'

She nodded again, her face pale, gaunt. I reached over and hugged her again. 'Thank you, Léa. Thank you so, so much.'

Xavier answered immediately when I called him. He sounded surprised when I explained who Léa was, but happy surprised. 'But this is *merveilleux,* Nicole,' he said.

'Can she come and see you now?'

'Yes, of course. Tell her I wait for her.'

I gave Léa my contact details before we parted, then I looked at my watch and saw that it was one o'clock. And I thought: *Shit! D'Artagnan!* But I wasn't too bothered because it was a minor problem. If Léa agreed to bring charges against Guillaume, I was certain we would have him. With or without the video, he would be well and truly *fucked.* And that made me feel very happy – triumphant, even.

***

The waiter showed me to our table and I slid into the chair opposite Guy after I'd kissed his cheek. He did not kiss me back.

He regarded me coolly. 'Why are you late, Nicole?'

I shook my head a little in mock exasperation. 'I'm so sorry, my darling, but the osteo was running late, and then the tram broke down and I had to wait for another one and it took so long to come... It was so frustrating. Anyway, I'm so sorry but I'm here now.' I reached across the table, touched his hand.

Slow blink. No smile. When he spoke, his voice was very quiet. 'Why are you lying to me, Nicole?'

I froze inside and I thought: *Shit, he knows. But what does he know? About the non-existent osteo appointment? About Xavier? About not taking the tram? About Lea? Which bit does he know I'm lying about?* My heart was beating fast.

I gazed at him as the thoughts raced through my head, then I made a quick decision to work backwards through the lies.

'I'm sorry, my darling. I was walking back from my osteo rendezvous and I bumped into Léa. You remember Guillaume's girlfriend? Ex-girlfriend? Well, she kind of grabbed me in the street and said she really needed to talk to me. She seemed quite upset.'

Guy blinked once, twice, but his expression didn't change. I was still getting Impenetrable Disapproval.

'So I went to a café and had a coffee with her.'

He nodded slowly. 'Yes. I see you having a coffee with her in the café.'

I let out an enormous, internal breath. Tah-dah! I had selected the right answer.

'I'm sorry,' I said. 'I should have told you the truth but I felt bad that I'd stopped for a coffee with her and it made me late for our lunch.' I reached across the table for his hand but he didn't move it.

'So, Nicole, tell me, what is young Léa so upset about? Because I see her crying while I am standing there watching you.' Now his eyes were slightly narrowed.

'Well, Guy, she's upset because Guillaume has dumped her. She's very young and she's hurt. I think *she* thinks she's still in love with him and she wants him back, and she wanted to talk to me about that.'

Apart from a marginally increased pout, which resulted in slightly more sunken cheeks, there was still no change in his expression. He stared straight into my eyes and his face was absolutely immobile. Finally, he said, 'Why you, Nicole? Why does she want to talk to you about that?'

The waiter came over and presented us with the menus with a flourish. I glanced up at him, smiled and said, '*Merci*.' He asked if we'd like an aperitif. I was tempted to ask for a double – or even a quadruple – whisky. Instead, I asked for a glass of Champagne. The waiter smiled and noted down my order. He turned to D'Artagnan. '*Monsieur?*'

'*La même*,' Guy said, without taking his eyes off mine. The waiter disappeared. 'Are you going to answer my question, Nicole?'

I held his gaze. I was starting to feel a bit peeved. I'd helped a young girl who was feeling a bit broken-hearted; it was a good story – what the fuck was so terrible about that?

'Because we bumped into one another. Maybe she talks to everyone she knows about it. That's what young girls do. Maybe she thinks I know him well and can help her get him to take her back?'

Long, cool gaze. 'So, Nicole, how do you know Guillaume?'

I froze. *Fuck. Fuck fuck fuck. There was more; he knew more.*

He leaned forward across the table. 'What I mean is, how well do you know Guillaume? Because I am starting to wonder when I see you there with this ex-girlfriend of his who is so upset... I wonder, is this why he no longer see this girl?'

I was completely confused. He knew something – or he thought he knew something – but maybe he didn't know what I thought he knew.

The waiter arrived with our glasses of Champagne. I picked up mine and went to touch it to Guy's. He picked up his glass but did not touch mine with it.

'Are you having an affair with Guillaume, Nicole?' he asked. 'Is this why his ex-girlfriend is so upset, why you are upset, why you must comfort her when she is crying? Why you must lie to me?'

I made a Herculean effort and banished the eyeroll. I banished the incredulous laugh, I banished the 'not in a gazillion fucking years would I be having an affair with Satan, you idiot!' that was right there on the tip of my tongue. Instead, I sipped my Champagne and tried to imagine what he had seen while I gazed at him steadily.

He had seen Léa and me sitting in the café. He had seen Léa crying and he had seen me hugging her. Perhaps he'd seen me giving her Xavier's card; perhaps he had even seen me calling Xavier to tell him she was coming to see him. But, on balance, I thought that he'd probably left by then because he would already have been seething with rage.

I put down my glass. 'No, Guy. I'm not having an affair with Guillaume. I'm not having an affair with anyone. I love you. I don't cheat on people I love.'

'But Nicole, you come to Bordeaux often for the rendezvous with the osteo, even though your back is fine now. For a long time now there is nothing wrong with your back. I see you with Nina, I see you outside planting the rosebushes you buy. We have sex, you have no pain.' He paused. 'Where are you going when you say you go to the osteo, Nicole?'

I really hated myself in that moment, a real, visceral hatred, as I formed and polished another lie. 'The reason why I don't have any back problems is *because* I go for regular appointments with the osteopath. That *is* where I go. And that *is* why my back is so much better.'

The waiter had come to hover again. D'Artagnan glanced at him and made a dismissive movement with his hand to indicate we were not yet ready to order. He gazed back at me. 'Give me the number of the osteopath.'

I shrugged. 'Okay.' I reached into my bag and pulled out my phone. I lifted my eyes to his. 'So good to know you trust me when I tell you something I didn't necessarily want to share.' I let only a hint of sarcasm into my voice.

He slammed his hand down, palm flat, onto the table. 'Why the fuck do you lie to me, Nicole?'

I slammed down my hand too. 'Because I felt bad that I had taken pity on a young, stupid girl who doesn't know anything about love and that I was late for our lunch as a result! But it's very clear to me, Guy, that you have absolutely zero fucking trust in me – and that's actually pretty horrible. Because if you knew anything about me, you'd know that I don't cheat on someone that I love!'

The tears in my eyes were completely genuine. Karl had cheated on me so many times but I had never cheated on him. I had loved him; the idea of cheating on him was never even on my radar.

Guy sat back in his chair. Finally, he took a deep breath and gave a little shrug. 'Okay,' he said. 'Maybe I believe you.'

'Oh gosh, D'Artagnan, please don't stretch your powers of credulity. I'd so hate for them to get distorted.' I held out my phone. 'Go on, ring the osteo – do you want me to dial for you?' Knowing full well that the osteopath's receptionist would be at lunch.

He started to look a little sheepish. '*Mais non*, Nicole, I say I believe you.' He took a sip of his Champagne.

I glared at him, took a sip of mine.

The waiter was hovering in my peripheral vision.

'You know, Guy, when I agreed to marry you—' I knew instantly that I should not have used that particular phrase. We both knew exactly when I had agreed to marry him; it had been intensely erotic '—when we were married,' I tried to ignore the little smile that was flickering at the edge of his mouth, 'we knew so little about each other. And sometimes that's frustrating. Of course sometimes it's quite lovely, discovering things we didn't know about each other – it is for me, anyway. But you have to know this: I love you and, unless you leave me, I will never love anyone else.'

He reached across the table and took my hand. His eyes were very serious. 'I am sorry, Nicole.' He kissed my hand softly. 'I am sorry I did not believe you, *mon amour*.' His eyes were full of remorse. 'I love you so much, Nicole. Please forgive me.'

Did I feel bad about that conversation, about lying so blatantly to him? Yes and no, because my lies were only to protect him from doing something stupid. Did we make it back to the Duchess for make-up sex? No, we did not; we had to go to a hotel. It was insanely hot.

Afterwards, when I was just about to collapse onto him and the throb of intense pleasure in every cell of my body was starting to recede, he whispered against my ear, 'Promise me that you will never lie to me again, Nicole.'

I placed my mouth against his ear and I whispered, 'I promise, my angel.'

And my heart felt like it was being wrung out like a dirty, wet dishcloth.

Chapter Fifteen

The resort in the Maldives was five star, of course, and it would have been worth twenty stars. Our luxurious suite was directly over the turquoise water, a celestial water haven. We could slip into the crystal-clear sea at any time from the semi-submerged bamboo ladder at the side of our deck.

We were at the very front of the run of waterfront suites so we had more privacy and I could sunbathe topless without fear of attracting displeasure. I had become very French in the short time I'd been living in France and could not be bothered with bikini tops any more. What was the point? Men didn't have to wear tops, why should women have to? It wasn't as if I were packing, FFS...

The sun shone every day with a soft, tropical, heat, that was so welcome after two months of autumn. We had left Bordeaux in the midst of an unexpected snowstorm – the weather had turned suddenly weird, very cold for late November.

Breakfast was delivered to our waterfront haven every morning at 9am: coffee, fresh fruit juice, exotic and unusual fruits, freshly baked breads, pastries, yoghurt, delicious nuts I'd never seen before. We ate on the terrace, gazing out over the ever-changing sea, watching the multi-coloured tropical fish darting in and out beneath our deck. After breakfast we put on our flippers, snorkels and goggles and slipped into the water. We snorkelled all over the atoll, gesticulating when we saw something bizarre, something beautiful, something extraordinary. There was a lot of gesticulating.

We were both suntanned, the ends of our hair light with sunshine by the end of the first week. At lunchtime we walked along the elevated bamboo boardwalk to the main resort building. We shared a bottle of white or rosé wine and then, lightly inebriated with sun and sea and wine, we wandered back and had slow, inquisitive sex, sex with questions that needed answers, murmured questions, breathless answers.

D'Artagnan was always more curious during afternoon sex, his desire aroused by affirmation that yes, *that* felt almost unbearably exquisite. The ceiling fan whirred hypnotically above us until finally the inquisitiveness became intolerable and had to be resolved. Afterwards we slumbered, our bodies moist with heat, one of his legs between mine, his hand damp on my hip, my hand damp against his chest, my lips touching his neck, his beard scratchy-soft against my forehead.

We did proper swimming in the late afternoon, racing each other across the bay. He always won, which was bloody annoying because I'm a good swimmer. I grew up swimming in the Indian Ocean and it's the only sport I'm any good at. (D'Artagnan laughingly informed me that yoga is definitely not a sport.) But he always beat me easily; he'd flip onto his back when he was five or ten metres ahead of me and taunt me, 'You're so slow, Nicole! You need to try harder.' Then he'd laugh as I tried to grab at him, flip back onto his front and draw away from me effortlessly until suddenly we'd find ourselves at the edge of the atoll, at the edge of the world.

The realization that we'd been swimming along the flat top of a very steep mountain terrified me: the sheer cliff, the unfathomably deep water falling away from it, harbouring who knew what evil, sharp-fanged creatures that were waiting to swallow us up. There was no way I could go further and, when we turned to swim back, I always swam that little bit faster to get away from the cliff edge.

As we were swimming back, Guy slowed down and let me draw alongside him. One day he reached over, put his hand on top of my head and pushed me down, held me under the water, which made me furious. I flailed at him and he pushed me away laughing, kicked his legs hard and swam away.

When I got back to the cabin, he was sitting on the deck, his legs dangling, grinning. 'Ah, Nicole, it's because you are only a fragile *princesse,* this is why you cannot swim properly.'

I held up a very long, very erect middle finger as I climbed the bamboo ladder out of the water.

We ate in the resort restaurant every night. The food was beautifully prepared, fresh, full of exotic flavours. We shared a bottle of wine, and some evenings it seemed to go more to my head than others.

It was one of those nights, after we'd been there for about a week, that I saw her. A family of four had just arrived. The mother was very beautiful, her skin the colour of gently baked biscuits. She had high cheekbones and her eyes sparkled when she laughed. Her husband had slightly darker skin and he was very good-looking. Their two children, a boy and a girl, were beautifully behaved; they sat politely at the table and chatted animatedly to their parents. Their parents engaged with them, asked them questions, listened to their answers. The children felt included, loved.

They were at a table slightly to our right on the edge of the terrace. The moonlight danced over the rippling ocean. My hand was on Guy's warm, bare thigh, the palm of his hand on the nape of my neck, his fingers in my hair.

When the family finished their meal and were getting ready to leave, the little girl got down from her chair. She stretched and yawned, but carefully, with her hand over her mouth like Jules' mum had taught me to do, because it was impolite to show the insides of our mouths in public. This gorgeous little girl, with a dark fringe like Nina's and skinny arms like Nina's, went over to her mum and slipped her arms around her neck. She pressed her face against her mum's ear and whispered something. Her mum smiled and slipped her arm around her daughter's little body, pulled her close and kissed her forehead. That kiss was so tender, so full of love.

I felt my heart shatter.

D'Artagnan was watching them, too. He glanced at me and saw the tears in my eyes. His voice was very gentle when he said, 'Do you want to say something, Nicole?'

The sound of the water lapping against the posts was quiet, soothing.

I tried to blink away the tears, and I thought: *I've got to say it, I can't just keep pushing this away every time it comes up.*

I took a very deep breath. I didn't look at him. 'I don't think... Guy, I'm so sorry but I don't think I can live happily without Nina in my life.'

He slipped his hand around the side of my face and turned my head so that I was gazing into his eyes. 'Tell me, Nicole. Tell me what you want.'

So I just said it out loud. 'I want us to adopt Nina.'

And he smiled the biggest, gentlest smile, slipped his arms around me and hugged me very, very tightly against him. When he finally let me go, he said, 'I have been waiting so long for you to say this, Nicole. Because I know for a very long time this is what you want. But you are so ... *timide* to ask for the things that you want, the things that are important to you.'

I stared at him. 'But you— Right at the very beginning, you said you didn't want any more children.'

A positively epic Gallic shrug with a *massive* eyeroll. '*Bah*, Nicole, I never say that. I told you that I cannot *give you* children. We never talk about adopting children.'

'Well I thought... I assumed... I mean, you never said—'

Eyebrows arched across his forehead, slightly annoyed expulsion of air. '*Pffff*, this is why I tell you, why I am always telling you to talk to me! Talk to me about what you are thinking, about what is in your head. Don't just think this is what I think!'

He stroked my cheek with his thumb. 'Sometime, *mon trésor*, I know we make a joke about it, but sometime you are very much like a *princesse* in your tower, locked away in the tower of your mind. You do not talk to me about what you are thinking.' His eyes were slightly narrowed, his tone gently exasperated.

'So I can see that you fall in love with Nina, I can see this so easily. And, you know, it might be possible to adopt her but you don't talk to me about this important thing, this thing that is causing pain for you in your heart. That make me sad because I love you, *mon amour*, and I will always try to make you happy. I will do anything for you, Nicole, because I love you so much. And I love Nina very much too. I want us to adopt Nina too.'

I slipped my arms around his neck and buried my face in his Dior-scented softness, and I cried then. I cried for all sorts of reasons, only one of them being the lurking guilt about Guillaume and my secret machinations to deal with that epic clusterfuck. All the other reasons I was crying were to do with love – how much I loved Nina, how much I loved D'Artagnan, how much love there was in my life now where previously there had been so little. My heart felt like it was made of tissue paper that had been submerged, was soaking in a thick, warm bath filled with pure joy at the thought that he loved Nina too, that he wanted to adopt Nina. It was almost frightening how much love there was in my life.

As we walked slowly back towards our celestial water haven, he said, 'There is only one thing I want to ask you about this, about the idea to adopt Nina. It is very important.' We stopped on the boardwalk. The night was warm and still and his face was serious in the moonlight.

'Ask me anything you need to, my darling. I know exactly how I feel about Nina.'

He gazed very intently at me. 'Do you want to adopt Nina because we can't have our own children? Is that why you want to adopt her?'

I snorted. It was a very unladylike sound and I think some snot may even have become dislodged. 'Of course not! Guy, I love Nina just because ... she's Nina! And I think she loves us, and I know she *needs* us – and I think we need her. I think she belongs with us. I can't imagine life without her, without watching her grow up.' I paused, wiped away a tear. 'It would be the most incredible, the most wonderful thing in the world if we could adopt her. Do you really think it's possible?'

His mouth curled into the loveliest smile as he reached out and tucked my hair back gently behind my ear. 'Yes, Nicole, it is possible. I already start the process. I already make the *demande d'agrément*.'

I stared at him. I don't think my eyes had ever been wider in my whole life. 'But... you already did what? What did you do? What's the *demande d'agrément*?'

He shrugged. 'It is some paperwork to start the process, to explain our situation *familiale*. And now I have a response, just before we leave on our *vacances*. So *mon ange*, when we get back we complete a lot more paperwork, we tell them all about us, we tell them about Nina, and we make a submission, very formal. Then we receive a date for a meeting with the *psychiatriste* to evaluate if we are acceptable to be parents. But—' and there was a classic D'Artagnan imperial sniff, a slightly arrogant shrug '— I think the procedure is just a formality. They will approve us. We will adopt Nina, but it might take some time because it's France and of course these thing take time.' Another shrug.

'How long do you think it will take? The whole procedure?' I hardly dared ask the question.

'*Bah*... I think it will be approved by the end of the summer next year. Maybe seven, eight months. Maybe a little bit longer. But it will happen.' He smiled at me then, the lovely, lazy smile. He slipped his hands under my head, tilted my mouth to his and kissed me very softly. 'So, next year, Nicole, you will be a mother finally, like you always want.'

I was quite familiar with D'Artagnan's *modus operandi* by now. I knew how his world functioned, how he made it function. I gazed into his beautiful eyes and I thought; *I trust him. He wants this as much as I want this*. And the surge of love I felt for him surpassed anything I'd previously felt for him.

***

It felt as if we'd never made love as intensely, as sensuously as we did that night, suspended over the Indian Ocean. Each time we were close, so close, closer even than that, we stopped. He distracted me, he distracted himself, his hands circled, stroked, caressed my body, my breasts, my stomach, my back, my thighs. I traced the muscles in his chest, in his arms, his stomach, his strong, smooth shoulders, and we waited until our breathing had calmed. And after several ... hours, days?…

Time was irrelevant; it ceased to exist until we were both glistening, slippery with sweat, the bedsheets tangled under us. Finally we could wait no longer. My body arched against him, craving him until he was deeply, fully inside me, and then he thrust again, so agonizingly, beautifully slowly, again and again, until we were both consumed, gasping, helpless as the orgasm invaded our bodies, and the cry that was wrung from me came from a place so deep, so primeval, it felt as if I were connected to the centre of the earth. And D'Artagnan, he roared, like a lion, and the sound of our ecstasy skidded out across the calm ocean, fled into the night – a moment of pure rapture, finally released.

Afterwards we slipped naked into the sea and he held me tightly against him. I whispered to him, my mouth pressed against his wet, salty ear, 'I never knew it was possible to love someone as much as I love you, my angel,' and he whispered back, 'I feel that every time I look at you, *mon amour*.'

And the water licked us both, it caressed us both: salty, silky, soft.

***

On the Wednesday afternoon after we arrived back, Nina came running at full pelt down the drive towards me. I caught her in my arms, her arms around my neck, her legs around my waist, and when we'd finally finished hugging each other she leaned back and looked at me. Her green eyes were wide, delighted, as she said '*T'as échangé beaucoup de bisous avec le soleil, Princesse Nicole*!'

You and the sun exchanged lots of kisses.

And that was just the loveliest thing I'd ever heard, and I hugged her again tightly until she started wriggling out of my arms. She took my hand and started running around the side of the château so that we could go and see Espiritu, the other love of both of our lives.

***

Xavier had submitted my and Léa's statements to the *procureur* while Guy and I were in the Maldives. He had also submitted the video evidence with a request that it be accepted for submission to the *juge d'instruction*. I didn't know about the submission until we returned, and then I tried very hard not to think about it all the time. The only thing that helped was thinking about Nina; whenever I did that, I found that I relaxed again and that I was inadvertently smiling. Then I'd remember that Satan's fate was being decided by a no doubt fully paid-up member of the Nietzsche Society somewhere in a dusty, probably windowless, mega-burrow in the depths of Bordeaux, and then .... *whooooosh*, down I would whizz on the roller-coaster. It was exhausting.

I went for my lesson with Bérengère the week after we returned, and she quizzed me about how much coffee I was drinking because my hands were shaking as we sat in her warm kitchen sipping our *Pineau*.

'It's not the caffeine, it's the anxiety, Bérengère!' I said crossly. 'I'm on bloody tenterhooks waiting to hear from Xavier!'

She blinked at me slowly, picked up half a roll-up in the ashtray and re-lit it. 'You are wasting a lot of energy on this,

Nicole. If the answer is no this time, well, you just have to find another way to bring this man to justice. But you are going to need to learn to be calm if you are going to be Nina's mother because your anxiety will make her anxious, and that is not good for any child.'

When I had told her about our decision to adopt Nina, she had given me a huge hug, her smile full of tenderness. 'I am so happy for you, Nicole. I know how much she means to you.'

I scowled at her and raised my glass of *Pineau*, spilling a drop as my hand shook again. 'Perhaps you should roll me a joint.'

She snorted. 'No, Nicole. Marijuana is for enhancing life's pleasures, not for hiding our anxieties. This is why you always have a problem with drugs. You take them for the wrong reasons.' She was annoyingly right.

***

But the day did arrive. Xavier had told us that the *procureur* would make his decision before the end of the year, and it was on the last Wednesday before Christmas that he rang Bérengère. She texted me immediately; all her text said was: '*C'est arrivé.*' It's happened.

My heart started beating rapidly when I saw her message. I'd been about to follow D'Artagnan and Nina outside, but I changed direction and went upstairs. I stood at the window at the top of the stairs and looked out over the paddocks. D'Artagnan had lifted Nina so that was sitting on the top paddock rail; his arms were around her as she leaned back against him while they chatted. I suddenly felt weak with love seeing them together like that.

I pressed dial and called Bérengère.

'Nicole,' she smiled down the line – down the digital signal? WTF is the terminology now? '*Ça va, ma belle?*'

'I'm fine thank you, lovely Bérengère. How are you?'

'I'm very well.'

D'Artagnan and Nina had gone into the tack room and emerged with a halter and Espiritu's grooming kit. Espiritu still looked at D'Artagnan slightly suspiciously; clearly his only experience before Camille had been with men, and it had not been good.

A pause. 'Did you get my SMS?'

'Yes, Bérengère, that's why I'm calling you. What is it? What's happened?'

A pause. You can never rush French people. Urgency is a thing that is peculiar only to *les Anglo-Saxons*.

'So Xavier call me today.'

'Uh-huh?' I had to consciously stop my feet from doing a little tap dance of impatience.

'Nicole, *le procureur* ... he is going to submit the video to the *juge d'instruction* and he is going to recommend to the *juge d'instruction* that a warrant is issued for the arrest of Guillaume.' Another pause. Then softly, 'You have done it, Nicole, you have succeeded. You are going to put that terrible man in prison. I am so, *so* proud of you *mon amie, ma superbe* Nicole.'

As I watched, D'Artagnan approached and stood next to Espiritu, scratching him in the favoured spot at the base of his neck underneath his thick mane. Nina was trying to get Espiritu's head into the halter; it was half across his nostrils, and he kept nudging his nose upwards to get the strap off, which pulled her arms up and unbalanced her. Even through the double-glazed windows I could hear her giggling, but she persevered. The halter went over his nose, then D'Artagnan helped her loop the strap over his head and she fastened it against his cheek.

I felt weak; I needed to sit down, but I didn't want to stop watching them, the two people and the horse I loved more than anything else in the world. 'Are you sure?' I finally asked, my voice faint.

I heard Bérengère smile down the phone. 'Yes, Nicole, it's real. Xavier sounded very – *bah*, happy? Very *positive*. He thinks that the *juge* will follow the *procureur's* recommendation.'

'How soon will we know?'

'Xavier thinks before the end of the year.' Another pause. 'I am so proud, so amazed at what you have done, Nicole. *Félicitations, ma belle, mon amie si forte. Je t'admire tellement.*'

'I couldn't have done it without you, Bérengère,' I whispered. 'And I have to go now, because I need to cry. Thank you so much for believing in me, I love you so much. *Gros, gros bisous.*'

I hung up and sat abruptly on the top stair. I covered my face with my hands and I sobbed heavy, hot tears for all of the shit that had happened in my life since that night in the Marble Villa in Hell. I knew that it was only the first step at the beginning of what would be an extremely unpleasant, traumatic quest for justice, but I felt enormous relief at having successfully cleared the first hurdle. That relief was exhausting; every muscle in my body, all the mental and physical tension, had turned to liquid.

Once Guillaume was in custody, I could explain everything to D'Artagnan. Although the thought of that conversation made me anxious, I was confident that he would understand why I had deceived him, why I couldn't tell him about it. He would be angry at first, but he would come to terms with it. He would accept that it was the best possible outcome, that I had made the right decision.

I took a deep breath, wiped my eyes, stood up and went downstairs. I went out of the back door and across the courtyard towards my wonderful husband and my lovely, soon-to-be daughter. They were chatting away, their voices carrying across the courtyard as they brushed and fussed the coat of the most beautiful horse in the world.

***

Later that afternoon, the day of the winter solstice, we walked Nina back up the hill to Marion and Thierry's house. Nina frowned that slightly hurt frown that she always wore when we took her back home and my heart ached as I watched her walk away from us. She ignored Marion's fond touch on her head as she brushed past her to go inside their house.

D'Artagnan held me close against his side as we walked back down the hill and watched the sun setting over the vines at the top of the valley. As we went up the drive towards the Duchess, the lights we'd left on in the dining hall and the salon beamed bright yellow shafts onto the chalkstone forecourt.

I had an urge to see the horses again because I knew that watching them for a while would block some of the hole in my heart that came from saying goodnight to Nina. We walked across the courtyard at the back and leaned side by side on the paddock rails. It wasn't a particularly cold evening; there was very little wind and, although it was cool, I felt warm after the walk up and down the hill. And I was wearing the 'Patagonian' duffle coat.

Guy and I watched Emperador and Espiritu munching on their hay and listened to the satisfying sound of their rhythmic chewing. Suddenly Espiritu stopped eating, turned his head and looked at us.

He walked over, stopped in front of me and nuzzled my hand with his velvety muzzle. He nodded his head and made a blowing noise, then he stood still again and blinked his big eyes at me.

'Nicole,' D'Artagnan said quietly. 'He is talking to you.'

I frowned. 'I don't know what he's saying, though.'

Espiritu touched my hand again and this time he mouthed the back of my hand with his thick, soft lips, as if he were trying to lift my hand.

'Go.' Guy's voice was very soft. 'Go into the paddock and stand next to him.'

I climbed under the paddock rail and stood next to Espiritu. I scratched him in that place at the base of his neck underneath his mane and he blew out again, a big blowy noise through his nostrils. His neck was very relaxed, his head low, and he blinked slowly as I gently scratched him.

Guy was behind me when the thought formed in my head, and when I turned to him and said, 'Do you think...?' He nodded and, even though the light was fading, I could see the smile in his eyes.

He leaned down. I bent my left knee and he lifted me effortlessly into the air.

And suddenly I was astride the most beautiful horse in the world. His body felt incredibly warm under me, solid, so strong. He didn't move at first, but after Guy stepped back Espiritu turned and nudged my foot with his nose. He nudged it gently and he gave a little snort, then he turned to face the front again.

I sat there on the most beautiful horse in the world and I felt absolutely invincible. And humble, too. I felt so grateful to Espiritu for allowing me to sit on his back. And then I thought: *Oh my God, I'm sitting on Espiritu!* and I felt an incredible surge of emotion, of power, of pride, of joy. I felt as if I were filled with stardust. So many emotions that I had never experienced so profoundly as I did that winter evening, sitting there quietly on the back of the most beautiful horse in the world.

After a while I leaned forward and slipped my arms around his neck, buried my face in his mane and breathed in his rich, intoxicating smell. I sat up again and slipped off him easily, landed lightly on the ground like I'd seen Camille do. Espiritu blew out again, turned and walked off back to his hay and started eating.

Guy's smile was tender, so full of love. He slipped his arms around me and I put my arms around his neck, then he picked me up and we spun slowly once, twice, three times in the winter moonlight. When he let me touch the ground again, we kissed and my heart felt like it was going to explode with love for all of the wonderful things that D'Artagnan, my musketeer, had brought into my life.

A grovelling plea, a thousand thanks and…further read

I really hope you enjoyed reading *Deceiving D'Artagnan*. I am fully aware that nowadays, every time we so much as fart we receive an email asking us to rate the fart experience. I'd estimate that 99% of us ignore them (me included).

But for a new author, feedback is like Tinkerbell. When we receive a comment, or even just a star rating, it means that someone out there *believes* in the world we've created, which makes that world more substantial, more real. It means we're not on our own transcribing the inside of our brains onto a computer screen that no-one cares about and that, quite possibly, we're actually a bit mad. Feedback is the Tinkerbell effect; it allows us to *believe*.

So, please leave a review on Amazon or Goodreads.com or visit my website at www.fiwhyms.com or Facebook at Fi Whyms, Author. Maybe you don't believe in Amazon (but it does exist…). Maybe you don't believe in reviews. Maybe you don't believe that authors need their egos inflated any more than they already are (newsflash: they're not, they're *incredibly* fragile). But if you believed in Nicole and Guy and their life in France, please tell me, and the more publicly, the better. Because then other people might start to believe in them too, and ultimately it helps me to believe in them and if I can do that, I can write about them and all of the other characters in my head.

And a thousand thanks to… my cheerleaders from the start of this wonderful journey; SC, Jonno, Flo, Jacqui, Bella, VMG, John, Karen, my kind, lonely OH and most of all, Zebedee-doodah and Skinny Kitty. And to all of you who left reviews for *Taming D'Artagnan: Mille-fois MERCI*!!! Seriously, thank you. Each and every one lifted my heart and made my day wonderful.

Beguiling D'Artagnan, the 3rd and last in the series is finished, it's being edited and it will blow your minds… I promise!!

Printed in Great Britain
by Amazon